DARZARADA

Dunyara Trilogy Book 2

DARZARADA

Dunyara Trilogy Book 2

Melinda J. Lewis

Copyright © 2020 Melinda J. Lewis
All rights reserved.

ISBN 13: 9798650954682

To my husband
*You were told not to take me
through the mud and the weeds,
but you did.
And I am a better woman for it.*

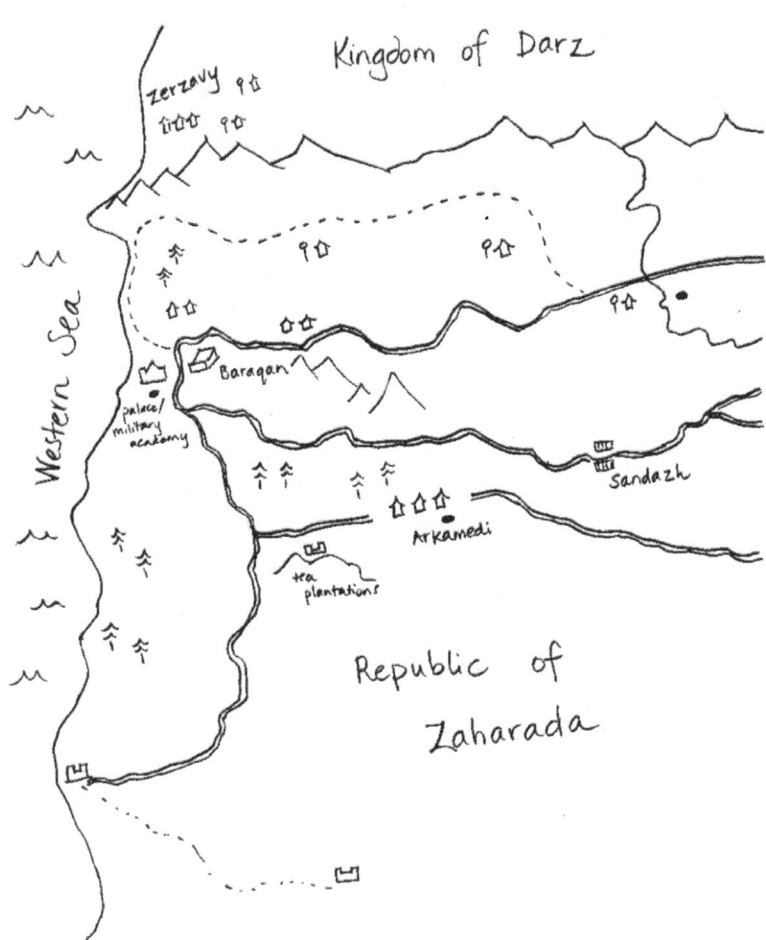

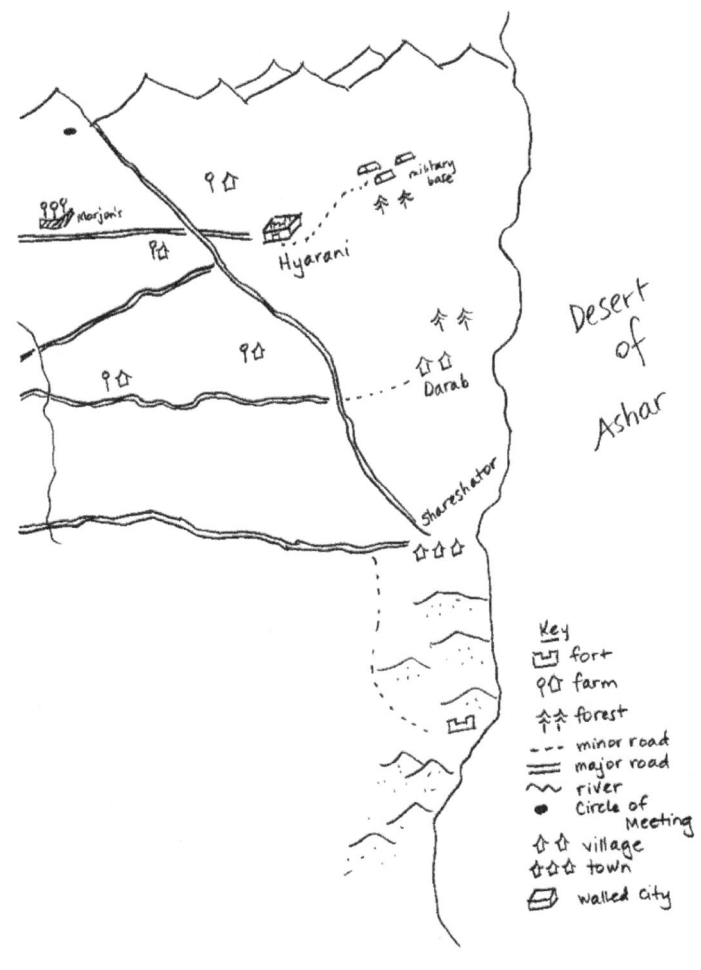

One

Zhelica understood why others in Zaharada slept after the mid-day meal: the sun beat down, radiating off the fields and roads. It was too hot to work. Her aunt, middle-aged and snoring in her own bed chamber, needed the rest. But Zhelica found lying on her own mattress, with scarcely a breeze whispering through the curtains at her window, punishment. She could not doze as she reclined in a pool of moisture.

Lately she had taken to stealing past her aunt's room, down the stairs and out into the orchard. Their employees returned home for the most intolerable hours of the day, so she had the grid of trees to herself. The air was cooler, fresher. Zhelica spread her blanket and stretched onto her belly, balancing on her forearms so she could read her favorite of the few books Marjon owned. It was an old volume, probably dating from her aunt's youth, including stories of the Zaharada that had been long ago. Part of the charm was imagining a time before clocks and guns, factories and banks, and even printed books like this one. But the stories themselves were what kept her coming back. Zhelica scrutinized each page illuminated with tiny inked drawings of castles and mountains and exquisite miniature waves crashing on the seashore. She cared for it like a newborn babe, tenderly turning each sheet as she read and wrapping the book in a clean scarf when she finished. Marjon did not know Zhelica had the book in her possession; her niece had found it in a cupboard months before, tucked behind a stack of rarely-used woolens. Someday she would return it. But for now, she kept it as her afternoon treat, relishing it in the temperate comfort of the orchard.

She knew that the workers would not be back for some time, so when the sound of a bell twinkling near the house caught her ear, she jumped in surprise. *It's no good if Marjon wakes up and finds me here,* she thought, sliding her toes into her sandals. She ran up the driveway used for carts hauling away the nuts and ripe fruit they sold.

The little viewing door in the metal gate was just above the level of her face, so Zhelica stood on tiptoe as she opened it.

"Hello!" came a friendly call from the other side, and a velvet muzzle pushed through the opening.

"Oh! Your horse," Zhelica said, gently pushing the animal away.

It backed up and Zhelica could tell by the thud on the other side of the gate that its owner had dismounted. "One moment!" came a cheerful voice. Zhelica waited patiently, and then where once there had been the nostrils of a quadruped, a human face appeared.

"Well, well," he said, his dark eyes wide. "You're not Marjon."

Zhelica covered her smile. "I'm not," she said through her fingers.

The eyes seemed to take her in, and then the face pulled back. Zhelica could see a young man, probably close to her own age. He was grinning broadly. "And who might you be?" he asked.

She hesitated. Aunt Marjon kept her indoors when the pickers worked the orchard. She had her wait in the carriage when they went into town. She felt sure that her aunt would not want Zhelica speaking with this unknown person. And yet...

"I'm Zhelica," she said. "Marjon is my aunt."

The young man whistled. "Well, that's something. She never told me she had a niece."

Zhelica stepped nearer the door. "And who are *you?*"

He had a cap the color of dirt and whipped it off with a flourish, revealing hair closely trimmed along the sides with a mop of curls on top. "I am Captain Yavan."

"Why would an army officer want my aunt?" Zhelica asked. She was beginning to wish she had not responded to the ringing at the gate.

"I am in charge of purchasing food for the local base," the captain told her. "Your aunt has the finest nuts and fruit in the region." He craned his neck as though to see more of her. "So, may I talk to your Auntie, Miss Zhelica?"

"You can't have done business with her long if you didn't know she always takes a nap after the noon meal," Zhelica said. And then, thinking of the hours she had been forced to honor that slot of time, she repeated, "Always."

Captain Yavan gave a little frown that brought out dimples in his cheeks. "I guess I'm early today," he said. He replaced his cap. "Say, it's hot out here. You wouldn't let me wait in the orchard, would you?"

Zhelica argued with herself. It made sense to let him in; Marjon knew him, did business with him. But on the other hand, if Zhelica was caught chatting with the captain, Marjon might lose her temper. Zhelica loved her aunt, but her anger was best kept at bay.

"I wish I could," she said apologetically, reaching for the little door. "Wait in the shade across the road for half an hour, and ring the bell again. Then my aunt will let you in."

"If I must," the captain sighed. As he turned to lead his horse away, Zhelica could see the look on the young man's face. He didn't seem displeased at all. She watched him for a moment, the little door opened a crack, and when he turned around and gave her a wink, she slammed it shut and latched it.

It was too risky now to remain outdoors. Zhelica bundled the precious book and shook dirt and leaves from her blanket before sneaking to her room. She smoothed the cover back onto the bed and sat down to wait. At last she heard her aunt cough, and then the creaking as she rose and headed down stairs.

The bell began jangling again – it was loudest near the house, where the long rope from the gate ended. Zhelica watched from her window as Marjon admitted Captain Yavan and his horse into the orchard.

Zhelica discovered as a child that if she moved stealthily through the trees, she was able to observe what was happening without being seen from the road or the gate. Slipping outside, she zigzagged from one trunk to the next until she could hear the conversation between her aunt and the captain.

"The apples won't be ready for at least another month," Marjon was saying. "We began picking plums this morning."

Captain Yavan seemed more businesslike now, an order book in hand. "Do you want me to send some men around to help with the harvest?"

She gave a sharp laugh. "Thank you, no," Marjon said. "I can only imagine the mischief they would stir up."

"Well, with just you here to manage. . ." Captain Yavan began. Zhelica wondered if he was trying to get Marjon to mention her.

"I have managed this farm for two decades on my own," she said, throwing her head back proudly. Zhelica chuckled. Despite her effort, her aunt, a little plump and unkempt, did not look imposing at all.

"Of course," said the captain, all charm. "So I should come back in two days?"

Marjon nodded. "Don't forget the carts."

The young man smiled. "Never fear," he said. He glanced over toward where Zhelica was standing, and she froze. Had he seen her? She thought not, but just to be sure, she tucked herself even tighter behind the tree.

Marjon opened the gate and Captain Yavan led his horse out. Zhelica waited for her aunt to return to the house before she skirted the building and began hauling water up from the well in the back.

The following morning the laborers arrived early. Marjon insisted Zhelica wrap a scarf around her hair whenever they appeared, even though she was not permitted to work with them. This day, however, Zhelica said, "Aunt Marjon, may I join the pickers? There's nothing to do indoors, and I know I could help."

Her aunt, busily plaiting her own salt-and-pepper hair into a single braid, stiffened. "You know how I feel about you out there with them."

"Yes," said Zhelica, "but I don't know *why*. I never get to talk to anyone my own age." It was the first time she had articulated the loneliness she felt. She didn't want to seem ungrateful to her aunt for all her care.

Marjon reached over to push a loose lock of hair under Zhelica's scarf. Her niece was startled by her expression: her brows bent upward in a look of tenderness, her mouth twitching with something fierce. She would not meet the girl's eyes.

"No," she said softly. Then more firmly, she said, "No, not this time. You make dinner, and I'll work outdoors. I don't want you to get sunburned," she added in what was clearly an afterthought.

Zhelica went to the kitchen at the back of the house and chopped vegetables for stew. She could see no one from here, only their garden and the high wall that surrounded the property. She was tired of what was starting to feel like captivity. Drying her hands, she ran upstairs and sat on the window seat in her bedroom, where she could hear the chatter of the pickers and occasionally see the dark-haired young women, their long dresses tied up at the knee so they could climb ladders to reach the uppermost branches of fruit. Once one glanced her way and called something down to a youth below, who stretched his head from behind the branches, took a look at Zhelica, and then laughed.

Why do they laugh? she wondered. It happened when she went to town, too. Sometimes rather than laughing they would mutter something she guessed was intended as an insult. Zhelica was afraid to mention it to her aunt, fearful that she would restrict her further. With a sigh, she returned to the kitchen and carried on preparing the meal.

Aunt Marjon looked hotter and more tired than usual when she returned at noon. Zhelica served her a bowl of stew and as soon as she finished, the older woman said, "Time for our rest," and left the room. By the time Zhelica had washed the dishes she could hear her aunt's rhythmic breathing. Today she would skip the pretense of sleep and walk in the orchard.

Boxes of plums rested at intervals under the trees. Looking up, Zhelica could see which branches had been plucked clean. A few pieces of discarded fruit lay in the dirt, ants already hard at work dismantling them and carrying fragments away. Zhelica wound slowly through the rows of plum trees until she came to the apples. One of the trees near the wall had a trunk perfectly split in a way that meant she could climb it with little effort. Imitating the pickers, she bound the side of her dress into a knot and clambered up until she found a place where she could look out.

It was an odd perspective, viewing the canopy of leaves from here. She gazed with interest across the orchard, and then turned to see how far down the road the view extended. To her surprise, a tiny figure was riding toward her. She watched as he came closer and saw the beige uniform of a soldier. She tried to lean down to remain invisible. The soldier slowed as he neared their orchard, and keeping his horse at a walk, he moved along the wall as though looking for something.

It was Captain Yavan.

Zhelica was so flustered, she shifted quickly and lost her footing. She let out a little shriek while catching herself, and the officer looked her way.

"Well, if it isn't Marjon's niece!" he said, stopping his horse right below where she sat. There was no reason to hide now, so Zhelica steadied herself and nodded.

"And she is – sleeping?" he guessed. His dimples were showing. "But not you."

"I – I just wanted to look around," Zhelica said. "Marjon isn't keen on me being out here while she's napping." She plucked at the leaves nearest her. As though accusing him, she said, "You weren't supposed to come back until tomorrow."

"I thought you might enjoy a visitor," he said. "I get the impression your aunt doesn't let you see many people." As he spoke, he tied his horse to a stump outside the wall. "May I come up?" he asked.

Without waiting for an answer, he deftly scaled the wall, settling himself on the top facing Zhelica.

"So what do you do with all your time?" Captain Yavan asked. "I mean when you aren't sitting in tree tops."

"Oh, I – " She stopped. What did she do all day? "I help Marjon with chores. When I have time, I read. When no one is here, I walk in the orchard."

"You like to read?" the captain asked, maneuvering until he found a better position on the wall. "What do you read?"

"We don't have many books," Zhelica said. "My favorite is full of stories about old Zaharada."

Captain Yavan's brown eyes glittered with interest. "You like the old stories? Which ones have you read?"

"Well," she began, "About how the Princess Yasneen of Bustaan saved the life of the king and then married Prince Sanjar."

"Very romantic," the captain said, raising his eyebrows teasingly.

Zhelica could feel her cheeks redden. She hurried on. "And stories about the exploits of the men of southern Zaharada," she said. "You know, like the one who was surrounded by leopards in the desert and managed to escape through a rocky path where they couldn't reach him."

"I like those stories, too," Yavan said. "Do you think they're true?"

Zhelica stared at him. "I thought they were. Aren't they?"

He smiled. "Some people think so. Most people think they are just myths, though. Just stories."

"I hope they're true," Zhelica said. "It sounded like a glorious time in Zaharada. Maybe it will be like that again someday."

"The golden age of our land," Captain Yavan suggested.

"Exactly."

He glanced down the empty road. "Does your aunt ever let you leave the orchard?"

Zhelica shook her head. "Well, not alone, anyway. We go to town sometimes."

"I might have to talk to her about that," Yavan said.

Zhelica reached out to grab his arm. As she did so, her scarf fell around her shoulders. "You must never tell her I spoke with you!" she cried.

Captain Yavan blinked as though the sun had suddenly flashed in his face. His mouth dropped open, and he murmured, "Oh."

Zhelica quickly wrapped her scarf around her head and neck. "I need to go," she said, and began to slide down the trunk.

"See you tomorrow," Yavan called. Zhelica stood below, watching the captain disappear from the wall before she ran back to the house.

The next morning after Marjon went out to help the workers, Zhelica stole into her aunt's room, scarf in hand. Standing before the small mirror that hung above her aunt's dresser, she braided her own hair, pinning it around her head like a crown. Then she took her scarf and wrapped it so that it covered her hair but not her neck. She took a deep breath, then hurried down the stairs and without stopping, burst through the front door.

No one looked up. They were all busy picking the last of the crop. She knew soldiers would arrive before noon to collect the boxes of plums that lined the road toward the gate. Seeing a group of women working a particular section of the orchard, Zhelica headed toward them.

The effect of her arrival was immediate. The pickers in the tree stopped, plums in hand. The young women on the ground also froze. Under her breath, one spoke to the worker next to her the word Zhelica had heard so often before: *"Alloy."*

Alloy. What did it mean? Whatever it was, once uttered, all the women melted back into activity. One laughed. Another said, "What are you doing here?"

"I came to help," Zhelica said.

The one who had called her the name leaned toward her and spoke, each word clipped. "We don't want your help."

They deliberately turned away and carried on with what they had been doing.

For a moment, Zhelica stood rooted. Why were they doing this? What was *wrong* with her?

Before she had a chance to return to the house, she heard another sharp voice.

"Zhelica!" It was Marjon. Zhelica turned to see her aunt marching toward her. The older woman's hair, disordered and sweaty around her scalp, bounced like a small bush. Her face was livid.

Zhelica moved to meet her. She reached to grasp her aunt's hands. They were shaking.

"It's all right, Aunt Marjon," she said, but her own voice was quavering. "I – I just wanted to see if I could help here."

Marjon pulled her toward herself and freed one hand so she could wrap her arm around Zhelica's shoulder. In a quiet but threatening voice, she said, "Go back to the house at once."

At that very moment the bell clattered and Marjon called a worker to open the gate. Once the bolts were lifted from the ground in the middle, both doors swung wide. Marjon shot her niece a warning look and headed toward the soldiers waiting up the hill.

Zhelica had always been compliant but today she stood her ground. Within her stirred a myriad of feelings: shock and pain at the rejection of the pickers, humiliation at her aunt insisting she return to the house, and a longing to see Captain Yavan.

He was there before his men and removed his cap to greet Marjon. Zhelica could see her aunt struggling to recover her composure as she motioned for the captain to back the carts into the orchard.

Zhelica, in full view, kept her place. The soldiers were busy positioning the carts, dropping the backs so they could load fruit. Captain Yavan moved among them, examining boxes of plums as they were stacked. Marjon walked beside him. She looked up and saw Zhelica still there. At the same moment, Captain Yavan glanced her direction.

Marjon's face blanched; the captain's lit up for an instant of recognition, then returned to its more professional expression. Still Zhelica did not move.

The plums loaded, soldiers latched the backs of the wagons and the captain gave the word for them to head back to base. Then he walked down the road with Marjon, his account book in hand.

He could not feign to miss Zhelica's presence.

When they came within a few feet of her, Captain Yavan turned calmly to Marjon and said, "Here is a new worker, I think."

Marjon said through gritted teeth, "She is not a worker, Captain Yavan. She is my niece."

He gasped as though surprised. "Why, Marjon, you never said you had a niece." He bowed to Zhelica. "So nice to meet you, Miss –"

"Zhelica," she and her aunt said simultaneously.

"And nice to meet you, as well, Captain –"

"Yavan," he said. He raised his eyebrows and Zhelica realized with a shiver that there was no way she would have known he was a captain without being told. Fortunately, Aunt Marjon was too upset to notice this gaffe.

"Zhelica, bring the captain and me some tea," she ordered.

They sat down at a table Marjon kept in front of the house, and Zhelica hastened indoors to heat water.

Her jubilance mingled with remorse. She had never openly defied her aunt before.

As soon as the tea was ready, she carried a tray with the pot and three cups out to the table. Marjon was speaking in low, urgent tones, but stopped as soon as Zhelica appeared.

"Just set it here and go back inside," Marjon said.

Captain Yavan seemed to be enjoying the apparent tension. "Come, Marjon, let your niece join us," he said, rising to pull out a chair for her. "Our business is finished."

A sack of coins lay near Marjon's hand, a confirmation of the captain's assertion. Marjon grumbled, "Fine." She watched attentively as Zhelica poured the amber liquid into a cup and handed it to her, and then poured a cup for Yavan. Zhelica avoided his eyes as she handed it to him.

"Thank you, Zhelica," he said. There was something about the way he said it that convinced Zhelica he was grinning. She looked up. He was.

"So," he said, sipping his tea, "where are you visiting from, Miss Zhelica?"

This question was so unexpected, she and Marjon gaped at each other. Finally, the older woman nodded, and Zhelica said, "I'm not visiting, Captain Yavan. I live here."

"Well, this is nice! I'm glad you won't have to be alone, Marjon," he said sweetly.

Zhelica's aunt was done with the game. "Zhelica has lived here for some time, Captain Yavan. But there did not seem a need for you to meet her."

He registered comprehension. "Of course," he said. "Why would I need to know your niece?" He dimpled at Zhelica. "Well, happy to meet you at last," he said.

Zhelica dropped her head, laughing silently.

Marjon fidgeted with her cup. Zhelica wasn't sure what to do next. Yavan resolved the awkwardness by polishing off his tea.

"I think we're done here," he said with a bow to each of the women. His eyes met Zhelica's, suppressed humor still apparent in them.

"Thank you for the tea and for your business, Marjon. I will return next week to talk about our fall order."

"Not next week," Marjon said. "Next month. The apples may be ripe by then."

He bowed. "All right, Marjon. I will be back in four weeks."

Yavan mounted his horse and tipped his hat toward Zhelica before leaving the orchard. Marjon handed a gold piece to each of the workers and they disappeared, chattering like a cloud of gnats. Single-handedly, she bolted the doors in place.

We are safe and alone again, Zhelica thought. She exhaled slowly and collected the teapot and cups.

Two

The next day Zhelica left her book behind when she escaped to the orchard. The nearly deafening sound of the cicadas thrumming in the afternoon air accompanied her as she wandered randomly under the trees. Arriving at the forked trunk, she knew she had been deceiving herself: Zhelica wanted to see if Captain Yavan, despite saying he would not be back for a month, would return.

She was not disappointed. He was already waiting at the foot of the wall, his horse tied across the road under a grove of pines. When her head appeared above the leaves, he hailed her.

"Marjon's niece! May I come up?"

Her heart leaped. "Of course," she said.

He mounted the wall and then said, "I think I can make it from here." With a leap, he landed on a sturdy branch near the edge of the property, and dropped to the ground. Standing beneath her, he said, "Come down."

As she lowered herself, he held out a hand to help her. Zhelica resisted and jumped beside him, brushing bits of bark from her skirt.

"Can we walk and talk here without waking your aunt?" Yavan asked.

"This way," Zhelica said. There was a path surrounding the trees near the wall. The captain whistled, occasionally stopping to pick up a stone and toss it against a high-hanging plum. When he knocked one loose, he caught it and handed it to Zhelica.

"Well, thank you very much," she said.

"My first gift to you," he replied, bowing.

"I'm glad you came back," Zhelica said, and then felt her face flush with embarrassment.

"Are you? Good. I plan on coming every day," he said. "You can't imagine how dull it gets only having other soldiers to talk to."

"Oh, I think I can," she replied softly.

Captain Yavan stepped in front of her, hands on his hips. "You find me dull?"

She laughed. "No, I just meant –" She shook her head. "I don't get to talk to anyone but my aunt. Needless to say, we don't have much new to discuss."

He nodded. "I can see that."

He didn't move, so Zhelica was forced to step around him. It was difficult not to notice his well-fitting uniform, his stance. The captain was a young man with a powerful presence.

He turned to follow her. "How long have you lived here with Marjon?" he asked.

"Since I was around six," she said. "My parents died and my aunt took me in, even though she was unmarried. She has raised me alone. I'm very grateful."

"I'm sure you are. If you don't mind me asking, how did your parents die?"

"I don't remember very much," Zhelica said. "They sent me to stay with Aunt Marjon when they got sick...some kind of plague going through the city at that time. A lot of people died. I never got to say goodbye," she added.

"That must have been hard," Captain Yavan said.

She nodded. Fragments of memories like crystals in a kaleidoscope rearranged themselves in her mind – a smile, a hand on her head, a song whose words were gone but with a tune that she found herself humming as she worked. No matter how hard she tried, she could never quite picture her mother and father. She cried a lot in the beginning, but over time life in the orchard seemed normal and her past with her parents like a dream.

She shook herself from her reflections. "Tell me about your family."

Captain Yavan spoke lightly. "I don't remember much about my parents, either," he said. "I was sent to the military boarding school when I was five years old, and they died shortly after that. I do remember the day when the headmaster called me into his office to tell me," he said, sobering. " 'Time to be a man, Yavan. You want a family? The army is your father and mother and brother.' " He shrugged, as though tossing off a painful memory. "And so it has been."

Zhelica had not had opportunity to read and interpret anyone besides her aunt. But instinctively she sensed that there was something here beyond Yavan's words. Without thinking, she extended her hand to touch his arm. "It must have been very difficult for you," she said. "The army doesn't seem like much of a replacement for family."

Before she realized what was happening, he grasped her hand and didn't let go. They walked on. Zhelica's mind was divided, half on what Yavan was saying, and half on the warmth of skin on skin. Her thoughts tugged from one to the other.

"I do have scattered recollections," he said. "You know – the scent of my mother. The tree in our backyard. My father was a carpenter; I remember watching him in the workshop."

"Why did they send you to military school?" Zhelica asked.

"That is what everyone in Baraqan did," Yavan said. "My best friend went, too. Afshar. And we both ended up based here. So I guess he is the closest thing to family for me." He kicked a branch out of their path. "Maybe sometime you can meet him."

"I'd like that," Zhelica said.

The hour passed quickly. Yavan said goodbye, squeezed her hand, and promised to return the next day.

Zhelica grew skilled at clandestine meetings, never letting a word escape to Marjon about what she and Yavan had discussed. It was as though she had been asleep and suddenly shaken awake. Every morning she rose excited at the prospect of that hour in the orchard with the captain. When she lay down at night, she closed her eyes and imagined what it would be like to run her fingers through his curly hair. Always in her mind Yavan was smiling.

One day he met her and said, "Can I take you for a ride?"

"You mean *outside* the walls?" Zhelica asked.

"Of course," he said. "We couldn't go very far in here. Plus I don't think I can lift Syah over the wall."

"Will we be back in time?" Zhelica asked. She had been so successful at hiding their rendezvous from Marjon she did not want to jeopardize them.

"Yes," he said. "I want to take you to one of my favorite places near here."

A few weeks before Zhelica would have been horrified at her own behavior. Meeting a man in secret, riding off to who-knew-where with a soldier: it sounded like the stuff of the old book she read in private. But the more time she spent with Yavan, the more she craved. With a nod of assent, she allowed him to help her over the wall and onto his horse.

"You'll have to wrap your arms around me," he said.

"Oh, I don't know. . ." she protested.

"The alternative is to fall off when the horse starts galloping," Yavan told her. Zhelica obediently embraced him, and with no notice, the captain dug his heels into Syah's side, and off they went.

At first, Zhelica clenched her eyes closed. Riding in the carriage was nothing like being on horseback. The air rushing past, the beat of hooves on the gravel road, the bouncing – it was terrifying. But when it seemed there was no risk she would fly off, Zhelica dared to peek around Yavan's shoulder.

They were headed the opposite direction of the town but did not go far before the captain slowed and turned off on a path into the forest. Zhelica did not even know there was a forest here. Between their orchard and town she had only seen fields of various crops, trees in mere clumps around houses.

The air was cooler even than the orchard, and much darker. Creeping plants and ferns covered the ground. As they descended, the air became moister. Yavan pulled up to a stop at the edge of a clearing.

"How was that?" he asked. Zhelica dropped her arms.

"I liked it," she said. "Once I got over my dread of being thrown from the horse."

He swung out of the saddle and lifted her down. "Have you ever been here before?"

She looked around. They were standing in a circle with a mosaic floor surrounded by trees. The tiny pieces of glass seemed to tell a story, with a castle beat by waves, a man standing in a garden, a crown lying on an island in the middle of a sea.

"It seems familiar, but I don't think so. What kind of place is this?"

Yavan wanted her to see it, yet he was evasive when it came to explaining. "Oh, it's one of the ancient places," he said. "Maybe the story is in your book."

Zhelica walked around the circle. She had a strange sensation: there was something significant about this place, but she did not know what. Simultaneously she sensed both that someone was there and that someone was missing. Sadness swept over her.

"I'll show you the river," Yavan said. He held out his hand, and she took it, as she always did now. There was something safe and reassuring about being connected to him that way.

A mist rose from the river as it crashed over rocks. Near the shore was a stone building with gaping windows and a doorway but no door.

"What a lovely place!" Zhelica said. "Why doesn't anyone live here anymore?"

"Why, indeed?" Yavan asked. He did not speak as though it was a mystery, however. They walked through the doorway into the simple home. It was completely bare. Zhelica leaned down near the window, and brushed her fingers along the stone. When she brought them up to the light, her hand was blackened.

"There must have been a fire," she said.

Yavan nodded. "That would explain why no one is here."

As they were leaving, Zhelica glanced up. "Yavan, look."

Over the doorway, they could see that once there had been words, but they had been mutilated, chiseled away, leaving gashes in the stone. Zhelica shivered. "I think something terrible must have happened here."

Yavan scanned her face and his whole mood changed. "Race you back to Syah!" he cried, and dropped her hand. He let out a gleeful laugh and ran up the trail. Zhelica forgot her feelings of foreboding and chased him. There was no way to pass him on the narrow path, and when they arrived back at the horse, he caught her up and swung her around.

"Beat you!" he said.

She felt dizzy, but not only as a result of being whirled. Yavan lifted her back onto Syah and settled himself in front of her. "Hang on," he said. "Back we go."

He rode with abandon, and Zhelica held on with a new consciousness, feeling his muscles tense as the horse's feet rose and fell on the road. When it was time to return to the orchard, she did not want to let go.

"I'll see you tomorrow," Yavan whispered. "I have a meeting with Marjon."

He helped her over the wall and back to the ground before disappearing.

Zhelica stood for a few moments after he left. The tingling of his presence was harder to shake off than it had ever been before.

A month had passed, and true to his word, Yavan returned to meet with Marjon. He arrived at the front gate in the afternoon. He had not come early to meet with Zhelica, and she was mystified. When Marjon approached the door, Zhelica hid among the trees to eavesdrop.

"Come sit by the house," Marjon said, guiding him down the path.

Captain Yavan asked, "Will your niece be joining us again?"

Marjon stopped abruptly. "Yavan, I saw the way you were looking at her the last time you were here. Stay away from her."

He threw out his hands innocently. "Marjon, you know me! What danger am I?"

Even from the distance at which she stood, Zhelica could see fire in her aunt's eyes. "You ask me that?" she hissed.

Zhelica felt every fiber awake. *What did that mean?*

"Fair enough," Yavan said. "But I have to be honest with you. I can't get her out of my mind."

Marjon stomped down the path. Yavan followed her in the open, Zhelica beneath the trees.

Her aunt slid into one of the chairs at the table in front of the house. Yavan did the same. Zhelica could see (with relief) that her aunt had already set out the tea.

"Yavan, she is like my own daughter," Marjon said. "Why do you think that I would let her spend time with a man like you?"

He folded his hands on the table in front of him. "Have you any complaints about my character?" Although his comments were often tinged with amusement, he seemed dead serious now.

"No, not your character," Marjon said, one hand on the teapot. "Not your character."

"You can't protect her forever," Yavan said. "You can't keep her like a canary in a cage, singing for your enjoyment until – what? What will happen when you're gone?"

Marjon's face dropped. "I don't know," she said mournfully. "She is safe here. Maybe she will take over the orchard."

Yavan laughed but not in his typically carefree way. "And then instead of dealing with one soldier who loves her, she will have to do business with several who view her either as a potential conquest or an enemy."

Marjon looked up at him. "Love her?" she repeated sharply. "How dare you say that? You have only seen her once."

It was Yavan's turn to look uncomfortable. "Dear Marjon," he said. They seemed, Zhelica thought, to be more than business associates; he spoke as though to an old friend. "She made such an impression on me. I couldn't resist."

Marjon started as though to rise, but he reached out and patted her arm. "Calm down," he said, not in a patronizing way, but to reassure her. "I've been speaking with her every day since I first saw her. I come after the noon meal when you are asleep."

Now Marjon did jump up. She was visibly quaking, and Zhelica recognized the rage in her face. "How could you! How could *she!*" She turned toward the house. "Zhelica!" she called. "Come out here right now!"

Zhelica was trembling, too. She emerged from the trees, so that by the time her aunt turned around, she was standing uncertainly behind Yavan.

Marjon rushed to her and began shaking her. "Zhelica! How could you! You have been sneaking around behind my back...with a *soldier*...like a common —"

She worked outside and was a strong woman. Zhelica, who would never think of harming her aunt, did not resist as Marjon grasped her shoulders and jerked her back and forth. "No, Auntie," she gasped, tears rushing to her eyes. "No, you don't understand."

Yavan did not wait. He pulled Marjon away. "Stop this!" he demanded. "Your niece has done nothing wrong."

Marjon was a wreck. She ran her hands over her always disordered hair, and swayed back and forth like a woman in grief. Yavan seemed uncertain which female to comfort, as they were both crying now.

"You come to my home," Marjon said to him. "I trusted you, and you have gone behind my back."

"I should have spoken to you," Yavan said. "But I knew you would say no."

"Aunt Marjon," Zhelica said. "We have only talked. He has always been kind and respectful toward me. He never insults me like other people do."

Marjon let out another sob. "The world is a hard place, Zhelica."

"I know," Zhelica said. "But Captain Yavan's right, Auntie. I can't be kept here forever away from it."

As soon as she said this, Zhelica's own tears slowed. She joined Yavan, who was near Marjon. The older woman still seemed in anguish, and Zhelica wrapped her arms around her. "Auntie, I love you. I will always love you."

"I promised your parents," Marjon moaned. "I promised I would protect you."

"And so you have," Zhelica said.

Forever after, Zhelica associated the ripening of apples with a turning in her own life. Marjon insisted that Yavan no longer appear during the lunch hour and instead come at night. Sometimes he joined them for dinner, and afterward they would walk at twilight in the orchard. One evening, Zhelica reached up and weighed an early-ripening apple in her palm before letting it bounce back in place.

"What does *'alloy'* mean?" she asked. It had fretted her since the worker spat it out so venomously.

Yavan took her chin in his hand, turning her face so he could look into her eyes. Apparently satisfied by what he saw, he let go, walking on as he explained. "An alloy is made by mixing two kinds of metal together," he said. "For example, brass. The smith takes copper and adds zinc, and you end up with a metal that can be shaped for different items – plates or doorknobs – which is better and stronger than either substance alone. Copper added to gold gives it a reddish color; if it's added to silver it makes it sturdier."

"So," Zhelica spoke softly, thinking carefully about what he had said, "An alloy is a good thing? Making something better than it would have been if you had kept the metals separate?"

Yavan took her hand. "Definitely better."

Zhelica had not asked her aunt about her experience. But Yavan would surely answer. "So why did the girls in the orchard call me *'alloy'*?"

Yavan's grasp tightened. The sky had darkened enough now so that it was harder to make out his expression. "It has to do with your family history," he said.

Zhelica waited, but he said nothing more.

"What about my family history?" she persisted.

Yavan cleared his throat. "This would be a good conversation to have with your Aunt," he said. "She'll know the whole story."

They headed back toward the house. "Zhelica, I have to leave town for a few days. I have some business up in the mountains."

"Oh." Even Zhelica could hear the disappointment in her own voice.

Yavan laughed. "Do not fear, my love," he said. "I'll be back. And when I come," he added, "I'll bring Afshar to meet you."

Her heart lifted at this news. "I'll be glad to finally meet him."

"Yes, you will," Yavan said with a grin. "He's my opposite. Well-behaved, quiet. Even Marjon will like him."

Before they entered the house, he gently kissed her forehead. "I will be back."

The following nights the two women sat quietly, mending clothes by the light of lanterns hung around their front room. It felt cozy, with the evenings cooling as autumn approached. Periodically Zhelica glanced up at her aunt. She had been uncharacteristically accepting of Yavan once he began coming in earnest to see her niece. Zhelica hated to break the gentle peace of the hour before bed, but she *had* to know the answer to her question.

"Aunt Marjon," she began, trying to sound nonchalant, "Yavan was telling me about how alloys are made."

Marjon dropped the garment she had been working on. She looked as though someone had slapped her.

"How did that come up?" she asked.

"Sometimes," Zhelica began, considering each word with care, "I have heard people say *'alloy'* when they see me. In town, or in the orchard."

Her aunt bit her lip, and finding her needle, resumed her work without looking at Zhelica.

"So what did Yavan tell you?"

Zhelica mindlessly crushed and released the dress she held between her fingers. "He explained about metals," she said. "Mixing copper with gold or silver. Making brass." She paused. "But when I asked him why people said *'alloy'* to me, he told me it had something to do with my family history, and I should ask you."

Marjon seemed surprised by this, and a little smile played at the corners of her often-severe mouth. "Well, good for Yavan," she said. She kept stitching.

"So," Zhelica continued, "I was wondering if you could tell me more about our family."

Marjon completely abandoned her sewing. She pinned the needle safely into place, folded the tattered leggings she had been fixing, and set them into a basket beside her. Zhelica watched as her aunt went to a drawer of the cabinet nearby. She pulled out a small mirror and came and sat down next to Zhelica. Leaning close to her niece, she held the mirror so that both their faces reflected back. Zhelica was puzzled.

"What do you notice when you look at us?" Marjon asked.

Zhelica scrutinized the images facing them. "Well," she began, "I am younger than you."

"Go on," her aunt urged her.

"Your skin," Zhelica said. "It's darker than mine, like other people here." She had thought it before, but never said it aloud.

"Yes," Marjon said.

"And your hair – it's dark brown, except where it has turned white," Zhelica said, turning from the mirror to touch the wisps that haloed her aunt's face.

"And *your* hair?" Marjon prompted.

"It is. . ." Zhelica gazed into the mirror. How would she describe it? Not like an apple or even a peach. More like one of the dark carrots they brought from the bazaar. "It's orange," she said.

"Most people would call it 'red'," Marjon told her. "There is another thing – do you see what it is?"

How many times Zhelica had glanced in the mirror, and yet how little she knew herself! She pored over her own features. They were both women, both had ears, nose, mouth, eyes.

Her eyes.

"My eyes are not brown," she said.

"You're right," Marjon told her. "Your eyes are the beautiful green of the orchard in summer."

Zhelica grabbed the mirror and moved closer to one of the lanterns. Her own eyes stared back at her. What story did they tell?

"Why am I different?" she asked.

"Things changed here a few decades ago," Marjon said. "People immigrated from Darz and lived and worked in Zaharada. They married local men and women and had families. But their children weren't like other babies. Instead of having dark skin and bark-brown eyes like the Zaharadans, or blonde hair and blue eyes like the Darzians, they were all fair-skinned redheads with green eyes. Like you."

The room was silent. Zhelica's head was spinning. "So, one of my parents was Darzian?"

"Your father," Marjon said.

Zhelica collapsed into the nearest chair. It seemed like she would remember a blond father. All the imagined scenes of her with her parents had always involved dark-skinned, dark-eyed Zaharadans. The image of a mother rocking her to sleep, a father singing her a lullaby: they had been people like Marjon.

"And," she asked, "the term for people like me, people who have parents from the two countries?"

Marjon shook her head. "It isn't kind," she said. "But they call them *'alloys.'* To them, you are like a mix of two metals."

"But that's a good thing," Zhelica asserted, pulling herself upright. "An alloy is stronger than either metal on its own. That's what Yavan said."

Marjon's eyes softened. "That can be true. But sometimes an alloy is a mix of a valuable metal with a cheaper one. Like adding tin to copper to make the mugs we use for the workers. We don't worry if they get damaged, because they are inexpensive versions of the nicer mugs we use in the house."

The obvious nature of the insult now dawned on Zhelica. "I see," she said. "My Zaharadan blood is the copper. My Darzian side is tin." She held out her hands, as though examining their incriminating whiteness. "They can tell by looking what kind of person I am."

Marjon rose and put an arm around her. This was the most tender her aunt had been with her in a long time. When she looked up, she could see unspilled tears rimming the older woman's eyes.

"They make assumptions about you," Marjon said. "Of course they're untrue. But there are so few people like you here anymore ...most have moved away. . ." her voice trailed off.

"Is that why you have me wear scarves?"

Marjon nodded. "From a distance, they might not see that your skin is lighter, but your hair is like a beacon shining out your heritage." She smiled. "Your father was a remarkable person, Zhelica. He was a brave, big-hearted man. And he loved you."

"How did he meet my mother? What did your family think of them marrying?"

Marjon passed a hand over her face, wiping away the tears. "I'm tired, child," she said. "Why don't I answer your questions another time?"

The hours passed as Zhelica pondered on her window seat that night. She tried to visualize her dark-haired mother, someone like the beautiful young women working in the orchard.   And her father ...she had not seen a Darzian, only representations of them in Marjon's old book. What had it been like for him to live in a land where he was a minority, someone who stood out? This was something she had experienced a little already, despite her brief contact with the world outside.

And the nagging question: why would Captain Yavan of the army of Zaharada be interested in her, a mongrel person, a crossbred *alloy?* She slept fitfully that night, worrying.

Three

Arriving after his trip, Yavan allayed Zhelica's fears. Once he and his friend Afshar had led their horses inside and tied them to a hitching post, the captain caught Zhelica up and swung her around. She could not help laughing, and clutched her scarf to keep it from flying off her head.

"Put me down!" she cried, and Yavan complied, giving her an affectionate squeeze.

Afshar watched, neither laughing nor frowning. His eyes shifted from one to the other like a dog trying to guess whether his master had thrown the ball or still held it in his hand.

"Zhelica, as I promised, I have brought you my very best friend in all the world." He winked as he said it, as though to reassure her of her place in his heart. She inclined her head.

"I'm very glad to meet you, Afshar," she said.

He bowed awkwardly. Although the same age as the captain, his gangly limbs gave him a boyish appearance.

"Yavan has been talking about you day and night," he said. He managed a quick grin.

"Is that so? I hope we'll be friends anyway." She returned his smile. "Come down by the house and I'll bring you some tea."

While the sun shone, the days were still comfortable, and the soldiers stretched out on the chairs by Marjon's outdoor table. The gentle fragrance of ripe apples wafted toward them on a breeze. "About time to collect those," Yavan said, with a nod.

"Would you like me to pick you one?" Zhelica asked.

Yavan pulled her close to him. "No, stay here," he murmured. She wiggled free and poured them both cups of tea, then deliberately sat down across from Yavan. His dark eyes pleaded, but she shook her head firmly.

"So how long have you two known each other?" Zhelica asked Afshar.

He drummed his long fingers on the table and cleared his throat. "I don't know...since we were toddlers, maybe? Then we lived together at the military academy."

"Yes, I remember now...Yavan mentioned that," she said. "And your family – where are they?"

Afshar shot a look at Yavan and squirmed in his chair. Apparently getting no help from his friend, Afshar said, "Oh, kind of all over. I don't see them much." He appeared concerned with a crack in the table, running a finger over it as he spoke.

Zhelica looked at Yavan quizzically, but he just smiled and shrugged. "We didn't see anyone outside the academy often. We hardly ever left the school," the captain said. "Study, study, study."

At this Afshar bellowed, slapping the table. "What a liar!" he cried. "Is that what he told you? That we were good little boys?"

He leaned forward, spinning the cup around on its saucer. "Yavan was off campus as much as he could get away with."

"Not alone," Yavan said, his eyes sparkling.

"I had to go with you to make sure you didn't get into too much trouble," Afshar contended. "Did he ever tell you about the time we pushed over the statue?"

"Afshar. . ." Yavan began warningly.

"No, he didn't," Zhelica said, looking from one to the other. "That sounds like an interesting story."

"Afshar. . ." Yavan protested.

"The school is housed in the old palace, up in the mountains," Afshar began. He spoke like he moved, furtively, jerkily. "The walls are stone, and the windows have bars on them so the boys won't escape. But Yavan figured out a way to extract the pins that held the bars in place, and at night we would wait until everyone was asleep, and he'd pull those things out and we'd go exploring."

Afshar's face lit up with the memory of it. "One night, we made it all the way to Baraqan."

"How old were you at this point?" Zhelica asked.

Reluctantly, Yavan said, "Twelve or so."

Afshar continued. "In the center of the town square was this statue of the founder of the academy, General Semak. Frankly, we were pretty tired of school at that time. So Yavan climbs up and whispers down to me, 'Afshar, I think we can topple this thing.' Well, I'm not a troublemaker (I'm not! Don't believe him) and I tell him to get down. But Yavan has discovered that the statue is standing on a brick base, and he starts chiseling away. It took hours. But finally, he got enough loosened at the back.

" 'Afshar, come up here quick. We'll push him over and then run.' "

Afshar shook his head, whether in real or feigned disgust, Zhelica did not know. "You should have heard the crash," he said.

Yavan threw his head back and laughed. "What a noise that thing made! We didn't dare stick around to see what would happen. We ran all the way back to the academy, climbed in the window, and crawled into bed."

"Which would have been all right," Afshar added, "except Yavan forgot to put the bars back on the window."

Yavan gestured as though rubbing his back. "We got a beating for that."

"We sure did," Afshar grimaced. "And a welder came that day to make sure our bars never came off the window again."

"Did they figure out it was you that pushed the statue over?" Zhelica asked.

They both shook their heads. "No," Yavan said. "It might have been the end of our military career if they had." His dimples appeared, and he tried to reach out a foot to touch Zhelica's, but she tucked her own under her chair and shook a finger at him.

Marjon appeared and was introduced to Afshar. She did not seem inclined to join their party, but did tell Yavan they would start picking apples in the morning.

"Bring the cart in three days," she said. "They should all be boxed up by then."

"Good," Yavan said. He took a last drink from his cup and set it down. "We better get on our way," he said. "I just wanted to make sure you had an opportunity to meet Afshar."

Zhelica smiled at the lanky young man. "You're welcome any time," she said.

"Thank you," he answered, stumbling as he extricated his tangled limbs from the chair. "I'll probably be back, since I still need to keep an eye on Yavan."

Zhelica gave him a knowing smile and walked with them to the gate. Yavan was more circumspect now that Marjon was outside. He tipped his hat to Zhelica as she swung the doors shut. "See you soon!" he called.

The next morning, Marjon told Zhelica she wanted her to join the workers in the orchard.

"Really?"

Zhelica was washing the breakfast dishes, and she stopped, a plate in midair. Marjon never allowed her outside during harvesting, especially after her last attempt at helping.

"I have been thinking," the older woman said, her fingers deftly braiding her own hair as she spoke. "If you are going to mingle with others, you better get used to how they speak and act."

"Of course," Zhelica slowly replied. Although she had yearned to work alongside the young women, now that she had permission, she was scared. What if they did more than mock her? Would her aunt step in to rescue her? Or was she trying to force Zhelica into a corner, to make her see that a relationship with someone like Yavan was untenable?

She dried her hands and began tying a scarf around her hair.

"You won't need that," Marjon said quietly.

Zhelica's heart beat so loudly she thought her aunt would hear it. But the older woman continued organizing her work equipment – soft leather gloves, a basket, shears in case she needed to trim a branch.

"I'll be down in a minute," Zhelica said. She tripped up the stairs, knowing there was little time. The bell jangled as the first of the laborers arrived.

Zhelica imitated Marjon, arranging her hair into a single braid. She changed into a worn work dress and returned to the kitchen.

Marjon looked her over. "Good," she said. "Let's go."

Zhelica shadowed her aunt as she greeted the workers and assigned them sections of the orchard to pick. They went off in pairs, each with a basket. Every one of them gave Zhelica a poisonous look when Marjon turned away. Zhelica tried not to react, hoping they would see she was not threatened by them.

When all the workers had dispersed, leaving only young men who squatted by the house nailing boards together to form crates, Marjon said to Zhelica, "I am giving you the job reserved for those starting out." She swept her arm beneath the trees. "You see how many ripe apples have already fallen? Your responsibility is to retrieve those. If they are not bruised or damaged, put them in the nearest crate. If they are, collect them in your basket and put them in the bin by the house. We will make applesauce or cider from those."

How disappointing! Rather than the pleasure of plucking individual fruit, she would be bent over, traveling beneath one team after another, her hands in the dust. She sighed but dutifully shouldered the basket and began her work.

The apple orchard was off to the side of the house, where the pickers were invisible until someone stood next to their tree. Marjon was out of view within a moment. As Zhelica started on the first row, scanning the ground for fallen fruit, she heard the word.

"Alloy." It pelted down on her from the tree tops as she passed. Zhelica did not look up. Here was an apple, nearly perfect, with only a bruise on one side. She gently dropped it into the basket. There was a cracked one carried off in tiny chunks by a line of ants. She stepped over it. Some apples lay in groups, easily retrieved. Rarely were they undamaged. Zhelica became adept at assessing their quality as she collected them. Her burden grew heavy. If it were not for the words hurled at her, Zhelica might have enjoyed even this labor. But the pickers did not rest with calling her *alloy;* now they whispered questions like accusations.

"Where's your daddy, *alloy*?" one asked. "Did he run like a coward? Or did he drop dead when he saw your ugly face?"

Zhelica still did not look up as they taunted her. Her load tore at her shoulders, but she dared not turn back to empty the basket, not wanting them to get the gratification of apparently driving her from the orchard.

"Traitor!" one of the young men said in a voice loud enough only for her ears. Zhelica heard a guttural sound and suddenly realized a glob of saliva was running down her head.

This time she straightened up and her eyes met those of the worker. Curly hair, tan skin, brown eyes...it could have been Yavan's brother. The young man even grinned, but it was not a happy, affectionate smile. He was mimicking her, feigning to reach up to discover damp hair, something nasty running down his face. In her mind's eye, the worker suddenly transformed into a soldier.

Zhelica could not stay. She turned quickly and almost lost her balance with the weight of the apples at her back.

"Careful there, little *alloy*," the picker said. "Don't want to fall back down into the dirt from which you came."

She could not run, so she took steady, measured steps. Apparently someone else had been picking up the windfalls, too, so the bin was partially filled. Zhelica lowered herself to the ground and drew her arms from the basket's shoulder straps. As she tossed fruit into the bin, she realized her face was wet – not with spittle from an adversary, but from her own tears. She finished quickly and hurried into the house. No one must see her like this.

Zhelica was quiet during lunch. She was tired from the stooping, her heart mashed like an overripe apple by the incessant derision. But she would say nothing to Marjon about what had happened.

"I will see you after naps," her aunt said, and for once Zhelica followed, collapsing on her own bed. She did not know she could sleep in the afternoon – it had been so long – but weariness overcoming her, she dropped off so fast she was startled when Marjon sat down on the edge of the mattress.

Her aunt gently brushed the hair from Zhelica's forehead. "You must have been tired today," she said. "Do you want to stay in this afternoon?"

Zhelica shook her head as she sat up. "No, I want to work."

They slung on their baskets. "This time you can pick instead of collecting windfalls," Marjon said. She found the other girl who had been retrieving apples from the ground and showed them where she wanted them to start.

The other new laborer did not insult Zhelica, but she did not engage her in conversation, either. When she looked over to check on Zhelica's progress, she chided her.

"You are too rough with the apples," she said. "Treat them like eggs. Watch me." She reached for a red one and quickly twisted the stem. The apple dropped into her palm. "You can do two at once if you're careful." She demonstrated her technique, opening her hand to show two flawless globes nestled there. "And don't just toss them into the basket! They'll be as bashed as the windfalls if you do that." She showed Zhelica how she rested the fruit on top of what she had already collected. "I'll help you pack them when you get a few more."

Zhelica was so relieved to be treated civilly, she worked with new vigor. When the young man who had called her a traitor passed her, she watched him swiftly line a crate with fruit, tossing in hay to cushion it before packing another layer. He popped on a lid and returned to the orchard for more. When he saw Zhelica, he leaned to the side and let out a stream of spittle. Then he gave her one of his wicked smiles.

The afternoon went smoother than the morning. With only two working together, there was no opportunity for the others to harass her. After the pickers left for the day, she and Marjon walked through the orchard assessing what they had accomplished.

"I'm proud of you," Marjon said. "You're a hard worker."

"Thank you," Zhelica answered.

"Another day like that and we'll be done," her aunt said.

When the bell jangled from the front of the house, Zhelica said, "It must be Yavan."

Marjon sighed. "He is welcome to join us for dinner. Unless you are too tired."

"Not at all!" Zhelica answered, and to prove it, she ran through the trees to the gate. She peered through the little door, just to be sure, and her suspicions confirmed, she pulled up the bolts, opening the gates far enough to allow Yavan and Syah in.

"Well, look at you," Yavan said as he jumped down. His eyes twinkled. "My apple-picking maiden." He reached out and laid a hand on her head, and she shuddered. It was the very spot on which spit had landed. Yavan sensed her response. "What's wrong?"

"Just a little weary," she said. "Come down to the house. Aunt Marjon has invited you for dinner."

He did not move. "Wait, before we go in, let's watch the sun go down." He led her back to their old haunt, the tree near the wall. One of the bricks came loose as he stepped on it. He examined the wall. "This reminds me of a statue I saw once. I think with a little work we could push it over," he said with a laugh. He climbed up and then gave her a hand. The leaves were already changing, glowing golden against the darkening sky. They pushed through and settled onto the wall, their feet swinging over the road outside.

It was a glorious sunset – dazzling on the horizon, with beams shooting out shafts like a great crown. The few clouds were crimson melting into the purple and blue of the sky above.

Zhelica inched closer to Yavan, wanting the comfort of his thigh against hers on that cool wall. He put an arm around her, and her eyes smarted with tears stored up from the day. She brushed them away, hoping he would not see.

"You know what's more beautiful than this?" he whispered. He looked into her face. "*You* are, Zhelica."

He could see now that she was crying. "Oh, what's the matter?"

"It's nothing," she said, but having started, she was finding it difficult to stop. Finally, she managed, "One of the workers spit on me today."

Through her tears, she could see Yavan's face harden. "Who did this? Which one?"

Zhelica shrugged. "I don't know. It doesn't matter."

"Of course it matters," Yavan said. "I'll talk to Marjon."

Zhelica pressed a hand against his chest. "No, Yavan," she said, sniffling, desperate to control herself. "It will only convince her I'm not able to live outside these walls."

He drew her closer. The tears had run their course, and Zhelica rested in the afterglow of the sunset and her spent misery. They both watched until the clouds faded to gray.

"Zhelica," Yavan said, his voice as soft as the twilight, "Let's get married."

Confused, she pulled away. "Yavan, what are you saying?"

He laughed and squeezed her shoulder. "You'll survive outside the walls, Zhelica. You will be with me and I'll protect you. I love you, Zhelica."

The light was so dim now she could not see his dimples or the way his lashes hung over his dark eyes. But she reached up and laid her palm on his cheek.

"Really, Yavan? You would want to marry me – an *alloy*? Won't people hate you for loving me?"

"Never mind them, Zhelica," he said soothingly. "We will be our own fortress. We will be stronger together than either of us alone. I love you, Zhelica. Please say you will be my wife."

There, in the dark on the wall (even as the voice of Marjon winged over the orchards calling them to dinner), Zhelica and Yavan kissed. And she said yes.

It was hard to contain themselves during dinner. Yavan told Zhelica he would talk to Marjon alone before leaving. During the meal they merely exchanged glances, excited at their secret. Marjon, her aging body drooping from the day's labor, did not notice.

Finally, Yavan spoke. "Zhelica, would you excuse your aunt and me? I have some business I would like to discuss with her."

Zhelica rose. "Let me have your plates," she said, stacking them innocently before disappearing. But she could not resist listening; after setting the dishes in the sink she stood in the hallway close enough to hear.

"So," came the voice of Yavan. To Zhelica's surprise, it was not tinged with the humility of a supplicant asking for blessing on his marriage to her niece. He sounded ready to reprimand. "You sent her out a lamb into that pack of wild dogs?"

Marjon snorted. "There you go again! As though what I want for her is worse than what you have planned."

"Did what you had hoped happen? Was she so ill-treated that she begged to be locked away forever in this house?"

Marjon must have risen from the table; her voice sounded farther away now. "That's not fair. I only wanted to prepare her for what it would be like if she left home."

Yavan lowered his voice, apparently uninterested in following the older woman around the room. "She is not fragile," he said. "She can endure whatever they throw at her."

Marjon gave a bitter laugh. "Oh, Yavan, how easy it is for you to ask her to face that! She has been with me since she was a child. I care about her far more than you ever could. And I don't want her to have to endure things being thrown at her."

This must have been too much for the young soldier. The chair scraped against the carpet as he stood. "There are two kinds of love, Marjon. There is a love that possesses and holds back. And there is a love that gives freedom and life."

Marjon emitted what sounded like a sob. Zhelica's hand flew to her mouth. She could not bear to hear her aunt like this.

"Is that what you have to offer?" Marjon choked. "Freedom and life?"

"And love," Yavan answered. "I love her, Marjon, despite your conviction that mine was only a passing interest. She is not only the most beautiful woman I have ever seen. Her heart is like a fresh mountain spring. Let her go, Marjon. Let her marry me."

Zhelica could hardly breathe. For a moment, the only sound coming from the room was the gentle crash of embers buckling in the fireplace. Marjon cleared her throat.

"If she wants to marry you," she said sadly, "you have my permission. I only ask that you never tell her of our other connection. If you truly want to give her life and freedom, you will not speak of that."

More silence. And then Yavan replied. "Fine. If that is your wish."

"It is," Marjon said.

"Then let me call her back in here," Yavan said. "Zhelica!"

She hesitated so that they would not know she had been hovering beyond the doorway. And then she rushed in.

Yavan was holding out his hands to her, his dimples casting tiny shadows across his cheeks. Marjon stood by the mantel, clumsily smoothing her hair.

"She said yes!" Yavan said, clasping her hands in his. "We may marry!"

Knowing at what cost this concession had been granted, Zhelica quickly squeezed Yavan's hands and then dropped them, throwing her arms around Marjon. "Oh, thank you, Auntie," she whispered. "I love him so much. I know he will be a good husband to me and a good son to you."

But Marjon said nothing. She merely gave her niece a hug that felt strangely like a farewell.

Four

That night Zhelica could not sleep. She tried. She rearranged her covers; she threw them off. She stared at the black of the ceiling until fanciful patterns undulated before her eyes. She listened to Marjon's snoring and started up every time there was a longer-than-normal pause in its rhythm.

Finally, exhausted in body but alert in mind, she lit the lamp and softly closed her bedroom door. She would read. She went to the cupboard where she had hidden Marjon's storybook and drew it out. Sinking onto the floor next to the bed, she turned its pages, re-reading tales she had perused before.

She thought of Yavan's comment the first time they sat together on the orchard wall: "Some think they are myths." There was definitely something in the style of writing that reminded her of a good story. But they were not fantastic: every detail seemed authentic, every description beautiful but realistic. They seemed like true accounts.

She decided to read from that perspective. "There was a princess who came from Bustaan," she read. "She crossed the border of Zaharada in search of the king. When she was discovered, the men of Darab captured her and threw her into prison, fearing she was involved with a plot to overthrow the king. But then she had a dream . . ."

The dream was mysterious, hinting at magic. So perhaps this book *was* filled with tales created as entertainment for passing the long winter nights.

She remembered the mosaic circle in the forest where Yavan had taken her. The pictures on its floor reminded her of the book. She flipped through the pages and found an illustration of the castle. It looked just like the mosaic, including the waves that struck against the cliff next to the palace.

The story accompanying the picture was of a visit by the King of Darz. None of the figures in the painting had faces – everything was too small. But as Zhelica scanned the miniature crowd watching the King of Zaharada and the King of Darz shaking hands on the palace balcony, she began to notice details. Most of the tiny figures had dark hair, the men clad in dun tunics and the women in brightly colored dresses. But then, to her surprise, she noticed there were blond heads, too, among those standing below the leaders. And as she looked more closely, she saw that the depictions of children being held showed some with hair as red as her own.

Zhelica dropped the book into her lap and rubbed her eyes. Whether these were fiction or truth, they did confirm what Marjon had told her – there were others like her here at one time. *Where did they all go?* she wondered. She picked up the book again and instead of reading, she turned one page after another, trying to find more depictions of red-haired people. They were there, but always children; there were no adults.

She closed the book and ran her finger over the cover. *Tales of Zaharada* was imprinted in gold, and below was a circle stamped *25th anniversary reign of King Sanjar.*

Zhelica knew so little of her country. She must ask Yavan to tell her more. Somehow she sensed that Marjon would not be interested in talking about the past. That was probably why she kept this book buried in a cupboard.

Although her mind was now awhirl with questions, Zhelica's body told her to go to bed. She tucked the book away and climbed back under her covers. Her last thought in the state between waking and sleep was of the painting of the crowd. One of the red-haired children turned and she saw her own face smiling back.

When the first rooster crowed the next morning, Zhelica groaned. She was so tired. She urged herself to get up, but her body refused to cooperate. When Marjon opened the door, she managed to sit up.

"I'm sorry, Auntie," she said, stretching. "I had trouble sleeping last night."

Marjon nodded. She looked blanched, with purple rings under her eyes, as though she had not slept well, either. "And yet it is a picking day today. Do you want to work in the orchard or make applesauce?"

Zhelica felt vulnerable. She knew she would have trouble resisting tears if harassed by the other workers. "May I cook applesauce?"

Marjon nodded. "Come down when you're ready and I'll get you started."

Zhelica dressed slowly, her arms heavy. She realized it was not only staying up too late that was affecting her; her muscles were sore, too. Marjon must be even more worn out.

But they kept busy enough that day to scarcely think of anything else. Zhelica stood in the back garden near the apple peeler, which Marjon had attached to an old table. Her aunt showed her how to force the apple onto a central prong and crank the handle to turn the apple, dropping peels and cores.

These were saved for jelly and vinegar. The apples Zhelica threw into a massive kettle suspended over a pile of wood. When it was half filled, she scooped sugar and cinnamon into the kettle and one of the workers started a fire. Zhelica spent the afternoon mashing the mixture until it reached the perfect consistency. Then Marjon helped her ladle it into jars and lid them, lining the table with so much applesauce she wondered how they would ever get rid of it.

It amazed her to think that in the past Marjon had done all this herself. She had spent time and energy shielding Zhelica from the abuse of workers by keeping her indoors. Zhelica felt ashamed of her complaints against her aunt.

By evening not only were all the bruised apples converted to applesauce, but crates rested at the end of every row in that section of the orchard. As the light faded, the brightness of the freshly split wood made the boxes visible after the tree trunks melted into the dark.

"It's getting chilly," Zhelica said, rubbing her arms.

"Yes, let's go in," Marjon said.

Zhelica was waiting – she knew she was waiting – for Yavan to arrive. She walked slowly toward the house, wondering why he was so late tonight. She almost did not hear the tapping at the gate.

Marjon was already inside, and lantern light poured through the front window. Zhelica mustered strength to her limbs and walked as briskly as she could to the gate. She knew it would be too dark to recognize a face through the tiny door.

"Yes?" she asked loudly. "Is someone there?"

"It's me, Afshar," came the soldier's voice, quieter than Zhelica's.

Zhelica swiftly unbolted one side of the gate. She could see Afshar's thin form in the dim light from the house. Yavan was not with him.

"Come in," Zhelica said, and pushed the gate closed behind him without bolting it.

"Sorry to bother you," Afshar said. He fumbled with his jacket, pulling out a piece of paper. "Yavan asked me to bring you this."

There was no way to read it. "Did he want a response?" Zhelica asked, turning the note over in her hands.

"No. I need to go now," Afshar said. While speaking, he glanced around as though someone might be watching.

"Would you like to stay for dinner?"

"Thank you, but I really need to go," the soldier said. He had already stepped into the road. "Good night," he whispered.

"Good night," she said. He disappeared down the road and Zhelica carefully latched the gate.

When she entered the front room, Marjon was kneeling by the hearth, rekindling the morning's fire. The table was already set for dinner.

"Where have you been?" she asked.

"I'm sorry, Auntie," Zhelica apologized. "I didn't mean for you to do all the work. I heard something at the door, and Afshar brought me this." She held up the note.

Marjon rose, rubbing her lower spine. "What is it?"

Zhelica unfolded the note. She skimmed it, and then, instead of re-reading it to Marjon (there were terms of affection there her aunt might scorn), she said, "Yavan had some business in the mountains and will see me soon."

Marjon frowned. "He knows the apples are ready to pick up tomorrow," she said. "I hope he has made arrangements for them to be taken to the base."

They sat down to eat. Whether it was tiredness or something else, Marjon said nothing more.

"Let me clean up," Zhelica offered, and carried the dishes back to the kitchen. She washed as quickly as she could. When she returned to the front room, Marjon was seated in her favorite chair, rearranging the logs on the fire with her poker. She glanced up at Zhelica and still said nothing.

"Is something wrong?" Zhelica asked, dropping down at her aunt's feet.

Marjon put a hand on her cheek and gave a feeble smile. "I was just thinking about what it will be like when you are gone."

Zhelica put her hand over her aunt's. "It's not like I won't see you often," she said reassuringly. "We won't be far away, you know."

"You will need to live closer to the base. Maybe I can come once or twice a week to visit."

"I'm sure Yavan will bring me here, too. He likes your cooking," she added. They both laughed.

The next morning the women rose later. The pickers had been paid and would not return until the nut harvest in another month. In the meantime, Zhelica and her aunt had only to care for themselves and direct the soldiers who came to collect the fruit.

They arrived in the early afternoon, backing their carts into the orchard and retrieving crates of apples with wheelbarrows before stacking them securely to haul away. Zhelica had covered her hair again and hung back, watching the men work. She longed for Yavan to be among them. His assistant filled out the paperwork and handed Marjon money for the fruit. The older woman waved them out.

"Well, we have a little peace now," she said. Leaves had started falling from trees around the property, and they crackled as she and Zhelica walked along the rows, enjoying the sight of branches well-plucked.

"So, what should we do while we wait for the nuts to ripen?" Zhelica asked, dropping onto a rough bench between the plum and apple trees.

"Why don't we make a trip to town?" Marjon suggested. "We could sell the applesauce and start collecting your wedding clothes."

"Wedding clothes?" Zhelica had never heard of such a thing. "What sort of wedding clothes?"

Marjon shook her head. "How could I expect you to know? You need a special outfit for your wedding day, and it's customary to prepare a trunk of clothes to take with you to your new home."

This sounded promising. "Can we go tomorrow?"

The next day Marjon encouraged her to wear a scarf. "It is better not to draw too much attention to ourselves. I'll wear one, too."

They brought out the one horse Marjon kept for use around the orchard and for trips, and attached it to the carriage. "Let's both sit up front," she said.

It was a clear autumn day, and Zhelica relished the drive. They could see where winter wheat crops had recently been gathered, their sheaves propped like cones to dry. They passed vineyards where laborers were cutting off ripe grape clusters and laying them in baskets. They waved at the women as they rolled by.

Farmland went right up to the edge of Hyarani. Its brick buildings, more stylish than their own white-washed adobe house, were laid out in an orderly fashion. It was the first time Zhelica had traveled without the top up on the carriage. She noted the tidy, cobbled streets, and the trees shading front yards of shops and homes.

Something about the people, even though they were occupied with shopping and other business, made her self-conscious. She adjusted her scarf, tucking strands of hair beneath it as Marjon had often done before.

"There is a shop here that usually buys all the jars of applesauce I can bring," Marjon said, pulling up by a grocer's. "Wait here, and I'll get the boy to bring them in."

The pale fall sunlight felt good on her face, and Marjon was not long in reappearing. A boy clambered into the back of the carriage and handed down each golden jar to the shopkeeper, who carted them inside. When they were finished, he gave a purse full of coins to Marjon. Neither man nor boy noticed Zhelica.

Her aunt drove around the corner onto a busier street, stopping in front of a store with lace-curtained windows. "This is the fabric shop," she said.

Zhelica had never been allowed inside any stores on trips with Marjon. She marveled at the rows of fabric, bolts like volumes on shelves, arranged by type and color. She could not resist running her fingers over them – woolens, cheap cotton for work clothes, silks. When she looked up at Marjon, her aunt's face reflected her own pleasure at the variety and beauty she saw.

"First, you should pick out some silk," Marjon said. "I think with your hair color blue or green would look best on you."

The clerk came and pulled out the bolts they indicated, heaving them on to the counter and spreading the cloth so they could get a better idea of how each draped. Zhelica tried to ignore the woman's stares, leaning over to look closely at the fabric.

"I like this one," she said. Marjon held it up. The forest green silk shimmered as it moved, seeming to animate the pattern of leaping deer woven into it.

"Yes, that is very pretty," her aunt said. She turned to the clerk. "How much is this?"

"Three zahars for each length," the woman said.

"And for a wedding gown? How much would be required?"

The woman gave a little cough. "Red is the customary color for a wedding dress, madam," she said coolly.

Marjon stamped her foot. "I know that! But we want the green. How many lengths of cloth?"

"Five lengths," the clerk said.

Zhelica pulled Marjon's sleeve and stepped away from the counter. "Aunt Marjon, that's too expensive. I don't need such fine cloth."

Her aunt's eyes flashed. "You will have a magnificent dress," she insisted. "If you want the green, that's what you will have."

The clerk obediently cut the cloth while Zhelica and her aunt collected other bolts of more simple textiles for undergarments and other daily wear. In the end, a stack of new fabric folded into varying thicknesses lay at the end of the counter. The clerk wrote up the bill and handed it to Marjon.

"If you would like to pay in installments, we can make arrangements."

"Nonsense. I will pay now," Marjon said. And she did, counting coin after coin until her money purse was considerably lightened. The clerk wrapped the fabric in paper and tied it with a string.

"Good day, madam," she said, holding out the parcel.

"Hmph," Marjon responded. Zhelica gave a sheepish smile as they exited the shop.

"Auntie, you were a bit hard on her," she said.

Marjon was walking quickly, and Zhelica took the package to carry herself. "Rude, rude," her aunt muttered. "City people."

She seemed to know where she was going. The next stop was a tailor's. Zhelica's scarf was knocked askew as she maneuvered around a rack of hanging tunics and jackets, and she had to remove it before winding it around her head again. The tailor stiffened momentarily, and then worked professionally, measuring her and sketching out a simple design of what he intended for each piece of cloth.

"Two weeks," he said. Marjon paid half the final cost, and they now had little left.

"Let's get something to eat before we head home," she said to Zhelica.

They settled themselves in front of a café off the main road. Zhelica had replaced her scarf, but those who gave her more than a glance could see her white skin and there were some whispers as people looked her way. At least no one was openly deriding her for being an *alloy*.

They ordered tea and some flatbread and chicken. A white-haired woman carried the tray out and set the food on the table for them. When they thanked her, the woman looked down and a thrill shot through Zhelica. *Her eyes were green.*

Time seemed to stop. The older woman's eyebrows rose and she blinked twice as though to be sure of what she was seeing. She looked over at Marjon, who was already pouring tea, and back at Zhelica. She put a finger to her lips and Zhelica was surprised to see a single tear roll down her cheek. The old woman turned and was back inside before a word had been spoken.

"Marjon!" Zhelica whispered. Her aunt looked up in surprise.

"What is it?"

"Did you see the woman who served us?"

Marjon shook her head.

"She was like me, Marjon – with green eyes."

Marjon moved her chair to better search for the woman.

"No, don't look," Zhelica said. "She seemed to want to blend in here."

Marjon nodded. "We should respect that. There can be trouble for people like you." Her face contorted as she apparently considered what that would mean for Zhelica. But the expression passed. "Eat up," she said.

Zhelica kept hoping the old woman would return. She would love to talk to her about her life as an *alloy*. It was not until they had finished and were outside the café's fenced area that she saw her again, standing in the restaurant's doorway watching Zhelica and her aunt leaving. She did not smile or wave or acknowledge them in any way.

"It was so odd," Zhelica said as they rode home. "When she came to the table and looked at me, she started crying."

Marjon gave the horse's rein a shake. "As I said, it's better to let these things be."

That was always Marjon's way, Zhelica reflected. Keep hidden, don't attract attention, avoid trouble. It was amazing she had given her permission to marry Yavan.

By dinner time the captain still had not arrived, and both women felt his absence. Zhelica was lonely and distracted in her mending, having to pull thread out more than once when she accidentally sewed the front of a skirt and its back together. Marjon did not even attempt to fix clothing; she fidgeted with her hair, braiding and re-braiding it until she gave up, leaving an asymmetrical rope hanging down her back. She sighed as she stared into the fire.

Just as they were tidying up before bed, the bell outside rang softly. They both jumped.

"I'll go," Marjon said. "Just in case it's *not* him."

Zhelica waited, watching the last coals ripple with waves of orange heat. The gate scraped open and voices murmured outside. At last, the front door creaked and Yavan filled the doorway of the sitting room, ushering in the smell of the outdoors and a spirit of life that had been lacking.

"Hey, my girlie," he said, and picked her up. She clung to him. "What's the matter?" he asked, prying her arms from his neck.

"You were gone so long! We were getting worried."

He set her down and sank into an armchair. "Things to do up in the mountains," he said. "Is it too late for a hot drink?"

Marjon, back to her normal self, huffed. "I should say."

"Marjon, you go on up. I'll get Yavan some tea."

"Not on your life," Marjon said, and joined the soldier by the remains of the fire.

Zhelica rushed into the kitchen, fetched everything needed to make tea, and ran back to the sitting room. She hooked the kettle under the mantel, stoking the fire back into flames. While Yavan regaled them with tales of his travels, she sat on a stool nearby, steeping the tea.

"It's so beautiful up there now," he said, rubbing his free hand on his thigh. "But cold. There was a hint of snow as I was on my way back. Maybe we'll go up there after we're married for a little visit," he said with a wink.

"That's a terrible idea!" Marjon scoffed. "What would Zhelica have to do there? If she wants to sit under the trees, she can stay here."

Yavan chuckled. "Always looking out for my girl," he said so quietly that only Zhelica heard him.

"I got your note from Afshar," she said. "He looked nervous bringing it."

He ran a hand over her hair. "I told you we were opposites," he said. "Afshar hates to go out after dark."

"Well, there's some sense in that," Marjon said. "We were just about to go to bed. Why don't you come back for dinner tomorrow?"

Yavan downed his tea and handed the cup to Zhelica. "Good idea." He stood up and bowed toward each. "I would see myself out, but someone needs to latch the gate."

"I will," Zhelica said before Marjon could offer. As they walked up the path toward the road, their fingers interlaced, she said, "We went and picked out cloth for wedding clothes today."

"I'm glad. I realize we haven't known each other long, but I can't wait to stay under one roof." He pressed her hand tenderly.

"It's a good thing it's dark out here. Otherwise, you would see I'm blushing."

Yavan laughed. "A perk of being fair-skinned."

"I met an old lady with green eyes today," Zhelica said. "In town."

"Yes, there are a few. Did you talk with her?"

"No," she answered. "She just looked at me. She did cry a little, though."

Yavan said nothing. They had reached the gate.

"A little kiss for the road?" he asked.

"Why not?" she responded. Thoughts of shops, town, clothing, and little old ladies flew out of her head. There would be time later for a history lesson on Zaharada's redheads.

Five

By the third day, her muscles had recovered from apple picking. Yavan and Afshar showed up in the evening and the captain's friend kept Marjon engaged in conversation while Yavan and Zhelica whispered in the corner. The lanky soldier had a limitless appetite, and while Marjon complained that he was impossible to satisfy, Zhelica could see she was gratified to have an appreciative guest.

"Tomorrow I want to take you to town," Yavan said. "I've found a place for us to live, but I want you to see it before I sign an agreement with the owners."

Zhelica glanced at her aunt. "Do you think she'll let me go?"

"Marjon," Yavan called across the room, "may I take your niece to town tomorrow?"

She finished ladling a third serving of stew into Afshar's bowl. "Whatever for? We just went."

Yavan left his seat and stood next to the older woman. He draped an arm around her shoulder. "Well, Auntie, I want her to see her future home."

Marjon heaved a sigh. "You will be careful, won't you?" she asked, her face pleading.

Yavan dimpled. "We are just looking at rooms," he assured her. "With people I know. Good people. Nothing to worry about."

Marjon did not seem persuaded. "The kind of people *you* know," she began.

"A family," Yavan said. "Safe as a bank."

"Are you going to stay here after they are married, or move to town?" Afshar asked Marjon.

She began stacking dishes.

"I hadn't planned on moving," she said. "Why should I?"

Zhelica had not considered the implications of her aunt living alone. But apparently Yavan had.

"I was thinking, Marjon. What about hiring a watchman? He could keep an eye on the orchard, and send messages to town if you need us."

"I don't know," Marjon said doubtfully. "A stranger on my property?"

"Maybe one of the farms nearby has a young man who wouldn't mind earning some money," Yavan suggested.

"Oh, Auntie, there is that boy from the vineyard," Zhelica put in. "You know, he came to help with the last harvest." He had lodged in her memory because, unlike the other workers, he had not harassed her.

"Where would he stay? I can't have him in the house," Marjon said.

Afshar offered, "We could build a hut for him by the gate."

"Yes," Yavan said. "That would only be a day's work for us. Situated there, he'd be in the perfect position to question anyone showing up."

"Well," Marjon said, "let me talk to the boy first. It might be helpful to have someone around."

The following day Yavan was off duty. He arrived in uniform ("No day off from that when I'm in public," he said), carrying a bag of old clothes to wear while building the hut.

"You are counting on that boy working here, I see," Marjon said when he showed her his clothes.

"If you talk with him today, I'm sure he'll agree," Yavan answered. "When Zhelica and I get back from town, I'll start on the hut. Afshar said he'd come by later, after he's done with his duties on base."

Zhelica was ready for their trip to town, a scarf wrapped around her head. "Marjon thinks it's better if I don't attract attention," she explained. Yavan bowed to the older woman and helped Zhelica into the saddle. She remembered to put her arms around the captain before he kicked the sides of the animal and took off.

Again the exhilaration of the ride and the sweetness of having her beloved so near made the trip delightful in its own right. Instead of looking at the scenery, Zhelica clung on, with each bounce of the horse breathing in Yavan's distinctive smell, his rough jacket brushing her cheek.

The ride seemed short. They crossed to the far side of Hyarani, past shops she now recognized and down a side street near the ancient city wall. Yavan slowed the horse and dismounted, tying it to a post and lifting Zhelica down.

She had expected to see a house, but instead they were outside a restaurant, its front a row of low windows, tables visible inside.

"Come along," Yavan said, grabbing her hand.

"This doesn't look like a house!" Zhelica said.

"Exactly."

A bell tinkled as they entered. Zhelica looked around. It was a cozy room, despite its size. Many of the tables were set into private booths, gas lamps in wall sconces providing pockets of light in the dark room. A few men sat in one booth far from the door, busy with their meal. Closer, a family clustered around a table, the children glancing up with interest as the door fell closed behind Yavan and Zhelica. Two boys leaned over the booth to wave until their parents pulled them back into place.

To the left as they entered was a swinging door. "This way to the kitchen," Yavan said; he clearly knew his way around. Zhelica hesitated, so he tugged her along behind.

A woman stood at the stove, stirring something with one hand while she balanced a toddler on the opposite hip. As soon as the child saw Yavan, he squealed with delight and reached for the soldier. His mother looked up and gave a similar cry.

"Well, look who it is, Shoja!" the woman said to the little boy, laying aside her spoon and handing him to Yavan. The captain swung Shoja onto his shoulders, wincing as the child dug his fingers into his scalp.

"Hello, Nazhin," Yavan said. "I've brought my bride to meet you."

Zhelica could feel her face flush as the woman examined her and gave a nod of approval. "Welcome, my dear! Yavan described you as a great beauty. I see he was not exaggerating."

"Oh, thank you," Zhelica said. It was such a contrast to having *"alloy"* spewed at her.

Nazhin reached toward the pot she had been tending. "Let me set this aside and I'll show you the house."

A door in the far wall opened onto a staircase. "Up we go," Nazhin said, plucking her son from Yavan's shoulders before trotting ahead of them.

It was a narrow staircase, lit only by a beam of sunlight from the floor above. When they reached the hallway, Zhelica was astonished by the residence hidden there. Red carpets extended down the corridor, with doorways opening onto a number of rooms.

Nazhin opened the first door, and there was another outcry of young voices. Immediately, a trio of children ran and wrapped their arms around Yavan's legs. Nazhin released Shoja, who joined his siblings. There was so much laughter that the landlady pulled Zhelica aside so she could be heard.

"This is the sitting room," she said. "You are welcome in here any time."

She led her out and past the other bedrooms to the end of the hall. "This is the suite we are offering you and Yavan," Nazhin said.

It was larger than the other bedrooms and had a sitting area with a table and two chairs, a dresser, and a bed, as well as a private bath.

"I know it's nicer to have your own home," Nazhin said, "but Yavan is gone sometimes at night, and he thought you would get lonely. You can spend as much or little time with our family as you want, and your rent would include food. As you can tell, we eat well." She pinched her own waistline and giggled.

"It's wonderful," Zhelica said, glancing out the windows. The apartment was so much brighter than her room at home, and the lace curtains (plus a colorful quilt on the bed) gave it an elegance she was not used to.

Yavan leaned his head in. "Well, what do you think?" A child tumbled in beside him.

"Here, I'll let you two talk privately," Nazhin said. Then, in her sternest mother voice, she commanded, "Children! Leave Yavan alone."

There were groans and complaints, but the band disappeared down the hall.

"The room is so comfortable," Zhelica began. "And the family obviously adores you. But, Yavan, can we afford this?"

He pulled himself upright and donned an air of feigned pride. "I am an *officer,* Zhelica. Of course we can afford it."

She sat down in one of the chairs. Yavan joined her. She extended her hand, palm up, and he laid his on top. "Yes," she said. "Let's live here."

Without a break, Yavan said, "And they said we could get married in the restaurant. Nazhin will prepare the food as a gift to us. Who would you like to invite to our wedding?"

"Oh," Zhelica said. Who did she know? Besides Marjon, no one. "Well ...Afshar," she began. And then she said no more.

His face mirrored her own. "What's wrong?"

"I don't have any friends," she answered sadly.

He brushed this away. "Well, that's no surprise. Marjon has kept you locked up for so long! But don't worry, you will have many friends – *my* friends. Let's keep the wedding small. Marjon, Afshar, and Nazhin and Beyman's family. That should be enough. Oh, and I should probably invite my commanding officer."

"All right," Zhelica agreed. Then, tentatively, she asked, "And what date should we choose?"

"Well," he asked slyly, "When will your dress be done?"

"Two weeks," she said.

"I'll let Nazhin know," Yavan said. "Two weeks, and we will be married!"

The captain changed into his work clothes while Zhelica described their future housing situation to Marjon.

"Is the only way out through the kitchen?" Marjon asked.

"No," Zhelica told her, "There is a doorway on the other side of the stairwell that opens into the back alley."

This seemed to ease her mind somewhat. "What about all those children? Is that going to be too much for you?"

"They are darling. Even you'll like them, I think." She winked at Marjon before catching herself. Yavan was already changing the way she interacted.

While they were in town the bricks he had ordered were dumped outside the gate. With a wheelbarrow, he hauled them all inside. After mixing the proper mortar, the captain skillfully laid three walls, using the orchard perimeter as the fourth. The hut was spacious enough for a man to sit or stand in between visits to the gate and the house. When Afshar showed up later, he helped attach a simple flat roof.

"You should have put in a window," he told Yavan.

"He'll get light if he leaves the door open," the captain pointed out.

"Not going to be great in the winter, though," Afshar said, and looked to Zhelica for reinforcement. She merely smiled.

That night she wrapped herself in a blanket and sat gazing into the fire. There were still details to work out about the wedding day, she mused, but at least the food and clothing were taken care of. Zhelica did not notice that Marjon had settled into the chair nearby until her aunt cleared her throat. She was holding a small wooden chest Zhelica had never seen before.

"What's that?" she asked, leaning to look at the box.

Marjon ran a hand lovingly over it. "This contains a few of my treasures, Zhelica." The lid was a separate piece, and she removed it, handing it to Zhelica. Carved from sandalwood grown in southern Zaharada, the chest's aroma diffused when it was opened.

Marjon pulled out a necklace of glittering beads set on a silver chain. "This was a gift from my mother to me," she said, holding the necklace so the facets flashed in the firelight. "I guess she thought someday I'd marry and wear it at my wedding as she did. But that never happened. I would like you to have it."

"Oh, Marjon." She slipped the necklace over her fingers, turning the cool stones in her hand and marveling at the way the flames danced in miniature through the beads. "Thank you."

Her aunt cradled a piece of cloth in her hand. There was nothing extraordinary about it – it appeared a scrap torn from an old dress – but Marjon looked reverent as she balanced it on her palm. Finally, she spoke.

"Besides you, this is all I have of your parents," she said. She carefully unpeeled layers of fabric to reveal a tiny portrait. Zhelica did not dare reach for it. She carefully set the necklace on a table nearby and slid onto the floor at Marjon's feet. Her aunt held the painting down for Zhelica to examine.

There were five people in the portrait – two blond men on one side, and two women, both dark-skinned Zaharadans, on the other. Zhelica noted the features of the older woman and glanced up at her aunt. "Is that you?" she asked.

Marjon nodded. "This is your mother," she said, pointing to the woman in the center next to one of the fair-skinned men. Despite the size of the painting, the artist had managed to capture an expression of resilience on her mother's face, her arms crossed as though daring someone to challenge her.

"And my father?" Zhelica asked, almost breathless. He stood astride, his face turned not toward the artist, but smiling at a child standing between her mother and Marjon.

"Yes," Marjon said. "It's a very good likeness of them."

Zhelica pointed to the child. "Is that-"

"Yes," Marjon said tenderly. "That's you."

The girl was clearly fair-skinned, but her hair had been pulled back and a man's cap plunked jauntily on her head, hiding her red curls.

"This is amazing. Why have you never shown it to me before?"

Marjon sighed. "I was afraid you would have too many questions," she admitted. "But now that you know your father was from Darz, there is no point in hiding it."

Zhelica looked again at the painting. She observed now that at her father's side he held a stringed instrument. "Was my father a musician?"

"Yes. He brought that from the north. He often played and sang for us." She smiled again at the memory. "He painted his name on the its neck. 'Vaclav.' I think the artist managed to get it on there." She handed the portrait to Zhelica.

Zhelica turned the painting toward the firelight. She thought she could see the initial 'V' but the other letters had been too small to reproduce.

"I want you to have this now," Marjon said. "Take it with you to your new home and remember your family."

"But Marjon," she objected, "I don't want to take the only picture you have of your sister."

Marjon shrugged awkwardly. "No, you have it," she insisted. "I will cherish my memories."

Zhelica gazed on the faces of the adults. What had they been like? What were their dreams? Given the opportunity, what would they have said to their child before they passed away?

"Marjon, who is this other man?" Zhelica asked. Both Darzians were short compared to Zaharadan men, about the height of her mother and aunt. The handsome man beside him looked more serious.

"That was your father's best friend," she said.

"Did he get sick, too? Did he die from the plague?"

Marjon shook her head. "No, he went back to Darz. I have not seen him since your parents' death."

The fire burned low, and Zhelica yawned. "Let me wrap the picture, Auntie," she said. She carefully folded it in the scrap of fabric ("That was from your mother's dress," Marjon said) and laid it back in the box. While she had been looking at the painting, Marjon removed the few remaining items from the chest and tucked them in her pocket.

"You keep the box," she insisted. "I hope you will consider wearing my mother's necklace on your wedding day."

"Of course!" said Zhelica, laying it on top of the portrait. "My grandmother's," she murmured. "Thank you again, Marjon. These have been the most precious gifts anyone could have given me."

The neighbor agreed to the terms of employment Marjon and Yavan discussed with him. He would come from five in the afternoon until sun-up the next day. His mother agreed to send along an evening meal. Yavan promised to stack wood near the hut to keep the youth warm as the weather cooled.

"But don't forget you're working," he warned him. "Marjon needs to trust that you will answer the gate and do whatever she asks."

He was a shy teen; he nodded enthusiastically but said nothing. Pulling the old chair from his hut to the doorway, he sat down, waiting for the gate bell to ring.

The two weeks before the wedding passed both quickly and slowly, depending on the time of day. When Marjon and Zhelica were working together, collecting dead branches from the orchard, drawing water, or hanging clothes out to dry, the hours flew. In the evening, when Yavan came (or even when he sent word that he was on a trip), the clock seemed to stop. It felt so long since Yavan proposed and she said yes.

Finally, the day of the wedding, Afshar arrived at the orchard. His job, he told them, was to transport them both (plus Zhelica's belongings) to the restaurant. Zhelica had collected her new clothing the day before, trying on the dress at the tailor's. Her aunt was so enchanted by how beautiful Zhelica looked and how well the gown fit, she lost the will to bargain and cheerfully doled out every gold coin the tailor wanted. Despite his suppressed dislike of *alloys* (Zhelica was becoming adept at recognizing it), the tailor seemed content with his creations.

While Marjon was outside the day before, Zhelica reluctantly extracted her favorite book from its hiding place. She ran her fingers over the gold imprint on the cover as though to memorize it and then returned the volume to its original home. Perhaps, she thought, Yavan could get her other books to read.

The day was blustery, and they were all well-bundled as they drove to town. Even so, Zhelica shivered with cold and excitement. She could tell that Marjon did not share her joy; her aunt sat between the bride and driver on the front seat, her mouth in a grim line.

They stopped in the alley behind the restaurant. This must have been prearranged; the door was propped open. Nazhin greeted them in the tiny entry. "Go on upstairs," she insisted. "The men will bring your boxes up."

Beyman and Afshar managed to haul everything to the bedroom at the end of the corridor. Zhelica and Marjon were examining the room when they showed up, and quickly instructed the men on where to place things. Zhelica hung her wedding dress, wrapped in a clean blanket, from the window molding.

After the men left, she let out a sigh. "This is it, then," she said with a brave smile.

Marjon seemed to latch onto this moment of vulnerability. As though it were her last chance to keep Zhelica with her, to stop the inevitable transformation of their lives and relationship, she grabbed her shoulders and looked into her eyes. "It's not too late. If you've changed your mind – if you don't want to get married – we can go right back home."

For an instant Zhelica considered what that would mean. She shook her head and unwound the cloak she was wearing. "No, Marjon," she said quietly. "I love him. I'll miss seeing you every day, but I can't *wait* to be the wife of Captain Yavan."

With that settled, the women worked as a team, calling Nazhin to help Zhelica into her dress, carefully lacing the back. Marjon tenderly brushed through Zhelica's hair and braided it into a crown. Nazhin sent one of the children down to pick a few flowers from the restaurant's flowerpot. ("These are herbs, my sweet," she said, handing back a few green fronds.) Zhelica's new landlady wove the flowers together and set the circlet on her head.

"Only one thing lacking," Marjon said, after stepping back to evaluate the bride. Zhelica pointed to the dresser, and Marjon retrieved the carved chest and the bead necklace inside. She fastened the clasp and adjusted the jewelry on her niece's neck.

"It looks like we're ready," she said. No longer dismal at the prospect of Zhelica's wedding, she kissed her on the cheek. "Let's go."

It was a simple ceremony. Zhelica did not know until much later all that had been erased from Zaharada's ancient traditions – the couple sharing a glass of water from the Western Sea, the repetition of the First Words, the blessing bestowed by the ambassador. But beneath the spoken promises and the signed document that declared them legally married lay the weight of that past, and Zhelica could not help brushing away a tear of happiness as she faced her husband. Even he looked serious for a moment before breaking into one of his irresistible grins and kissing her in front of the little gathering.

A few disappointed patrons showed up for a meal that night only to find the door locked and a "closed" sign in the window. If they could have seen through the lace curtains, they might have been surprised at the sight: the young captain in his formal uniform, beige but with a green band across his chest and green epaulets at his shoulders, his wiry comrade at his side; the bride, glowing like a jewel in her green silk, her red hair topped with a whimsical arrangement of flowers; the proprietor of the establishment, his wife, and their four children dressed in their best clothes, the little ones wriggling in excitement at everything occurring; Marjon, whose hair had been reined in by Nazhin and a bowl of oil; and the local magistrate, a bland man just doing his job. Off to the side, his posture erect and his facial expression unreadable, stood a commanding officer of the Zaharadan army.

Zhelica felt shy and embarrassed as soon as she met him. She could barely look him in the face. She knew that he probably scorned Yavan for marrying an *alloy*. She inclined her head as he bowed stiffly and murmured the requisite congratulations. As they all sat down to enjoy a meal together, the commander took advantage of the magistrate's departure, apologizing for needing to excuse himself, and disappeared into the night.

After that they all seemed to breathe easier. Beyman and Afshar dragged tables together in the center of the room with places for all the guests, but Zhelica found she had lost her appetite. As she sat next to Yavan, she relished the liberty of slipping her hand onto his knee under the table, and listened with delight as he joked with

Afshar, made the children laugh, and complimented their landlord and landlady on the magnificence of the celebration.

The family let the newlyweds depart first. When Marjon gave Zhelica a hug, she could feel her aunt tremble. "I love you, Auntie," she whispered. "Don't worry."

Then she and Yavan slipped through the kitchen, up the narrow staircase, and down the hallway into their new life together.

Six

Each morning, Zhelica and Yavan joined the rest of the family in the common room for breakfast. Despite working at the restaurant all day, Beyman loved cooking for the family, and Zhelica marveled as they passed around dish after dish: fried eggs floating in a sea of oil; circles of thin bread hot from the griddle; whatever fruit was in season; and pots of tea. The children ate with surprising vigor, and Yavan – a little more serious in the morning hours as he downed his food – put away a hearty meal before heading off to the base.

"What should I do during the day?" Zhelica asked him as she picked lint off his coat the first morning.

"Hmm," he said, buttoning while looking into the mirror in their bedroom. "You can help Nazhin with the children. Or read."

"May I go outside?"

He laughed outright at this. "Yes, my dear wife," he said, kissing her on the forehead. "You are free to do whatever you like while I'm gone. But," he added, eyebrows together as though pleading, "it would be nice if you were here when I got back."

His hours were not as predictable as she had hoped, so Zhelica spent the afternoons home, playing with the children or tidying, ready to greet Yavan when he reappeared.

But growing up in the countryside made her restless for the outdoors. She took over the care of the plants Nazhin kept throughout their home; before the customers arrived, she hurried down to the restaurant to nip off dying leaves and check the soil moisture of the potted flowers and herbs. This did not satisfy her desire for fresh air, however.

After a few days upstairs, Zhelica took to traipsing the streets of the city, exploring shops and bazaars and getting a feel for the layout of the town. Yavan had assured her there was no need to cover her hair – there were others like her, he said. At first she felt naked without the scarf to hide beneath, but as the days passed, she grew more confident, twisting her hair into a bun or braiding it like the other women.

The city people paid little attention to her, although when her eyes met those of others, they often looked quickly away. There were no audible murmurs.

Hyarani, while surrounded by farmland, managed to sustain every kind of shop, although some were no larger than a pantry. Zhelica did not worry about food – Nazhin and Beyman did all the purchasing of everything for the restaurant and their home – but wandered through shops stacked with pots and pans, furniture, and cleaning supplies. One day she discovered the bookshop, tucked in a narrow side street, and stayed so long examining every shelf that she missed lunch and met Yavan at the door as he was returning from the base.

It was a revelation that there were so many books produced in Sandazh, the capital. They were mostly on practical topics – how to treat minor illnesses at home, cooking, building furniture. But Zhelica discovered in the bottom-most shelf at the back of the shop a few books on the history of Zaharada. When the owner saw her leaning against the wall, leafing through one of these, he snapped, "Are you just going to look, or are you going to buy anything?" She was obliged to tell him that she would have to come back with money another day.

"Yavan," she said that night, as she settled into bed, "I saw some interesting books at the store today."

He leaned on one elbow to gaze at her. "Yes? Did you see one that you wanted?"

She nodded. "I enjoyed that book that Marjon has. I think I'd like to read more about the history of Zaharada."

A troubled look flickered across his face, but he smiled. "I'm sure Nazhin has some good books," he said. "Let's ask her at breakfast."

Yavan seemed to have forgotten in the morning, but Zhelica did not. Nazhin glanced at the captain before answering, but told Zhelica she did have a few.

"They're really children's books," she apologized. "The boys like to look at the pictures." But even she seemed to overlook the request until Zhelica reminded her. Still she put her off. "I have a lot to do in the kitchen right now," she said. "I'll look for them tonight, if that's all right."

With Nazhin and Beyman both employed, Zhelica did not want to seem lazy. When she was in, she joined the children in the common room, playing games or reading stories to them. A girl a little younger than Zhelica came for a few hours in the morning to keep an eye on them, departing after lunch, so she did not feel bad leaving while this helper was there.

Keeping their own room clean took little time: it was small enough that making the bed and doing a quick dusting and sweeping kept it in order. In the late afternoons, Zhelica sat on the window seat and watched for Yavan and Syah to return from the base. There was a small stable near the back entrance to the restaurant, and after Yavan disappeared inside and then reappeared, he looked up and waved. At that point Zhelica hurried downstairs to greet him.

The day Nazhin finally handed Zhelica a stack of books on Zaharada, the younger woman disappeared into her room and settled in the chair by the fireplace. It seemed extravagant to burn a fire in their private quarters, but she permitted herself a small one. The days were cold now; the evening before she had seen a few flurries of snow.

As she nestled into the chair, tucking a blanket up around her feet and over her lap, Zhelica opened the first book. Nazhin was right: if the others were the same, they were clearly written for children. The artwork consisted of simple line drawings with one or two colors splashed across them.

The first was about the High Commander, the ruler of Zaharada. It showed him standing at a balcony (she thought perhaps it was the castle she had seen in Marjon's book) saluting a crowd of soldiers below. Most of the pages had pictures and text lauding the army and showing men marching, practicing shooting and lunging with bayonets, and exercising outside their tents. It was a dull read, and she suspected the children thought so, too: even though the publishing date was ten years before, the pages were unbent and without the usual smudges found in books for the young.

The next was only slightly more interesting. It covered cities of Zaharada, emphasizing how modern and efficiently they were run. (She did linger a bit on this one; she knew so little about the country that despite the primitive art work, showing how plants and buildings differed from region to region, it kept her engaged.)

The third book she picked up was different from the others. Its cover was bright blue, studded with gold stars. When Zhelica opened it, the spine crackled in a way that suggested it had never been read. On the title page *In the House of Shurash* was printed in glittering blue ink.

This volume had elaborate pictures, even more beautiful than in Marjon's book. It was written from the perspective of a boy going to visit a shrine. The child approached the building, a structure with blue spires on its corners, each covered (she decided, after looking closely) with tiny blue tiles, perhaps made of glass. (The artist had done an admirable job of depicting light glancing off the building, Zhelica thought.) The child entered the shrine, where braziers burned with something giving off blue smoke, which rose toward the high apex of the building. At the front of the room was a golden statue reaching to the ceiling. The figure was handsome, with waves of golden hair and the physique of a young man in his prime.

The striking thing about the statue, though, was what he held in his outstretched hands. Draped over each was what appeared to be a shackle with a severed chain, the finely crafted links falling uselessly from his palms.

In the narrative, the child prostrated himself before the statue. Men in blue robes surrounded him, clapping in happiness. In the last illustration, the boy was seen dancing with others under the stars. Blue fire burned from torches around the edge of the scene.

Zhelica was still looking over the detailed drawings when Yavan came in. He crossed the room and gave her a kiss on the cheek.

"I missed you downstairs," he said, rubbing her nose with his.

"I'm sorry! I lost track of the time looking at these books Nazhin lent me," she said. Zhelica realized now that the sun had set and the only light in the room came from the remains of the fire.

Yavan flipped over the book in her lap to see the title. "What's this one?"

She felt strangely embarrassed. "It's about some shrine," she said.

Yavan held out his hand and she gave him the book. He read through it quickly. In the glow of dying firelight, black furrows crossed his forehead.

"What garbage," he said softly. He snapped the book shut. "I'm surprised Nazhin is giving books like this to her kids," he said, laying it on the table.

"I don't think anyone but me has read it."

"Well, that's good," Yavan answered. He stared into the fire a moment. "Stories about Shurash...well, they aren't like the stories in Marjon's book. Frankly, they aren't worth your time. We'll find you something better to read."

He remained like this, his face hard but inscrutable for a moment. And then suddenly his dimples appeared, exaggerated in the low light. "The children told me there are two whole chickens for dinner tonight. Let's join them."

He picked her up and slung her over his shoulder like a bundle while she laughed, insisting he put her down. He nearly got his feet entangled in the blanket and was forced to set her upright. Given a moment's head start, she took off at a run down the passage, Yavan's mock roar echoing behind her.

It was a few weeks before Zhelica made it back to the bookstore. Yavan had given her money to spend as she wished, and she decided she wanted to know more about Shurash and how he fit into Zaharada's history.

She was disappointed when she reached the shop, however. A sign on the door read, "Closed for inventory." All the blinds had been pulled so she could not even peer in.

Zhelica rambled and found herself in front of the café where she and Marjon had eaten lunch a few months before. The tables had been moved under the awning, chairs upturned, waiting for spring. A breeze sent leaves scuttling across the pavement as the sun disappeared and the sky turned an even gray.

As she stood outside, not entering and not leaving, the door opened. To Zhelica's surprise, it was the other *alloy* (the only one she had seen, despite what Yavan had told her). The old woman was beckoning her.

Zhelica scurried up the walkway and slipped inside the restaurant. There were a couple of old men playing chess and drinking tea, but otherwise the room was empty. The proprietress led her through a doorway covered by a flowered curtain.

Clearly this was not part of the restaurant. A room about half the size of Zhelica's apartment contained a tiny round table and two chairs, a bed, and wardrobe.

As soon as the curtain had fallen, the old woman turned and Zhelica could see she was weeping again.

"Don't cry," she said soothingly, reaching to touch the woman's arm. The old lady brushed her tears away and then, to Zhelica's astonishment, grabbed both the young woman's shoulders and looked at her intently.

"Whose child are you?" she whispered.

"I don't know my mother's name," she answered. "My aunt raised me...My father's name was Vaclav. They both died in the plague."

"Oh, the plague," the old woman said, as though this were a new idea. "Is that what they're calling it now?" She shook her head sadly. "I thought maybe I'd recognize your parents in you."

"My father was from Darz," Zhelica offered. "And he played an instrument. I've seen a little painting of him."

The woman dropped down in one of the chairs, and motioned for Zhelica to sit opposite.

"Oh, I think I met him," she said. "Vaclav. Hmm. Who is your aunt? I don't remember her."

"Marjon. She owns a fruit and nut orchard less than an hour's drive from here."

The woman's green eyes lit up at this. "I know of Marjon. She sells to the army base. The best apples around," she added mournfully. "I can't afford them anymore."

What a sad creature! Zhelica thought. In an attempt to cheer her, she said, "I heard there are many *alloys* here. But you're the only one I've seen."

The restaurant owner said quietly but firmly, "I'm not an *alloy*. I'm a Zaharadan."

Before Zhelica could reply, the old woman reached across the table and grabbed her wrist. "It's not safe here," she said. "You're not safe here."

Zhelica tried to remove her hand, but the woman clutched harder.

"You mean in your restaurant?"

The old woman sniffed. "No, in Hyarani," she said. "You need to be more careful."

A chill ran through Zhelica. "Because I am an *alloy?*"

The old woman nodded. "The others are gone. I stayed...they know I am no danger. My husband, may he rest peacefully, loved this place too much to leave it when the ...the *plague*...when all the difficulties started. They've kept a close eye on me all these years. They know I am no danger. But who are you? Where did you come from? They will be watching you." She eased her grasp, and leaned back. "If you get into any trouble, I'll try to help you," she said. "My name is Azara. Come if you need me. But please do not loiter outside my restaurant again."

Zhelica fought panic as she exited through Azara's back door. She looked at the streets through the lens of apprehension. Who was watching? Could they see her now? Why would they view her as dangerous? She tried to walk quickly without arousing suspicions.

She was distracted now, and turned down an avenue she did not recognize. Snow had started falling in earnest while she was in the restaurant, and she pulled her cloak around her, wishing she had brought a scarf to cover her blazing hair. It was a relief when she turned a corner and realized she was looking down the back alley on which her home lay.

Nazhin met her below the stairs as she closed the door behind her. The bustle in the kitchen, the light and warmth and smell of hearty food and the voices of men, muffled as they were by the restaurant door: it was all reassuring and safe.

"Look at you! Pale as an icicle," Nazhin said, throwing an arm around her. "Run upstairs. There should be a good fire going."

The children rushed to her when she entered the common room, and that warmed her, too. It was just the way they greeted Yavan the first time he had shown her the rooms.

"Did you see the snow?" Zhelica asked. Hanging her wet cloak by the door, she went to the window and pulled back the lace. The children shouted with pleasure, crowding onto the window seat. Even Shoja toddled near, whimpering until Zhelica picked him up so he could join the fun.

"We should build a snowman!" one of the boys cried.

Zhelica laughed. "There's not enough yet," she said. "We might have to wait until tomorrow."

The hired girl served them all soup and the children sat around the table telling Zhelica about their morning, what they played while she was away. Despite sitting with her back to the door, she knew immediately who had entered when the whole group broke into cheers.

"Yavan!" Zhelica cried. She started to rise, but was stopped short by the hired girl's order to the children to sit down. Remembering *she* was not obligated to obey, she jumped up and gave him a hug. "What are you doing home at this hour?"

He had a way of showing her affection while extending it to the entire room. "I left early because of the snow," he said. Then, more quietly, "I have to make a trip up to the mountains tonight."

Her joy at seeing him was dampened by this news.

"You're all wet," he said suddenly, patting her hair. "Were you out in the snow?"

She nodded, and the memory of her fear and Azara's warning returned. Her eyes began to sting and she looked away.

"Children, keep eating. I'm going to take Zhelica to get some dry clothes. We'll be back in a few minutes,"

Yavan said. He guided her out of the common room and down the hall. Once they were in their apartment with the door closed, he asked, "What's the matter?"

She felt reluctant to tell him. As though it were the main issue, and not the secondary one, she said, "I wish you didn't have to leave."

He laughed. "That is an impressive pout, my dear. I thought you were really upset about something."

She turned and went to the dresser, retrieved a dry dress, and slipped out of her wet one. The room was cold, and she shivered as she hurriedly yanked it over her head. "Will you tie the back?" she asked, and he did so. Zhelica was beginning to manage her feelings, and decided not to tell him about her visit to Azara.

"We haven't been married very long," Zhelica said. "It doesn't seem fair they'd send you away so soon."

He sat down in one of the armchairs by the fireplace and pulled her onto his lap. "I know," he said, kissing her forehead. "I wish I didn't have to go, but I do."

"Where exactly will you be? What are you doing?" she asked, running her fingers through his short curls.

"I'm going to Baraqan, where Afshar and I went to school," he said. "The generals want to meet with the provision officers from all the bases and talk about the food situation."

"How long will you be away?" she asked, nestling down. She could feel his chest rise and fall. There was something soothing about his heart beating against her side.

"A few days. Hopefully it won't take long." He enfolded her in his arms; his body heat crept through her clothing. She imagined it touching that place in her heart where the cold lump of fear still lay. "I'll have time to visit my favorite old tutor," he said. "He sent me a note and told me to come by his home when I'm in town."

"Don't knock over any statues," she said.

"I won't," he promised.

If left to themselves a few minutes longer, they might have forgotten lunch, but there was a knock on their door. "Zhelica? Yavan? Did you want to eat?"

Yavan let out a groan so low only Zhelica could hear it. Then he called, "We're coming, Nazhin. We'll be out in a minute."

Zhelica did not want to move, and burrowed down against him. "I'm not hungry," she murmured.

"That's because you already had something to eat," he said, lightly but softly. He kissed her and said, "But unless you want me to starve on my journey, I think I better get some food."

This time she gave him a deliberate pout, and he kissed her again. "Up we go," he said, and lifted her with him from the comfort of the chair.

It was a moment she would never forget.

After lunch they returned to their room. While Yavan stuffed changes of clothing into his knapsack, Zhelica hovered nearby. She glanced at the small table near the armchair and noticed its bare surface.

"Nazhin's books are gone," she said.

Yavan dimpled. "I knew you were done with them, so I gave them back." Then, as though in afterthought, he added, "Wait – you *were* done with them, weren't you?"

"Yes," she said. "I went by the bookstore to find something else to read, but it was closed."

"That's too bad," he said. "I know – why don't I drop you at Marjon's? I'm going that direction, and I could pick you up when I return. That will give you more time to read that book of hers you love."

Her aunt had only visited a couple of times since the wedding, and Zhelica admitted to herself (with some guilt) that she did not miss her as much as she thought she would. But now the orchard sounded like a good place to hide for a few days, in case anyone *was* watching her.

"You won't forget to bring me home, will you?" she asked, already extracting some thick garments from the dresser to take with her.

"Are you joking? I'll be thinking about you the whole time I'm gone," he said.

It did not take long to get all their travel essentials together, inform Nazhin of their plans, and say goodbye to the family. One of the boys whined, "But we were going to play that game you like!"

Yavan shook a finger at him. "You know better than that," he said in a mock-parent voice.

The children insisted on watching them from the window until they rode out of sight. Yavan and Zhelica, outfitted with their warmest gear, their bundles tied on Syah, made sure to wave at them before disappearing into the gray swirling snowflakes.

Marjon's new watchman was there, they could tell: a wisp of smoke curled above the little hut Yavan and

Afshar had constructed near the front wall. But the captain had to beat twice on the gate before the boy's face appeared. The snow had stopped, but the air was brisk, and like them, the watchman was wrapped in layers of wool.

"Yes?" he asked, his voice muted by the scarf across his face.

"It's me, Captain Yavan. Open up. I'm leaving my wife here for a visit with Marjon."

The gate scraped open. Yavan dismounted and helped Zhelica down, untying her bag.

"I must go, my love," he said. "Tell Marjon I'll visit when I return in a few days."

He gave her a bear hug and a quick kiss on the part of her cheek exposed to the air, then quickly remounted and was off in an instant. The boy, stamping in the cold, eagerly slammed the gate shut and disappeared inside his shelter.

Any snow the orchard received had already melted, and Zhelica sought out the drier patches of ground along the cart path toward the house. Marjon, who looked out to see who was arriving, met her at the door, pulling her inside before all the heat escaped.

"Oh, Zhelica," Marjon clucked, unwinding her layers and hanging them on hooks beside the front door. By the time they could embrace, Zhelica's regret at not visiting sooner welled up within her.

"Marjon! I am so sorry I have not been back," she said. She followed her aunt into the sitting room. A fire was blazing and Marjon hurriedly set the kettle of water on to make tea. The older woman radiated happiness.

"Well, you *are* a new bride," Marjon said. "I certainly didn't imagine you'd choose a day like this to come see me. The weather is terrible."

Zhelica held out her hands to the fire. "It was snowing heavily in town. Did you get much here?"

Marjon shook her head. "We are a little lower," she said. "And a bit warmer."

"So how are you, Auntie? What have you been doing with all your time?"

Marjon was pouring water into the pot now, agitating it so the tea leaves would infuse it with flavor. "I started a quilt," she said. "Look." She set down the teapot and fetched a large square of fabric from her basket. The scraps of material looked familiar; Zhelica realized they were from her own old clothes.

"I remember that dress," Zhelica said wistfully, pointing to a calico.

"Do you? You were only six when I made it," Marjon said. "The first dress I ever sewed for you."

"I must have been nine by the time I outgrew it!" Zhelica laughed, poking the worn cloth.

"And what have *you* been doing? How do you fill your days at the restaurant?"

The way Marjon asked it ("at the restaurant") made it sound as though Zhelica had left for employment. Perhaps, she thought, Marjon was not yet able to refer to the place her niece lived now as "home."

"I spend time with the family," Zhelica said. "There's not much housework, and Nazhin won't let me help in the kitchen. So I keep our room tidy, and I often go out."

She was sorry she had said it, because Marjon asked sharply, "Out? What do you mean?"

"I walk around town," Zhelica said. "I'm getting to know my way around, although there are a few streets I haven't been down."

"Why would you want to do that? Go out alone?"

Zhelica felt transported back. She was muddled, and she thought to herself, *I did get married, didn't I?* For a moment she thought it had all been a dream.

"Well, Aunt Marjon, I get tired of being indoors all the time," she said.

"What does Yavan think of you wandering around like that?"

She handed a cup of tea to Zhelica, and the younger woman held it between both hands, staring into the dark liquid, not looking at her aunt.

"My husband," she said, lingering over the word, "says I am free to do what I like."

Something like a clicking of her tongue escaped Marjon, and Zhelica turned toward her.

"Have you had any trouble?" her aunt asked, more subdued.

Although she had met Yavan without Marjon's knowledge, she had never out-and-out lied to her before. Taking a deep breath, Zhelica answered, "No, Marjon. Living in Hyarani is fine. No one even notices me."

Marjon seemed to study her before taking a sip from her own cup. The tension between them lessened, but Zhelica was conscious of a struggle of her own. The truth was, she thought, that she had not had any trouble. She had only been *warned* of trouble. So maybe she was not lying.

"How long can you stay?" Marjon asked.

"If it's all right with you," Zhelica said, "Yavan had to make a trip to the mountains and will pick me up on his way back in a few days."

Her aunt lit up at this. "Oh, it will be like old times!" she said. "Of course you are welcome to stay." She set down her cup. "I'm just going to open your room to take the chill off. You wait here."

While her aunt was upstairs, Zhelica thought to herself, *I can't* wait *until Yavan comes back.* The first hour dragged slower than she imagined time could pass.

Seven

Zhelica took her first opportunity to retrieve the beloved 25th anniversary volume from the cupboard. She had only read and re-read the first few stories before marrying Yavan; now, alone with the book in her old bedroom, she determined to finish it.

She knew she was looking for something on the cult of Shurash, but as she worked her way through the stories, she saw no evidence of the beautiful blue shrine and its golden figure. The only mystical thing she discovered was a reference to the ambassador, a man who seemed to speak to the ruler on behalf of the distant Overking. The messages included warnings and occasional instructions. To her disappointment, Zhelica found little elaboration on these interchanges. What she did notice, however, was that in one drawing, the ambassador was shown standing on a mosaic circle similar to the one she had seen in the forest with Yavan. A white light illumined his face as he stood in the darkness, apparently speaking with the Overking.

Zhelica skipped through the pages once more when she had finished reading every story. There was no mention of Shurash.

The days at the orchard were strangely blank. When she woke, Zhelica reached for Yavan, but her hand fell on the edge of the narrow mattress. When she sat at the table, the voices of the children, the laughter of her husband – all were missing. There was only Marjon, looking a little grayer and less interesting than before. The evenings stretched endlessly before them. Zhelica felt trapped in a life she thought she had escaped.

The snow did not reappear, but the days were still cold. There was no work to do in the orchard now, but Zhelica slipped out each afternoon to walk the perimeter of the walled property. She thought of the first day she had answered the gate to meet Yavan. This brightened her spirits a little.

Finally, on the fourth day, he returned. As soon as she heard the bell, Zhelica threw on her cloak and ran to meet him. He jumped down, tied up Syah, and gave Zhelica a kiss that assured her he had missed his wife as much as she had missed him.

"Come in," she said, pulling him toward the house. "Aunt Marjon wants to see you before we leave."

They both knew it would not be as easy as a mere chat. Marjon insisted on serving dinner and wanted to hear all about Yavan's trip.

"Well," he began, "during the day we all met and talked about this year's supplies – what we still had in storage, how the crops and prices had been. We discussed ways to share food at bases around the country so that soldiers everywhere can get a good variety.

"In the evenings," he continued, "I went to my old tutor's house to stay. I mentioned him to you," he said to Zhelica, while reaching for the ladle to scoop more beans onto his plate.

"Yes," she said. "But you never told me why you needed a tutor. I thought you said you were a good student."

"I was a good student when I *tried*," he corrected her. "History was my weakest subject. I just couldn't see how it related to the modern world." He smiled at Marjon. "So the school arranged for me to meet with Mr. Koosha. It was great, because he lived off the academy grounds. He treated me like a little gentleman rather than just a schoolboy – always serving me tea and letting me sit across from him in his study in a big, high-backed chair. He made learning history fun. We've kept up writing to one another and when I go to the mountains, I often take the opportunity to stay with him."

Marjon had stopped eating, Zhelica noticed, listening intently to what Yavan was saying. She relaxed when he finished, returning to her food.

"Did you tell him you're married now?" Zhelica asked, sidling nearer.

"Of course," Yavan grinned. "He sends you his greetings."

"Did you mention that I am an *alloy?*"

"Zhelica!" her aunt reproved her. "Don't call yourself that."

"What should I say?" Zhelica asked, stirring her food around on the plate and not meeting Marjon's eyes. She remembered Azara's words. "Should I just call myself 'Zaharadan'?"

"Of course," Yavan said soothingly, putting a hand on hers. "That's what you are, after all."

The air was tight with the strain between aunt and niece, and Zhelica stubbornly refused to ease it. Yavan, however, broke in with a story about how Syah was spooked on the first night as they traveled up the mountainside.

"He stopped right in the middle of the trail and would not go forward. I couldn't see anything, and when I finally urged him on, I noticed the glint of mountain lion eyes peering back at us from the side of the trail."

Zhelica shivered. "Well, good thing Syah's looking out for you."

"Best horse ever," Yavan agreed. "And he's surefooted, even on the most treacherous trail or in the worst weather."

Shifting their thoughts to Syah and Yavan's travels changed the mood in the room. The captain quickly finished his food and pushed his plate away. "Ah, Marjon, you are such a good cook!" he said. "We really should come more often."

She patted her disordered hair. "Well, you are welcome any time. You know that."

"Indeed we do," Yavan said. Then he turned to Zhelica. "Is your bag packed?"

"It will only take me a minute."

She hurried up the stairs. She was tempted to take Marjon's book, but dutifully returned it to its cupboard before heading back down. The relief at leaving her childhood home was like a spring of water rushing down the steps behind her.

"Thank you for letting me stay, Auntie," she said, kissing her cheek with more warmth than she had felt during her stay. "We'll try to come again soon."

"I'll be in town next week, so I might drop by for a visit."

"Good," Zhelica said. And then she added, "Afternoons are best. I am often out in the mornings."

She could not resist this last opportunity to remind her aunt of her new-found freedom.

"I have to travel more during the winter," Yavan explained a week later as he was again packing. "This is when we arrange contracts with our suppliers and pick up any dried food we might need to get the troops through until spring."

Zhelica wiped away a tear. "I had no idea you were going to be gone so much," she said.

Yavan dropped the socks he was holding into his bag and leaned over to kiss her on the forehead. "I'm sorry," he said. "Would you have said 'no' to my marriage proposal if you had known?"

She shook her head vigorously. "Of course not," she said. "But it makes me sad."

"You're sure you don't want to go stay with Marjon?"

"Our home is here," she said. "I'll wait for you here."

It was while he was away on this second long trip that Zhelica discovered more about the mystery of Shurash. She put away her fear of being observed and resumed her daily walks. One morning she stayed away from home longer than usual, ending up in a section of town she had never been to before. It was a crowded bazaar with closely packed shops, chickens hanging from the butcher's stall, open bins of grains and legumes, and the few expensive fruits shipped from southern Zaharada.

Caught up in the throng of humanity, Zhelica stumbled along, trying to take in the sights and smells of this neighborhood. It was in the middle of a long block that she saw, tucked between two shops, a small shrine. It was an alcove painted blue; set into the back was a gold statue about the length of her arm.

Struggling to break free of the people around her, Zhelica came to a stop before the figure of Shurash. It looked just like the picture in Nazhin's book. A few faded flowers had been tossed at its feet. A blue candleholder stood off to one side, its flame flickering as people passed.

"He's beautiful, isn't he?" a shopper asked. When she turned to look at Zhelica, however, she jumped, startled, and pulled her bags close before disappearing into the crowd.

Zhelica did not know what to think. The shrine, honoring a person this way – it was beyond anything in her experience. She stood a moment longer and then made her way to the nearest side-street and walked home.

She had missed lunch, and Nazhin was sitting with the youngest children reading a story when Zhelica entered the common room. They looked up and waved at her, not wanting to interrupt the tale. Zhelica knelt on the floor next to the older boys, who were constructing a tower of wooden blocks. Since they were also listening to the story, they wordlessly indicated the fine points of their building. She nodded encouragingly.

When Nazhin finished, she set Shoja on the floor. He headed toward his brothers' block tower to wreak havoc. Nazhin asked, "Did you want something to eat?"

The table had been cleared, so Zhelica shook her head. "No, I can wait until dinner," she said. "But I want to ask you something."

"You look serious," Nazhin said. "Come sit over here."

Zhelica joined her on one of the window seats. She wasn't sure what she wanted to ask, or how, so she just blurted out, "Nazhin, tell me about Shurash."

Nazhin reached behind Zhelica and gave a quick pull to the lace curtain, which was askew. "We don't talk much about him," she said in a low voice.

"But who is – or was – he?" Zhelica persisted.

"He was...he was the Great Ambassador," her landlady said softly. "Didn't your aunt ever tell you about him?"

Zhelica shook her head. "I saw that picture in the book you gave me, and then today I went by a shrine dedicated to him."

Nazhin looked toward the children. "I'm sorry I gave you that book."

Zhelica did not respond. She hoped Nazhin would say more, but her friend seemed relieved at the silence. She took the opportunity to call the toddler, who turned in his travels and crab-walked eagerly to his mother, stopping at her feet and extending his arms with a grunt. Nazhin scooped him up and smoothed his tiny curls. Zhelica realized with dismay that the conversation had effectively ended.

"I'm a little tired," she said. "I think I'll go lie down for a while."

"All right," Nazhin said. Her forehead crinkled in concern. "Are you unwell?"

"No, I'm fine," Zhelica said with a smile. "I'll see you all later."

Her room was cold, but Zhelica felt too weary to make a fire. She removed her cloak and lay it over the bedspread and then crawled under the covers. She shivered as the bed warmed up, and then fell asleep.

She had been exhausted lately. She wondered if it was from walking more while Yavan was gone. She decided the next day she would stay in.

At dinner Zhelica noticed Beyman kept glancing her way. Even so, it was comforting to be here with the others. She was glad she had not gone to Marjon's.

It was fortuitous that she stayed in that day, she thought later. Marjon sent a message with her watchman that she would be coming before lunch and would take Zhelica out to eat.

"We can eat here," Zhelica said. She felt sluggish even after a good night's sleep.

"Nonsense," Marjon said. "The family probably needs some time without us."

She had parked her carriage in the alley and she and Zhelica rode a few blocks away, to the part of the town where the tailor was located. Zhelica thought for a moment she would suggest Azara's restaurant, but reconsidered. Marjon took her to a diner where they ordered a thick soup with bread. She talked as though she had not seen Zhelica in weeks.

"My quilt is coming along. I need to get some more fabric, though. That was why I came to town."

"I see," Zhelica answered, nodding. She realized she was resting her chin on her palm, something Marjon would never tolerate at home. She dropped her hands into her lap.

"You're not eating much," Marjon noted. "Are you all right?"

"I'm fine. They serve such a big breakfast, I'm not usually very hungry at noon."

Marjon had made an effort to look more tidy than usual, but when she reached her hand across to pat Zhelica's, her niece noticed how rough and worn it looked. A pang of guilt shot through her.

"Are you all right, Auntie? There is so much work for you there alone."

Her eyes creased warmly. "There is hardly any work right now. That's why I'm spending so much time quilting. When will Yavan return?"

"Oh, day after tomorrow," Zhelica said a little mournfully.

"Where is he this time?"

"Somewhere in the mountains again."

"He seems to be gone a lot," Marjon observed.

Zhelica nodded. "That's why he rented a room at Nazhin's for us. So I wouldn't be lonely."

"Right," Marjon said.

There was nothing more to talk about, so her aunt paid the bill and they walked together to the fabric store. Zhelica thought of asking her aunt about the shrine she had seen, but suddenly felt reticent. By the time they were finished and back at Nazhin's restaurant, she was ready for a nap.

"I didn't sleep well last night," she told Marjon. She wasn't sure that was true, but what other reason could there be for her tiredness? "I think I'll have a little rest."

Marjon put a hand to her forehead. "You aren't feverish," she said. "Well, I have a couple more errands to run, so I'll just head out now. See you soon," she said, and gave her niece a hug. "You rest up," she added.

The next morning Zhelica was woken not by the sounds of pots banging in the kitchen or the cries of little people wanting their mother, but by a wave of nausea. She sat up, immediately collapsing again on the pillow. She lay one hand on her abdomen. *I guess I am sick,* she thought miserably.

She lay still until she heard a timid knock on the door. "Zhelica?"

"Come in," she called.

Nazhin hesitated in the doorway. "Are you all right?"

Before Zhelica could respond, her landlady hurried to the bedside. Like Marjon, she put a hand to Zhelica's forehead.

"My stomach is unsettled," Zhelica said.

"Well, you hardly ate anything yesterday," Nazhin said. "Let me bring you some tea."

She returned a few minutes. On the tray she carried sat a small teapot and a plate with an unadorned slab of white bread. "Can you sit up?"

Zhelica pulled herself upright, leaning against the headboard. "Oh, I feel terrible," she said, clutching her belly again.

Why is she smiling? she thought as Nazhin sat down next to her. Never had she struck Zhelica as the kind of person who would relish another's agony.

"Have a little tea and try a bite of bread," her landlady said.

"I'm afraid I'll vomit."

"Just try it," Nazhin urged her.

Zhelica took a tiny sip and a small bite of bread and then reclined. She waited a moment. Instead of feeling worse, she actually did feel slightly less nauseated. "You must be magic."

Nazhin smiled again. "It only works for some kinds of illness," she told her.

"I've never felt quite like this before," Zhelica told her. "Usually I only get sick if Marjon's sick. And she was fine."

Nazhin started quaking with silent laughter and then suddenly exploded. "Really, Zhelica? You have no idea why you're feeling this way?"

Zhelica just stared at her friend. She was totally mystified.

"How long have you been married? Two months?" Nazhin crossed her arms. They rose and fell as she continued to laugh. "My first took longer than that," she said.

"Your first - ?" Zhelica stopped. "Wait, do you think I'm -?"

Nazhin let out a happy sigh. "Well, we'll see," she said. "I just know that whenever I'm pregnant, nothing soothes my stomach like a little tea and plain bread first thing in the morning. That explains your tiredness," Nazhin added. "That will pass after another month or so."

She rose. "I need to get back to my own brood. We'll see you whenever you feel up to joining us." She leaned down and whispered, "Don't worry – I won't tell anyone."

As the day wore on, Zhelica improved. By evening she decided that she would not mention anything to Yavan for a while.

She had a repeat of morning sickness the next day but fended it off with Nazhin's help and determined that she would keep a small piece of bread in the room to nibble on before rising each morning.

Days later Yavan swept in like a summer breeze, brightening everyone and showering them with gifts: for the children, a wooden puzzle he had bought in the bazaar in Baraqan; for their parents, a box full of fine candies imprinted with "Chocolatier of Zaharada" on its lid.

"I didn't find anything for you," he apologized to Zhelica. "But my friend Mr. Koosha sent a present."

He handed her the elegant box, cardboard molded into an oval and painted with gold patterns on the top. She lifted the lid. "To the wife of Captain Yavan" was written in cursive script on an envelope inside. She pulled out the card. This, too, was covered with gold flourishes. It read,

My dear Zhelica,

How happy to hear that Yavan has found a worthy bride! He has always been like a son to me, so my pleasure is complete. I hope that you will visit me one day. Until then, please accept the enclosed. From what your husband told me, you cannot be improved by ornamentation. But most women enjoy beautiful things.

Yours,
P. Koosha

Pushing aside the tissue paper, Zhelica lifted a silk scarf. It was in the style of old Zahardan clothing, a delicately embroidered peacock extending across a jade green background. It was exquisite.

"Look at this," she said, standing so that she could display the whole scarf. Everyone gasped. Zhelica tossed it over her head and wound it around so that its splendor encompassed her.

She looked at Yavan. "Did he send this because you told him...about me?" She knew he understood what she meant: that she was an *alloy*. He wanted to help her cover her red hair.

Yavan laughed. "He had it wrapped and waiting when I arrived. It is enough to be the wife of Captain Yavan," he said, and took her in his arms. Nazhin and Beyman's older girl squealed in anticipation of a passionate embrace; the boys turned away in disgust. Yavan pulled the edge of the scarf to block them from view before kissing Zhelica.

That night they dined alone in their room, ordering from the restaurant's menu. Yavan built a fire so big they needed no other light as they ate at the little table. He told Zhelica about the magnificent snowfall and the way the trees sparkled in the moonlight. He recounted his discussion with Mr. Koosha about the war years.

"I wish you'd explain Zaharadan history to me," Zhelica said, poking at her meal. Her appetite was again dampened, but she did not want Yavan to notice. "I can't seem to get hold of any good books."

Yavan leaned back and stretched his legs before the fire, tucking his arms behind his head. "What do you want to know, my love?"

Zhelica stopped playing with her food and leaned over the arm of her chair. "Tell me about the ambassadors."

His eyebrows shot up in surprise. "The ambassadors?" he repeated. "What do you know about them already?"

"Not much," Zhelica admitted. "I saw a picture in Marjon's book of one standing on this tile circle like the one we saw in the forest by the burned-out house." She shivered in recollection, and then went on. "And I heard that Shurash was the Great Ambassador."

Yavan shook his head, lowering his arms and pulling his feet in. "That's what *he* called himself," he said. "But he wasn't a real ambassador."

"Who *were* the ambassadors?" She was desperate for answers, but tried not to look too eager, for fear that Yavan would stop talking.

He stared thoughtfully into the fire. It seemed like a straightforward question, but he was clearly choosing words carefully.

"Have you ever heard of the Overking?" he asked.

"He was mentioned in Marjon's book," she said. "but he wasn't described or anything."

"Well, he lives on an island on the far side of Dunyara," Yavan said. "He is the one who appoints rulers and helps when there is trouble. The ambassadors are the people who communicate with him."

"That's right," Zhelica said. "I guess there was something about that in the story I read."

Yavan sighed as though his words were taking a lot of effort. "Well, Shurash said *he* was the greatest ambassador of all, and he banished the other ambassadors. He said he alone would speak to the Overking on behalf of the people."

"But why would he do that?"

Yavan shrugged. His countenance changed, and Zhelica knew that he would not yield any more information. "Who knows? It was a long time ago." He reached over the divide between their chairs. "I'm tired," he said, rubbing her nose with his. "Let's go to bed."

She had so many questions! Zhelica wondered if they would ever be answered. But the appeal of her new husband overrode her curiosity, and she said, "I've had to warm it myself the last few nights. You get in first, and let me know when it's not cold."

He threw off his uniform and dived between the sheets, letting out a yell of anguish. Then he spoke sweetly, using every term of affection he could think of, even promising to let her warm her feet on his back, tempting her to join him. And she did.

Eight

"Hey, are you getting up today?"

Yavan was standing near the bed, and Zhelica rolled over on her side facing away. "I'm tired," she murmured. *And my belly is roiling.*

"Nazhin's not very good about saving breakfast," Yavan said, buttoning his shirt. "Do you want me to bring something back for you?"

"No, thanks." She wanted to get up, but her limbs felt pinned by weights.

"All right, my love," Yavan said, kissing her cheek. "Are you sick?"

She shook her head. "I'll be all right. Just let me lie in bed for a few minutes."

Zhelica waited until the door closed behind him, and then she reached into her bedside table for the bread she had left there the day before. She took a small bite, hoping it would stay down, wishing she had tea to drink with it.

There was a knock at the door, and Nazhin peered in. "I've brought a hot pot for you," she said, scurrying in. Setting the teapot on the bedside table, she quickly poured a cup.

"Did Yavan see you?" Zhelica asked.

"No. But I need to get back before I'm missed. I'll check on you soon." Her landlady vanished and Zhelica sipped the soothing brew.

By the time Yavan returned, she was out of bed and dressed. He stood behind her at the mirror as she combed and plaited her hair. "You are looking a little pale. Do you want me to get a doctor?"

"I'm an *alloy,*" she laughed. "Of course I'm pale." She turned. "You don't really mind if I call myself that, do you?"

He frowned in a way that made his dimples prominent. "It depends on *why* you're saying it. Do you feel like cheap metal mixed with the better stuff? Or like strengthened gold?"

"Gold, of course," she said. "Especially being married to you."

This ended in a kiss. "I have a busy day today, so I might be back a bit late," he said. "If I'm not here for dinner, eat without me."

As soon as he was gone, Zhelica carried the teapot and cup down to the kitchen. Nazhin and Beyman were already at work preparing breakfast for the first customers of the day. Nazhin beamed when she saw her.

"Better?" she asked as Zhelica set the dishes in the sink.

She nodded.

"How long are you going to keep this from Yavan?" Nazhin asked.

Zhelica shrugged and smiled. "I don't know. Maybe until he can see my swelling belly."

Even though she was tired, she decided to go for a walk. The distant mountains were caked with snow but Hyarani glowed under the thin sunlight of a winter day. Zhelica covered her head to protect her ears. She headed for the bookshop; it was open now, but to her disappointment, the history section had been removed.

"There's no market for those books," the owner told her. "They were just taking up shelf space."

She turned through street after street as though she were wandering aimlessly, but she knew where she was going. Soon she stood before a shop in the busy bazaar.

"Can I help you?" a man clutching a small broom asked. Zhelica made a show of looking through his stacks of scarves.

"You don't have any with embroidery, do you?" she asked, thinking of her own new peacock covering.

"Nobody does that anymore," the shopkeeper said. "Too much effort. The days of that kind of handiwork are over."

Zhelica moved on, edging toward the shrine. She felt a strange attraction to the golden statue. She gazed at it. It was just a lump of metal, she knew, but there was something mesmerizing about it. She wanted to leave, but could not stop staring at the figure, the candlelight bouncing off the gold, the hues of blue varying as the moving crowd cast shadows across the alcove. *Was Shurash good or evil?* she wondered. Yavan and Nazhin seemed unwilling to talk about him, and when her husband did, he was scornful. *But how could anyone so beautiful be bad?*

The spell was broken by a voice behind her. It was the first time it had happened in the city. *"Alloy!"* came a boy's voice.

Zhelica turned. The youth yanked down her scarf before diving into the mass of shoppers. Zhelica hastily pulled it up, but not before others had caught sight of her. Suddenly self-conscious, she headed for the nearest alley and hurried home.

As the day progressed, the weather turned. Clouds rolled in, the temperature dropped, and it began to rain – first a light drizzle, but by late afternoon, it was all-out pouring.

The common room was so dark, Nazhin lit the gas lamps and the children played near the fireplace. Yavan had warned Zhelica he might be home late, but she waited by the window until the last minute, watching for some sign of Syah trotting up the alley. At last she abandoned her post and joined the family around the table.

The children were testy; they had been indoors too long. Usually the hired girl took them for a half hour to a park nearby to run around, but she had a cold and had taken the day off. The older two kicked each other under the table, and Shoja (whose molars were about to erupt) screamed until Nazhin removed him from his high chair and held him on her lap, massaging his tender gums. Zhelica was not nauseated but felt overwhelmed at her future as a mother. She wondered when she should let Yavan know she was pregnant.

When the captain finally appeared, everything changed. The children pushed him down and then proceeded to climb on him, slap hands, pinch his cheek, and tell predictable jokes. Nazhin relaxed, Beyman cleared up the dinner dishes, and a happy family scene filled the common room.

After the children were sated with their fill of Yavan, he joined Zhelica at the table.

"Sorry I'm so late," he said. "We had a shipment of flour slide off a bridge into a creek, and I had to send men out to get it. Most of it was salvageable, but some of it got wet and froze. Anyway, it's all in the warehouse now." He smiled and arranged a curl on her forehead. "What have you been up to today?"

"I went out for a walk in the morning," she said. "Otherwise, I've been here. The children have been little monsters."

Yavan glanced at them, his brown eyes softening. "But you have to love them, don't you?" He reached over and squeezed her hand, and she wondered if he had figured out her news already.

"Yavan! Come help with the puzzle," the younger girl said, dragging him away from Zhelica. "It's too hard for us."

He shrugged helplessly toward his wife and joined the others on the floor by the fireplace. Zhelica sat on the couch next to Nazhin, who was still soothing Shoja, and watched her husband.

The next day, and for many days after, she wished they had spent their evening differently.

Everyone went to bed at the usual time. Yavan was clearly tired, and Zhelica, too, so they flopped into bed, quickly falling asleep.

Sometime in the middle of the night, Zhelica woke. The room was dark but one curtain had been pulled aside. Muted light from the overcast sky showed the outline of her husband at the window.

"What is it?" he called down to the street in a loud whisper.

"I'm sorry, sir," came a voice below. "There's been an emergency at the base, and they need you to come."

He groaned. "Are you sure it can't wait until morning?"

"The commander told me to send for you, sir. I am heading back now, so I will see you there."

"I'll come as soon as I get my boots on," Yavan said. He closed and latched the window. Zhelica was already shivering from the outdoor air.

"Yavan? Are you leaving?"

He bent over her. "I'm sorry to wake you, my love. Look, there's some emergency at the base. I can't imagine what could be so critical at this time of night, but I have to go." He tucked the blanket around her. "Go to sleep, and I'll be back before you know it."

She listened, but could not see, as he pulled on his trousers and jacket and boots. The bedroom door opened and closed, and he was gone.

Zhelica wanted to get out of bed and watch him ride away, but now that the window was closed, she felt deliciously warm, and was afraid to move. "I'll just stay awake until he gets back," she told herself, trying to keep her eyes open. But it was hopeless. Within a few minutes, she was back asleep.

The sky was still dark when she next awoke. Light poured under the door, and she could hear the sound of voices in the hallway.

"Zhelica?" The door opened a crack, and Nazhin stood before her, a lantern in hand.

"What is it?" Zhelica asked, sitting up. Nazhin opened the door wider, and in stepped a soldier. But it was not Yavan – it was Afshar.

"My apologies," he said. His voice was shaking and his hands, clasping and unclasping in front of him, were doing the same. "There's been an accident."

Zhelica jumped out of bed. Afshar averted his eyes; she was, after all, in her nightgown. But Zhelica grabbed his arms.

"What happened?"

"Zhelica, let's get you dressed," Nazhin said, stepping forward. "Afshar wants to take you to the base to see Yavan."

Her husband's friend went out to wait with Beyman, who had heard the young soldier banging on the alley door.

"Is he all right?" Zhelica asked, complying as Nazhin dropped her dress over her head. "What happened?"

"There's no point in speculating," Nazhin said soothingly. She laced up the dress in back. "Where's your cloak? You will need it."

Zhelica pointed to the wardrobe. Nazhin wrapped her up, scooping her hair into the hood. "Afshar's going to let you ride with him. It will be faster than taking a carriage." She put a hand on each cheek of the younger woman. "Don't be afraid. Yavan needs you to be strong so you can help him."

Zhelica nodded, choking back tears. She was vaguely conscious of the knotting in her stomach, but hurried after Afshar, both skipping steps as they rushed down the staircase and out the back door. "Hold on," he said, and gave his horse a kick that sent it at a run down the street.

They stopped once, to rouse the guard at the gate and wait for it to be opened. They shot into the countryside, opposite the direction of Marjon's orchard. The horse's hooves ground strangely on the wet road, deftly maneuvering around patches of ice which glistened along the way.

Afshar slowed as they approached a bridge. He turned to Zhelica and said softly, "This is where the accident happened. They said Syah lost his footing and slipped, landing on top of Yavan." He dismounted and led his horse carefully, examining the place where one of the boards was knocked loose from the railing: apparently they had struck here. Afshar reached down and touched something dark on the road, and then stood up, staring at his hand. "Blood," he said, looking at Zhelica.

"Oh, hurry," she said, fighting tears.

Afshar jumped back on the horse. Although the bridge had a few wet spots that had iced over, his animal seemed to move without difficulty. It was strange,

Zhelica thought, that Syah would lose his footing. Yavan had boasted recently about the animal's surefootedness.

They arrived at the gate to the base. A guard approached, lantern in hand.

"Who goes there?" he asked, lifting the light.

"It's me – Captain Afshar," the soldier answered. "I need in. Quickly."

"Who's that with you, sir?" asked the guard, walking to the side to illuminate Zhelica. She was glad that the hood shielded her face.

"It's Captain Yavan's wife," Afshar said. "Now open the gate, soldier, or you will have to answer to me in the morning."

"Yes, sir," he said, and lifted the cross-beam that served as a barricade. Afshar wasted no time steering his horse into the infirmary grounds and tying him to a post.

"Come along," Afshar said. Zhelica followed him inside the infirmary.

The night nurse rose from his desk. "How can I help you, sir?"

"I heard that Captain Yavan had an accident," Afshar said. Despite his nervousness around her, Zhelica noticed that with military men he spoke confidently. "Take us to him."

"Civilians aren't allowed on the ward, sir," the nurse said.

"This is Captain Yavan's wife," Afshar said. "I will answer for her presence."

"Yes, sir," the nurse said, and led them through the dark corridor.

Most of the patients were asleep in the rooms they passed. The nurse stopped outside a door near the end of the passage. "Captain Yavan is in here."

"Give me your lantern," Afshar said. The nurse complied, but Zhelica could see he was not happy. "You may go," Afshar told him. The man turned and (one hand on the wall so he would not trip in the near darkness) felt his way back to the entrance.

The room was small, with only one pallet in it. Lowering the lantern so he could see better, Afshar sucked in his breath in a way that frightened Zhelica. She pushed him aside so she could see the patient's face.

It was her husband, but his normally vibrant features were blank, his skin a strange gray, his lips parted, and short, rasping breaths coming out.

"Oh, Yavan!" Zhelica cried, putting a hand on his cheek.

"Quiet, Zhelica," Afshar warned her.

Yavan's eyes fluttered open but while he appeared to be looking at his wife, there seemed no recognition.

"He needs water," she said, and turned to look around the tiny room. She realized now that they were in a linen closet. She stepped back into the hallway; in the light from the lantern she could just make out a tank with a spigot. She filled a cup with water and carried it back into the room. Afshar had thrown back the blanket and was frozen in place.

"What is it?" Zhelica whispered.

The side of Yavan's uniform was drenched with blood, as was the mattress beneath him. It was more than would come from merely falling, even if Syah had pinned him. Afshar, his fingers quaking, lifted up Yavan's jacket and shirt and they both saw the wound.

It was small and straight. The work of a blade.

Yavan let out a heavy sigh and Afshar dropped his shirt. Zhelica skirted the pallet so she could reach her husband without going around Afshar. It was too late. He was no longer breathing.

Frantically, Zhelica began shaking his shoulder. "Yavan," she begged, "Yavan, wake up. Open your eyes." Her voice started to rise. "Yavan."

"Zhelica." Afshar spoke quietly but so sharply that she could not help but look at him. "We need to get out of here *now.*"

He drew her away from the pallet, keeping one hand firmly on her shoulder while covering Zhelica's mouth with the other. She was not struggling, but they could both tell a wail was waiting beneath that palm. They pushed through the door and stood outside in the dark, in the cold, both shaking.

"Zhelica, you must not make any noise, or we are both done for," Afshar whispered. "I want you to wait here while I get the horse."

She felt his long fingers slide away from her mouth and she let out one gasp but nodded her cooperation. Her teeth were chattering; she pushed her fist into her mouth. Zhelica could not think. All her concentration was focused on staying quiet and still.

Afshar explained later that he had gone to the nurse with a story that Captain Yavan's wife had been ill at the smell of the ward and he had taken her out back. He told the nurse that the captain seemed to be resting and he would return in the morning.

Zhelica was almost catatonic and mounted the horse with difficulty. Afshar eased himself up. "Raise your hood," he urged her, and then returned to the gate. Feigning good humor, he waved at the guard as they left.

"How's Captain Yavan, sir?" the man called to him as he moved the barricade.

"I think he'll be much better with rest," Afshar said. "Good night."

He deliberately walked the horse beyond the entrance and cantered away, not wanting to appear too eager to escape. When they reached the bridge, he slowed again. It was just past dawn now, and the increasing light showed where Syah's hooves had scraped across the muddy planks. He must have been injured, too, when Yavan was attacked.

They returned to the restaurant. Nazhin and Beyman had waited up for them in the kitchen, and the four of them huddled together there, talking in low voices so they would not rouse the children. Zhelica wept openly now, and Nazhin held her as Afshar told them the story that *he* had been told: Yavan had been going too fast on the icy bridge, Syah lost his footing, they both had fallen, and Yavan had been crushed under the horse.

Everything had happened so quickly, Zhelica felt like she could not grasp the story. Had Yavan been attacked on his way to the base or the way back? Who would hurt him? Did they *mean* to kill him, or had there been some kind of struggle that had gotten out of control?

His rasping breath echoed in her mind and the sight of Afshar lifting his uniform, showing her the wound, replayed itself. Her lips were parched, and when Beyman handed her a cup of water, she thought of her own scramble to get a drink to Yavan. It was too late. She had been too late.

The same wail that had been suppressed at the base was still there, waiting to push out. She longed to give it freedom, but surrounded by the others, she could only cry.

Afshar answered Beyman's questions, the same questions rephrased and discussed until there was nothing new to say.

"He was like a brother to me," Afshar said at last. He looked almost as pale as Zhelica.

"I feel the same way, even though I have not known him as long as you," Nazhin said, repeatedly wiping her eyes. "And the children! I don't know how they will cope without him."

"He was a good man," Beyman said. "What a loss to us all. Especially you, Zhelica."

She was numb, exhausted from crying, her mind now empty. It was too hard to think of what had happened and what it meant. Nazhin put an arm around her shoulder and pulled her close. "Poor thing," she murmured in her friend's ear.

They might have sat like that all day, but one of the boys found them. "Shoja's crying," he said. "What are you all doing down here?"

No one was ready to tell the children, so they returned to their normal pattern of life, cooking breakfast for the little ones (none of the adults could eat), and getting ready to open the restaurant for the day.

Somehow they made it through the morning. The girl who stayed with the children was still sick, so they were left upstairs, the adults taking turns watching them. The little ones could sense something was wrong, and from the tiniest up, they all showed their affection for Zhelica in little ways, so that by the afternoon, she felt both emotionally raw and tenderly cared for.

Afshar managed to head back to the base, but not before prohibiting Zhelica from discussing what they had seen. "Something's going on, something bad," he said. "I'm not sure what it is. I don't know who would want to –" he couldn't say it, and his voice trailed off. "I'll try to find out what I can, but in the meantime, you need to stick to the story I told."

Zhelica nodded, biting her lip. She lay a hand on Afshar's arm. "Come back when you can," she choked.

She felt at a total loss of what to do. Fortunately, Nazhin stepped in like an older sister. "We need to send word to Marjon. Do you want to write her a note?"

Zhelica dreaded sharing the news. But she dutifully sat down at the table with the paper and pen her landlady provided.

Dearest Marjon,

There was a terrible accident last night. Syah slipped and Yavan was crushed. (She became teary as she wrote it.) *Afshar and I were able to see him in the infirmary before the end. Oh, Marjon! I can't believe he's gone.*

Zhelica

She did not have the strength either to ask Marjon to come or urge her to stay away. She wanted nothing, no one. Her one desire was to wake up and find that it had all been a terrible nightmare.

Marjon appeared a few hours later. She did not knock on Zhelica's bedroom door but threw herself inside, not even removing her winter cloak before embracing her niece. Zhelica could see by her bloodshot eyes that she, too, had been crying.

"I had the watchman drive me," she said, looking around the room as though she had left something there. "He'll wait while you get your things."

Zhelica cried, "No, Aunt Marjon! No! I cannot leave now." She began hyperventilating, and her aunt quickly settled her in one of the chairs.

"I didn't think you'd want to stay here alone," Marjon said. She appeared hurt by her niece's vehemence. Zhelica dropped her head in her hands and wept.

"Oh, Auntie," she sobbed. "He was gone most of yesterday and got home late. And then he spent the evening playing with the children. When he got up to leave for the base, I had no idea he wouldn't...I didn't even get up to see him off. . ."

"Dear Zhelica," her aunt said, rubbing her back. "You should not blame yourself for that. You couldn't have known he wouldn't return."

"And Afshar took me to the base," Zhelica gasped.

"Yes, Nazhin told me everything," Marjon said soothingly. "There, just sit quietly. Let me get some tea for you."

The children had been kept in the common room, but they sensed the anguish of their friend, and tiptoed through the hall as though ready to help at a moment's notice. When Marjon opened the door, she called the oldest one to her. "Get your mother to send some tea up for Zhelica. She is not feeling well."

The boy strained to glance behind her but Marjon blocked his view, so he gave up and headed down to the kitchen. The others stared at her with big eyes. She forced a smile and gently closed the door.

"Zhelica," she said, sitting next to her, "did Yavan say anything to you before he . . . ?"

She shook her head. "He had lost too much blood."

Marjon looked startled by this. To have broken his back might have killed him; but there would not have been much blood.

"We need to get you away from here," she said firmly.

"No, I'm not going," Zhelica said. She looked wildly about their little apartment. There were hints of Yavan everywhere: his extra trousers and shirt hanging in the wardrobe, which had been left open; a book he had been reading on the bedside table. She would not leave this room.

Marjon seemed frightened. "Zhelica, I'm not sure it's safe here for you."

"The family will take care of me, Marjon. I'm not ready to leave yet," she begged her aunt. She felt like a little child, pleading to get her way. Marjon watched her.

"Maybe I could stay the night, then," she suggested.

"Yes, please do," Zhelica said. This was an option she could agree to.

The darkness settled in early again. Marjon busied herself by keeping the fire blazing and coming and going with food. Zhelica was not hungry. She tried not to think about the baby, now so tiny its presence was mainly manifested by an upset stomach. *If only I had told Yavan about the baby,* she thought miserably. *Maybe he'd be alive now, if he'd known he is a father.*

Afshar reappeared after dark. He was surprised to find Marjon in the room. He awkwardly hovered over the women until Marjon went out to get a chair for him. While she was gone, he quickly knelt by Zhelica.

"The rumor going around the base is that Yavan was a spy," he whispered.

"A spy! For who?" The idea was ridiculous, but everything that had happened over the last day seemed so surreal, that Zhelica did not know what to do except be carried along with the tumbling current of strangeness.

"They're saying for Darz," Afshar said. He shook his head and ran his long fingers through his hair.

"I can't believe it," Zhelica whispered back. "I never saw any sign of him spying."

"He *was* a risk taker. I mean, it wouldn't be a total shock to me if he was spying, but if he was, he didn't ever let on to me."

Marjon returned with the chair for Afshar, and this part of the conversation was over. Zhelica felt lightheaded. She leaned back in the armchair. Could it be true? Could Yavan have been a spy?

Afshar composed himself. "I only came to say that I am sorry. Yavan was my best friend in all the world...I can't believe he's gone." He wiped a tear away. "The funeral will be tomorrow afternoon. I would be glad to drive you there."

His face belied his words. He was worried now: if Yavan had been a spy, Zhelica was suspect, too...and so was Afshar himself. It would be better to have some distance from Zhelica.

Marjon anticipated her niece's response. "No, thank you, Afshar. We will come ourselves. But thank you for letting us know."

He rose. "Well, then, I should probably get back to the base."

"Ride carefully," Zhelica said, tears again brimming over.

"I will," Afshar told her. He bowed to them both, and when he lifted his head, Zhelica could see apprehension swirling in his dark eyes.

Nine

If she had not been pregnant, Zhelica probably would not have slept at all. But despite dropping off in exhaustion, in the middle of the night she found herself awake in the blackness, disoriented. Next to her someone was snoring, but it was not Yavan. Marjon: she was sharing her bed. Suddenly Zhelica's chest felt like an empty cavern. The ache of loss, and the knowledge that haunted her before she was conscious of it, overwhelmed her. Yavan was dead.

She could not sleep now. Curled in a fetal position, clutching her knees, yearning for relief from the pain, she drenched her pillow with noiseless tears. After what seemed hours, Zhelica gave up and climbed out of bed.

She knew where everything was in this little room which had been their first – their only – home together. As quietly as she could, she slipped into her dress (there was no one to lace it tight; she did her best). She pulled on her shoes and felt on the wall for the hook where she had hung her cloak. She wrapped it around her and carefully - anticipating the point at which the wood would creak - opened her bedroom door. Marjon did not stir. Zhelica gently pulled the door shut and stood a moment in the hallway.

All houses groan in the night as they shift, expand and contract. This one was no different. The occupants were still, their doors all closed. But the walls and roof occasionally wheezed, causing Zhelica to stop her journey down the corridor. Once she figured out what was happening, she hurried to the stairs and tip-toed down.

It was too dark to go out yet. She sat on the lowest step, her back pressed against the wall so she could watch the window on the side door. Zhelica never knew a night could last so long. At last, when she blinked, she recognized the dim light of dawn showing through that small pane of glass.

She did not have a key to the door. When she was out during the day, Nazhin left it open. Even though she did not like leaving the family unsecured while they slept, there seemed no option. She turned the bolt and slipped out into the early morning air.

The alley and the streets beyond looked odd in their vacant state. Zhelica felt like a ghost floating unseen from corner to corner. The sky lightened as she went. By the time she reached the café, it was definitely morning.

Azara was awake; Zhelica could see her stirring something on the stove in the open kitchen, her hair wrapped in a scarf.

Zhelica knocked and then relaxed her forehead against the window. Azara jumped when she saw the white face peering in, but she quickly unlocked the door, grabbed Zhelica and tugged her inside, relocking the door behind her.

Azara led her back to her private quarters, pulling the curtain aside. "Go on in," she said.

She had not yet made her bed and reached to yank wrinkled clothes off one of the chairs. "Sit down."

Zhelica dropped limply into the seat.

"You look like you haven't slept in days," Azara noted with a frown.

"You said if I needed help, I could come to you," Zhelica said. "Azara, I don't know what to do."

"What's happened?"

Zhelica sighed. She was so tired. "My husband was murdered," she said, her voice dwindling so low that it took the old woman a minute to register the last word.

"Oh no, oh no," Azara clucked. She dabbed her own eyes with the end of her scarf. "Who would kill him? Why?"

"I don't know," Zhelica said. "One of the other soldiers told me there was a rumor that he was a spy. But that doesn't make any sense to me." She rested her head on her hand, tears splashing unhindered on the table.

Azara did not answer; finally, Zhelica looked up. To her astonishment, the old woman was breathing heavily, her pale cheeks flushed. "The idiot!" she finally burst out. "The idiot! What did he think? Of course, marrying you...that makes sense now. . ."

Zhelica straightened in her chair, sniffling. "What do you mean?"

"Well," Azara said, "you are a pretty girl, no doubt about that. But the risk of marrying an *alloy* (yes, I know

I told you I don't call myself that, but it describes what we are)...Who would take that risk? Either someone who wanted to cut himself off from the world, or someone who wanted to hide in plain sight. It was too obvious! Idiot!"

Zhelica slapped the table. "Stop calling my husband an idiot!" she cried. And then she sat back, wrapping her arms around herself, rocking in her chair. "I don't understand what's going on," she murmured.

"How much do you know about the history of Zaharada?" Azara asked.

"Very little. I tried to find books, but the bookstore closed and the history section disappeared."

"Did you tell your husband you were looking there?" Azara asked.

Zhelica nodded.

"He probably arranged for those books to vanish."

Zhelica could not hide her shock. "What do you mean? Why?"

"He didn't *want* you to know about the past," Azara said. "Oh, don't look so stunned. He was probably trying to protect you. Did he ever talk about what had happened here?"

Zhelica shook her head.

"I'll tell you now. But you must not breathe a word of this to anyone." Azara leaned in. "It is very dangerous to discuss these things, but you and I of all people should know the truth."

In a soft voice, the old woman began her tale.

"We had a lovely queen. She came here from Bustaan. They called her Yasneen the Just; she revolutionized our laws and our court system."

"I read something about *her,*" Zhelica said. "In a storybook."

"Hmph," Azara snorted. "That was no storybook then. Because she was a *real* queen. And the king, Sanjar the Innovator he was called. He invented things like a way to print books by machine and how to spin thread using steam power. He also hosted an annual fair where other inventors could bring their ideas to the palace and he would choose which to finance. He brought Zaharada into the modern world. So clever and good! Those were happy days in this land. We were prosperous and at peace with the world. There were craftsmen from Bustaan brought in to put glass in our windows and sell gold jewelry...such fine stuff, so delicate and intricate! My mother left me some. Ah!"

She became lost in thought, a smile playing at the edges of her lips. Then she glanced at Zhelica and shook herself.

"My father came here from Darz. He was a weaver, and he thought, *Why not make clothing and scarves on commission?* So he set up a shop here in Hyarani, and the fine ladies of the town came and ordered the most beautiful cloth, with golden threads and elegant patterns. My mother was the daughter of one of those wealthy families. When my father saw her, he said he fell in love with her right away." She gave a chuckle of delight. There was a rich story there, but she seemed to realize now was not the time to tell it.

"Life was going on well, but there was one great sadness throughout the land. Years went by, and the king and queen did not have any children. It didn't make them bitter like it would some. They say that when they were in public they were tender and affectionate with each other. But people started worrying about who would rule after the king died. His brother had married into a family in Bustaan and moved there. It was clear he had no interest in returning.

"Back in those days, the Overking sent messages through men called ambassadors. One day the ambassador in Baraqan went to the king and told him that he was to make the royal gardener his prince and heir.

"King Sanjar was puzzled by this. But the queen often went to the gardens and talked with the young man; she wholly approved of the plan. The gardener moved from the shed where he lived on the castle grounds into the palace.

"I saw him once," Azara said. "He was nothing special to look at. But there was something noble about him. And even when he became prince, he didn't put on airs. He walked around the capital every day when he was there, like a normal citizen. When he traveled around the country, he didn't take a retinue. He'd just ride in on his horse, tie it up in the town square, and walk around, talking to everyone. The people loved him. He seemed to really listen to their concerns, even the children. And whenever he saw a plant that wasn't thriving," she said, laughing at the memory, "why, he'd take a minute and snip off dead leaves, or untangle the branches, or just tell the owner what needed to be done to help it."

"How curious," Zhelica murmured.

"The king and queen loved him like a son. When the king died and he took the throne in his place, things got even better. He didn't spend time inventing things like King Sanjar. But he had such a way about him – such wisdom. People would come from all over to bring him gifts or ask him for advice.

"Well, the people of Darz, who were mostly farmers and woodsmen, heard tales about Zaharada and how it was thriving. Pretty soon they started coming here to work in the shops and do carpentry. They married Zaharadan women. And one day the King of Darz came himself. He said, 'We would like to join our kingdom to yours. We will be your loyal subjects.'

"There were celebrations and parades and our king went to Darz. The people there loved him, too. They crowned him emperor of the new country, which was called Darzarada. A road was carved through the mountains joining the two old countries. The emperor built a new palace there looking down on what used to be Darz to the north and Zaharada to the south."

"Darzarada," Zhelica whispered. "I wonder if my father came during that time?"

"Oh, probably," Azara nodded. "Lots of young men did. The emperor wanted the people of Darz and Zaharada to learn each other's customs. He wanted us all to see ourselves as one country.

"Of course there were plenty of *alloys* after that. So much intermarriage, so many children! And no one hated us – we were like a symbol, a badge of what the unity of the countries meant."

"So what happened?" Zhelica asked.

Azara stood up, and peeked through the curtain. "I guess I have a little more time before customers start arriving," she said, settling back into her chair. "Well, not everyone was happy with this new empire."

"Bustaan?" Zhelica suggested.

"No, it wasn't from outside that the trouble came," Azara told her. "An man appeared one day in Baraqan while the emperor was traveling. He said he was the High Ambassador. He announced that the other ambassadors were no longer needed. He claimed that was what the Overking had said."

"What was his name?" Zhelica asked, suspicious.

"He called himself Shurash. I saw *him* once, too. He was so handsome! The emperor looked plain next to him. But there was something about him that didn't seem right."

"How so?"

Azara shifted uncomfortably. "I don't know how to explain it. His words were like honey, but the effects were poisonous. He began speaking to the generals of the army. They were taking recruits from Darz at that time. He said the Overking didn't want that happening, so they were sent home. Shurash gained more and more control over the military. Finally he persuaded them that they needed to destroy the emperor and rid Zaharada of all Darzians.

"It was terrible," Azara said, and her eyes filled with tears. She clutched her throat. "The emperor was ambushed. They had a military trial and sentenced him to death."

"On what charge?" Zhelica asked. She was so caught up in the story, she had almost forgotten why she came.

"They said he was a traitor. He had broken faith with the Overking. He'd seized too much power by combining the kingdoms. It was a travesty – trying him at night and then executing him in the morning. Just to mock him for being the former gardener, they hanged him from a tree in the palace garden."

Azara shook her head sadly.

Zhelica was exhausted and hungry. She had come emotionally depleted and this story heaped on her personal tragedy seemed too much. She started weeping and said, "Why are you telling me this?"

Azara snuffled, wiping her nose and eyes with the edge of her apron. "A resistance sprang up inside Zaharada. There were plenty of people who wanted to keep Darzarada alive. There were even reports that the emperor was not actually dead. I don't know how that could be, but some believed it. Anyway, these cells of people were meeting. There were former Darzians and Zaharadans and even displaced ambassadors all trying to overthrow Shurash and the new military government. His response was ruthless. He seized all the boys in Baraqan and created a military academy there before killing their parents. And he had any suspected members of the Restoration (that's what the members of the resistance called themselves) rounded up and shot.

"There was no plague," she added.

No plague. Zhelica's thoughts went nowhere.

"Your parents," Azara said pointedly. "They weren't killed in a plague. Like your husband, they must have been part of the Restoration."

The combination of morning sickness and horror sent waves of nausea through Zhelica. She stumbled to the sink and heaved up the little food she had not fully digested. And then bile. And then she just stood by the sink, shaking.

Azara was beside her in an instant. "I'm sorry, my dear. That was too much at once."

She poured a glass of water and supported her while Zhelica swished. There were no more tears now: she had cried herself out.

"I still don't know what to do," she said, despair creeping into her voice.

"There's only one thing to do," Azara said, suddenly firm. "The only way to protect yourself is to show that you are not connected with the Restoration. You must go to the base and ask for a job."

"Work for the military?" Zhelica asked. She could hear her own voice, and she sounded like a madwoman. "Are you crazy? They are probably planning on killing me next."

Azara said quietly, "Not if you show that you are a loyal citizen. You have no means of support; your husband was a soldier. You want to serve because he no longer can. If you work for them, they can be sure you aren't a spy."

There was a sound from the restaurant, someone trying to open the door.

"Wash your face, my dear, and let yourself out through the back. And let me know how it goes." Azara gave her a grandmotherly kiss and disappeared into the restaurant.

Zhelica walked slowly back to Nazhin's. Azara's plan sounded dangerous. Or was it the best choice? Should *she* try to hide in plain sight? It had not worked very well for Yavan.

She kicked a piece of chipped brick off the sidewalk. How could he do this to her? Yavan had hidden who he really was from her...They had been in the most intimate relationship possible, and yet he had not told her anything of who he was or what he was really doing. He had put her at risk by his actions. And now he would never know their child because somehow he had been found out...

She instinctively put a hand on her belly as she walked, anger mingling with her sorrow. She did not know what she would do in the long term, but for now she would take Azara's advice and ask for work at the base.

When she turned down the alley toward the restaurant, she saw Beyman at the door, glancing worriedly up and down the street. When he saw her, his face relaxed.

"I'm sorry for leaving the door unlocked," Zhelica said. Her lips felt dry from crying without drinking enough water. "I had to walk."

His eyes softened. "We're all fine. Go on up and get some breakfast."

The children and Nazhin were at the table, but Marjon was pacing the floor when Zhelica entered. Her hair and expression made her look like she had escaped a whirlwind. She rushed to her niece and wrapped her arms around her. "Oh, Zhelica," she said, her voice catching. "I was so worried about you."

Zhelica hugged her briefly and then slipped out of her grasp. "I needed to think."

"Come, have something to eat," Nazhin urged, sending a child to another chair so that her friend could sit next to her. Zhelica could not bear to look at Marjon. If what Azara had said was true, Marjon had lied about her parents.

"Afshar let us know that the funeral will be this afternoon," Nazhin said softly. "I don't want the children to...to see ...so I will keep them here and Beyman will take you. I hope you understand."

"Of course," Zhelica said, reaching for a piece of toast. There was no point in subjecting the children to unnecessary grief.

"Are you sure you are up to going?" Marjon asked.

Zhelica's look seemed to silence the older woman. "I have to go."

By the time they were ready to leave, both were dressed somberly. "This was left from when my own mother died," Nazhin said, patting a black scarf affectionately before handing it to Zhelica. "My thoughts will be with you during the funeral."

They were allowed to drive onto the base after Beyman explained that Yavan's wife was in his carriage. Chairs had been set up on the parade ground. It looked like every soldier on base had chosen (or been required) to attend the ceremony. Beyman spoke with one of the officers, and he, Marjon, and Zhelica were escorted to the front of the assembly.

Zhelica could feel eyes inspecting her as she walked up the aisle. There were a few audible gasps: even though she had covered her hair, they were close enough to see her ivory skin. "See, I told you," one soldier whispered to another as she passed. She sat as upright in the chair as she could. If they wanted to see she was an *alloy,* she would not deprive them of the opportunity.

Marjon fidgeted nervously next to her. She was clearly not comfortable being on the base, even though she had been selling fruit and nuts to them for years. When the commander came over to offer his condolences, he began with her.

"So sorry about the tragic accident which claimed such a fine young officer," he said, bowing stiffly. Marjon murmured some response. The commander moved on to Zhelica. "Your husband was a brave man."

She dared to look him in the face. "Thank you." A tear rolled down her cheek. "My loss is almost too much to bear." The commander's face twitched (was it sympathy? regret?) and he bowed and moved on to Beyman. "Thank you for coming," the commander said, and Nazhin's husband nodded.

The ceremony was brief. Six officers (including Afshar) carried the coffin to the front of the crowd and rested it on a raised platform so they could all see it. Yavan's sword was drawn from its scabbard and laid on top of the coffin. The commander read from the military handbook. " 'And now we lay this soldier to rest. . .' "

It seemed unreal. Zhelica wanted to pry the lid off that box and confirm her husband was there. She wondered what she would say if she could talk to him right now: Would she kiss him or slap him in wrath? Would life ever return to any kind of normal? Would she ever be happy again?

When it was over, the crowd dispersed. None of the soldiers approached her to offer a word of consolation or praise for her fallen husband. Marjon lay a hand on her back. "Let's go," she said softly.

"One moment," Zhelica said. "I need to do something."

She went up to the commander and stood patiently while he finished giving instructions to one of his men. When he turned, a contemptuous look flickered across his face before he brought it back under stern control.

"What can I do for you, ma'am?"

"Well, commander, I don't know if Captain Yavan told you, but I am an orphan."

"No, that did not come up in any conversations."

"I need a means of supporting myself now," she said. "I can cook or clean and I am able to read and write."

He nodded toward Marjon. "Won't she provide for you?" he asked.

Zhelica smiled weakly. "After tasting freedom, I don't think I can go back to the orchard," she confided.

"Yes, I can imagine." He stood looking at her a moment, clearly weighing something, his eyes narrowed.

Then he told her, "We have a few civilians working on the base, but no women."

"Please, just give me a chance," Zhelica pleaded. "I am a hard worker, and it would mean a lot to me to support what meant so much to my husband."

One of the commander's eyebrows rose at this. If Zhelica believed in her husband's devotion to the military, she must be ignorant Yavan was a spy.

At last, he answered. "Fine. How soon can you come?"

"Tomorrow," she said. "There is nothing preventing me from starting immediately."

"Be here at eight in the morning. I will have my assistant give you a work detail."

"Thank you, sir," she said. "You will not regret hiring me."

"Hmm," he said, scratching his head. "That remains to be seen."

Marjon looked more astonished than the commander when Zhelica told her what she had done. "But Zhelica, why in the world would you want to work on the base? You know you always have a home with me."

They were sitting at the little table in Zhelica's room. Nazhin had sent tea in, and Zhelica poured her aunt a cup.

"Auntie," Zhelica said, "I know that you love me and have always taken good care of me. But the day I married Yavan, everything changed. I can never return to being a child in your house."

"Of course not," her aunt said, her hands trembling as she set down the cup and saucer. "I would not expect that. But I can train you to take over the orchard, and you'll be safe."

"Safe!" Zhelica shook her head. "I will never feel safe again."

There must have been some finality in the way she said this. Marjon did not broach the subject again.

"Nazhin and Beyman are allowing me to keep my room here," Zhelica said. "Since Syah was put down after the fall, I'll walk to the base, at least until the weather gets too hot. Please don't worry about me," she said, and reached over to give her aunt's hand a reassuring squeeze. "I will be fine."

She heard Marjon stop and exchange a few words with the landlords on her way out. But she seemed to have accepted Zhelica's choice. Her countenance when she turned before descending the stairs, however, was heavy with concern.

"Well, now, Zhelica," Nazhin said, collecting up the tea tray. "Beyman said he'd give you a ride in tomorrow, since it's your first day." She smiled encouragingly. "I think Yavan would be proud of you for what you are doing."

"Thank you," Zhelica said. She looked at the clock over the fireplace: it was still early, but she was feeling the previous night's lack of sleep. "Nazhin, I think I might just go to bed now. Thank you for your kind help today. I am glad I can stay here. Oh, wait," she asked. "Could you loosen my ties?"

"Of course," Nazhin said. She gently undid the back of Zhelica's dress. "Sleep well."

Zhelica slipped into her nightgown and wrapped a blanket around herself, sitting before the fire until it had burned down to coals. She crawled into bed when she felt she could no longer keep her eyes open, quickly dropping off to sleep.

When she awoke the next morning, the heaviness of loss hung in the cold air, and she turned on her pillow to look at that place where Yavan used to lie. The bedclothes were as smooth as when she had slipped under the covers. She sighed and got up.

It was strange after having so many days to spend as she pleased to suddenly have responsibilities. Zhelica joined the family for breakfast but did not linger. Beyman kissed his wife goodbye, and with the young widow next to him, drove to the base. Zhelica jumped down and said to the guard, "I am working here. Please admit me."

The guard went back into his booth and returned. "I have a note here about you," he said, holding up a sheet of paper. "You may enter." He held the bar aloft and Zhelica passed under it. "Go to the administration building. It's next to the parade ground, where the funeral was."

The administration building was a dull place, painted dun outside and in. Zhelica stepped to the desk, where a soldier about her age was filling out paperwork. He feigned busyness for a moment and then glanced up.

"Captain Yavan's wife, isn't it?" he said. "What can I do for you?"

"I'm here to see the commander's assistant about my work assignment."

The young man's jaw dropped. "Just a minute," he said, and ducked into the nearest office. Zhelica heard voices but could not distinguish what they were saying. The soldier returned.

"You are to report to the mailroom."

"Where's that?" Zhelica asked.

"Just go outside and turn right. It's a small brick building with bars on the windows." He gave her a half-smile that was almost cheering. "Good luck," he said.

His description was apt. The other structures matched the administration building, but the mailroom stood off by itself, a red brick box surrounded by bushes. Zhelica went up to the door and knocked. No one answered. A couple of soldiers walked by, and one called out, "It's open. Just go in."

She did.

Inside was a high wooden counter. Zhelica peered over to see what was on the other side. A fireplace blazed in one corner, a couple chairs in front of it. The rest of the room was filled with tables and cubbyholes for the letters. A soldier, his back to her, was leaning over, tightening the string on a parcel. She waited patiently until he was done.

"So, you're the help they sent," he said, as he turned and leaned against the table, crossing his arms.

The first thing that struck Zhelica was the soldier's hair. It was not the neat-and-tidy trim that Yavan and Afshar wore. Curls tumbled down his forehead and over his ears – massive black curls. He tossed his head to move the hair from his eyes. They were not friendly, but flashed with lightning, which seemed appropriate for a face like a storm cloud. He had a strong jaw, which he clenched and unclenched as he stared at Zhelica.

"Yes, I'm – " she began.

"I know who you are," the soldier said. "Mrs. Yavan."

The next thing Zhelica noticed was how massive the man was. He approached the counter, which was shoulder-height to Zhelica; his upper body towered over it.

He flipped up a section of the counter. "Come through," he said.

Zhelica felt years younger as she passed the man. He let the counter section bang back in place, and Zhelica jumped.

"I hope you're not the nervous type," the soldier said, his eyes sparking through the curls that fell back over them.

"Not at all," she said. Drawing on a courage she did not feel, she said, "My name is Zhelica. If you will explain what you want me to do, I'll get to work."

This seemed to amuse him, and he gave a quick smile before returning to his normal state. "Well, Zhelica, my name is Rakshan. Not *Captain* Rakshan," he said, his voice tinged with bitterness. "*Lieutenant* Rakshan. Despite this building being small, every piece of mail that moves through Zaharada is processed here."

"Why is that?" Zhelica asked. It explained the stacks of correspondence piled on every surface.

"Part of our job is to censor what comes in," Rakshan said. "We don't have to read it all, but we should be on the lookout for anything threatening to our country. You know, spy correspondence, that sort of thing." He gave her a meaningful look, probably some reference to Yavan. Zhelica decided to ignore his implication.

"How do you know which are suspicious?" she asked, plucking a letter from the top of a mound.

"That's *my* job," Rakshan said. "Your job is just to sort. First, you pull out all the military mail and put any items for this base in the cubbyholes for the soldiers here." He nodded toward the wall. "The other military mail is then put in bags for the academy in Baraqan, and for the other two bases. The rest is sorted by city into separate bags."

"I can see why you needed help," Zhelica said. "Why didn't they assign another soldier to this office?"

"Why, indeed?" he asked. "Guess this job isn't considered important enough."

Rakshan pointed to one of the tables that already showed signs of organization. "You can start putting those in the cubbyholes," he said. "The soldiers are listed alphabetically by last name."

Zhelica picked up a handful of letters. They were not yet alphabetized. At first she wandered back and forth along the wall, sliding the envelopes into the holes. With the second stack, she rapidly arranged the letters in order first, and then distributed them. When the table was cleared, she said, "Lieutenant? I'm finished. What now?"

The soldier walked along the wall and randomly pulled out letters to make sure they were correctly filed. His expression softened slightly.

"Well, that was pretty fast," he acknowledged. "Who knows? Maybe with your help we can get on top of this mess."

She smiled. It felt good to have her mind and fingers occupied, and there was a slight gratification in the brooding soldier's praise.

"Why don't we work together?" he suggested. "I'll separate the military from the nonmilitary mail, and you can bag them by base." He showed her where to find the base name in the address. Zhelica marveled at his large hands. *Sorting mail seems like odd work to give a man built like him,* she thought.

By noon they had figured out how to work together without getting in each other's way. It was not intellectually difficult, Zhelica admitted to herself, but distracting enough to allow her to forget about her own pain for a few minutes at a time. Her heart did leap when she caught a glimpse of Rakshan's arm extended for more mail, the color of his uniform bringing forth a primal happiness suggesting Yavan was near. *"He's not here,"* she kept telling herself. *"He's not coming through the door, he's not on the base, he's not going to show up."*

"Did you bring food?" Rakshan asked. "Or do you want me to get something from the mess hall for you?"

"I've got my lunch," Zhelica said. She pulled out vegetables wrapped in flatbread and sat down by the fireplace.

"I'll be back in a few minutes," the lieutenant told her.

He was so tall that Zhelica could see him far down the road, his shoulders bobbing as he took giant steps, his hair bouncing as he walked. *A strange young man,* she thought as she took a bite of food. But so far, her job was going well.

Ten

During the afternoon, they got into a good rhythm in their work. By quitting time, Rakshan seemed pleased with what they had accomplished.

"Look around," he said. Of the four sorting tables, only one had stacks of letters on it. Mail bags, their cords pulled tight, sat in a row by the front door, each labeled with its destination.

"Not bad," Zhelica agreed. "So may I go, then?"

"Unless you'd like to celebrate with me," Rakshan said. He opened the door of one of the many small cupboards built below the front counter and held aloft a bottle. "A little wine to toast our first day?"

Zhelica had seen wine in Beyman and Nazhin's restaurant. Marjon never kept it at the orchard (in fact, she had warned Zhelica about its effects). Her landlords never served it at family meals.

"I think I should go," Zhelica said, apologetically. "It's a long walk home for me."

Rakshan shrugged, setting the bottle on the floor near the fireplace. "Never mind. I'm fine celebrating alone."

He folded his long body into a chair, stretching out his feet toward the fire, combing curls away from his face before uncorking the wine.

"Well, good night then," Zhelica said. "I'll see you tomorrow."

"Right," Rakshan answered without turning.

Zhelica ducked under the counter and let herself out.

The sun had already set and the sky was streaked with pale pink clouds. Zhelica wrapped her cloak around herself, pulling up the hood. A few soldiers glanced her way as she left, but no one said anything to her. The shift had changed and the afternoon guard looked a bit startled, but opened the barricade with only a, "Good evening, miss."

The road was edged with leafless trees, Zhelica's only companions a few small birds darting through the underbrush. Her mind kept busy on the tasks of the day, on the unexpected pleasure of having work to do in the wider world. She thought of her strange co-worker and compared him to Yavan. Taller. Moodier. He scarcely smiled and his jokes were cynical. But he had not made any references to her being an *alloy*, which was some relief. Perhaps Azara had been right suggesting that Zhelica make her living on the base.

When she reached home, she walked past the front entrance of the restaurant. The sky had darkened considerably, and the light spilling out across the street gave a warm glow. Zhelica could see groups of men who had just finished their work eating at one table. A family sat together at another. The father was spooning food into the mouth of an infant compliantly poised in his high chair, his arms waving excitedly at the prospect of mashed vegetables. Zhelica pressed her hand to her abdomen. Who was this little person Yavan had left her? What would become of them? She sighed aloud before heading upstairs through the alley door.

"Zhelica!" the children practically pounced on her when she entered the common room. Nazhin was just setting a pot of stew on the table.

"Children," she reprimanded. "You can't jump on her like she's ...she's a *man.*"

They all stopped, as though frozen. Zhelica knew everyone was thinking the same thing. *You can't jump on me like I'm Yavan.*

She tossed her cloak onto the rack by the door. "It smells amazing in here," she said, inhaling deeply.

"Everyone come to the table," Nazhin said. Beyman popped in after they had started.

"We're so busy downstairs, I can't eat with you right now. How was your first day, Zhelica?"

She smiled. "Not bad. I'm in the mailroom. It's warm and there's only one soldier working with me, so not too much trouble."

"You must be hungry," one of the children said, watching her down her stew.

"I am!" she laughed. "I haven't worked that hard in ages."

Nazhin looked cheered by Zhelica's manner. "We missed you around here, though. The children were a handful after our helper left this morning."

Zhelica looked around and gratefulness welled up within her. Marjon had returned home. Yavan was gone. But he had chosen wisely when finding lodging for her. Zhelica brushed away a tear.

"You don't have to spend the evening with us," Nazhin said quickly, responding to Zhelica's apparent unhappiness. "We could send dessert to your room."

"No, I am glad to be here with you all." She turned to the boy next to her. "Maybe we could work on your puzzle tonight."

They did. After dinner, the children pushed the couches far from the fireplace and dumped jigsaw pieces on the floor. While their parents watched, the children sorted, tested the placement of various shapes, and tumbled over each other in an effort to complete the picture. Zhelica basked in the love of the family while trying not to think about the empty room that awaited her.

One by one, the children were led off to bed. Finally, Nazhin said with a yawn, "I'm afraid I'm done for today. Good night, Zhelica."

Beyman banked the fire. Zhelica knew she would have to leave. "Well, goodnight. Thank you for dinner."

Her own room was cold. There had been no fire there during the day, since she was gone, and none lit in the evening. Zhelica chose a dress from her wardrobe and lay it over the back of one of the chairs for the next day. She thought of bathing, but was too tired. Flinging off her dress and stepping out of her shoes, she crawled between the chilly sheets and shivered until she dropped off to sleep.

The thing about death, Zhelica realized, was that it was always there. In the morning, it hung in the corner of her room, reminding her of its presence. When she walked, they were companions. When, after minutes of distraction at work or with the children, her mind was uncluttered, death seeped in. *Yavan is gone. Dead and gone. You are alone.* It weighed on her even when she was not thinking about it.

She felt tired. At first she thought it was working all day, but as the weeks passed, she realized it was a combination of physical demands (standing and sorting, plus pregnancy) and yearning for Yavan. After the first night without Marjon, she admitted to herself there was no point in putting off bedtime: it was no easier to go to bed when Nazhin and Beyman left the common room first than it was to go earlier, warming her room and bathing before sleep.

"You seem sluggish today," Rakshan noted one morning as she moved slower than usual.

"I'm sorry," Zhelica said. "I guess I'm not feeling myself."

The soldier pushed the hair away from his bright eyes and looked closely. "Let's figure out a way you can sit while you work."

He dragged one of the chairs from the fireplace over to a table and pushed a pile of letters toward her. Then he got a broom from the corner and slid it between bars under the table so that it jutted out, hanging an open mail bag on it. "First sort the mail for the capital, and when that's done, I'll bring you another bag."

She smiled appreciatively. In the days they had spent together, she had grown to understand Rakshan better. He was, he told her, the son of one of the top generals. "I never wanted to be a soldier," he confessed. "But I was not given a choice. My father had me sent here and given a position where I interact with almost no one. (He's afraid I'll stir up discontent. Imagine.) The one perk," he added, "is that as long as I shave, I can keep the hair." He grabbed a handful and let it fall around his ears. "All the other soldiers have to get theirs cut short."

"Did you go to the military school?" Zhelica asked.

"I *lived* there," Rakshan said. "My father used it as his headquarters. I hated that place," he added gazing thoughtfully at the ceiling. "I think the feeling was mutual."

"Did you. . ." she began hesitantly.

"Did I what?"

"Did you know my husband at school?" Her cheeks burned as she asked, and she reached for a handful of letters to sort.

He stopped what he was doing and leaned against the table opposite her. "Little Mister Perfect Yavan?" He saw her expression change from embarrassment to pain, and changed the trajectory of his speech. "Yavan and I were classmates all the way through. Yes – he was front of the class, that kid who always had his hand up to answer questions. The teachers loved him. Everybody loved him," Rakshan admitted. "As you can imagine, I was more back-of-the-class."

Zhelica looked at him thoughtfully. "But you did well anyway," she guessed.

He chuckled. "I did well when I wanted to. I'm actually quite good at math."

"I'm surprised they didn't use that when choosing a job for you," Zhelica reflected.

"Well, like I told you, they wanted to keep me out of the way. And I'm fine here," he said, gesturing to his little world. "Nobody bothers me. And now I've got you here to help."

After showing consideration for her that day, Rakshan began helping her in other ways. He brought food at lunch, even when she said she had some. He repositioned her when the fire seemed too hot. He lifted the heavier mail bags so she did not have to.

This kindness was not lost on Zhelica. Since most of her days were spent with Rakshan, it felt good to be treated well.

On a day off, she dressed discreetly and dropped into Azara's restaurant between meals. The older lady let her sit at a corner table where they could both see the door.

"Tell me," she said, grasping Zhelica's hands. "What are you doing now? How are you?"

"I took your advice, Azara," she said. "I'm working in the mailroom at the base."

"The mailroom!" her friend responded. "Well, they must trust you if they put you there."

"Why do you say that?"

Azara moved closer. "Well, you could steal letters."

"I would never do that!" Zhelica said.

"Of course not," Azara said. "I'm glad it's worked out for you. And the men? How do they treat you?"

"They mostly ignore me," Zhelica said. "Maybe someone told them not to talk to me." She pulled out a purse filled with coins and jingled it. "It's not the most interesting work, but it fills the days and my pocket."

"I'm so glad," Azara said. She nodded toward the door. "Look, some customers are coming. Do you mind?"

"I'll head out the back," Zhelica said.

"Thank you." Azara stood up and put a hand on her shoulder. "You be careful, my dear."

"Don't worry," Zhelica said. "They barely notice me."

A few weeks later, Afshar surprised everyone by showing up. Beyman sent him upstairs, and the children, who recognized him as Yavan's friend, hung on him, some grabbing his hands while others jumped onto his back. Nazhin reproved them, but Afshar assured her the attention was fine with him.

"I hardly see you anymore," he said.

"Let me get some tea," Nazhin said. "You sit here and catch up with Zhelica."

As they talked, the children wandered off, playing in another area of the room.

"I'm sorry I haven't been by to check on you," Afshar said. "I was afraid of being seen with you at the base."

"I'm glad you've come by now," she said. Suddenly she noticed the sadness in his eyes. "How are *you* doing, Afshar?"

His ever-moving hands squeezed the arms of the couch and then smoothed out the slipcovers over them. "I miss Yavan so much."

"Me, too," Zhelica whispered.

"I know it's not right to burden you with *my* loss," Afshar said. "But I don't think anyone else understands like you."

She nodded. "I don't really talk about it."

Afshar let out a heavy sigh. "He was my best friend in the whole world."

Zhelica did not know how to respond to this; "Mine, too," seemed like it would either minimize Afshar's comment or remind him that as Yavan's wife, she was closer than his old friend.

"And I've been thinking," Afshar said, glancing at the children. "I've never met anyone like Yavan. I mean, he was a good man. He was the best person I have ever met."

"With all I've discovered about him," Zhelica said, "I'm not sure I really knew him as well as I should have."

"Well, how could you? He was hiding half his life from you."

"Maybe more," she said sadly.

"Look, I've been thinking," Afshar began. But Nazhin entered the room with the tea tray, and he dropped whatever he was going to say. The landlady sat down next to Zhelica and poured tea for them both.

"Have some cake, Afshar," she said, cutting him a slice.

"Thank you," he said. "The food here is so much better than on the base."

"You're right there," Zhelica agreed. As she took a piece of cake, the children clustered around, begging for some. Nazhin ended up serving them all, asking Afshar questions about life and work as she distributed the food. Everyone seemed settled now, and eating, when Shoja started crying.

"Oh, the little one's awake," she said with a smile. "Excuse me."

As soon as she was gone, Afshar said quietly, "I need to talk to you in private."

She looked around. "How can we do that?"

"What if I take you to see your aunt? We will have time on the way."

Zhelica squirmed at this. She had been avoiding Marjon. She had not been able to shake off the knowledge that her guardian deceived her about her parents, and she did not know how to bring the subject up. But it had been days since she had seen her. "I suppose that would work," she said.

"Why don't we go now? We'll make it in time for dinner"- his eyes lit up at this prospect - "and then I'll bring you back."

"All right," Zhelica said. "Let me get my cloak and tell Nazhin we're leaving."

She stopped by her landlady's room. Nazhin was rocking the toddler.

"Nazhin, Afshar offered to take me to see Marjon."

"What a lovely idea," Nazhin said. "When will you be back?"

"Later tonight," Zhelica said. "Don't wait up for me."

After Yavan's death and the beginning of Zhelica's employment, Beyman got a key made for Zhelica so that she could come and go without leaving the family vulnerable to thieves. She plucked it off her table and retrieved her cloak, pulling up the hood and tucking her hair well back into it. Afshar was waiting in the corridor. "Let's go."

Once they were beyond the city gates, he slowed. "First I want to take you somewhere we can talk. Marjon is not expecting us, so we won't be late."

He turned on a side road that led near the same river where Yavan had once taken Zhelica. He left his horse tied under a tree and they walked near the shore. The current moved more slowly here and a family of ducks swam past, periodically dipping and diving.

"I've been thinking a lot about Yavan," Afshar began. "Here he was, the best friend and person I have ever known. And what did he give his life for? The Restoration. The reunification of Zaharada and Darz." He shook his head, as though mystified by this. "He risked – and lost – *everything* for this cause. I know he seemed like a fun-loving man -"

"Which he was," Zhelica interjected.

"Which he was," Afshar agreed. "But that was not *all* he was. If Yavan was a spy," he dropped his voice as he said this, even though no one was around, "he gave it a lot of thought beforehand. He never talked with me about it...he could probably tell I'm not as brave as he was...but he must have considered long and hard before joining the Restoration."

Zhelica asked, "But why didn't he let us know?"

"He loved us," Afshar said. "He loved us too much to put us at risk."

Zhelica was no longer crying every day, but she did now. Dropping her face into her hands, she wept, "I wish he had loved us enough to not put *himself* at risk."

Afshar stood shuffling his feet awkwardly, his arms at his sides. Zhelica could see his long fingers trembling. "It was hard to find materials about Darzarada, but I've read enough to understand a little. And I've decided, Zhelica. If the cause was so important to him, I don't want his death to be for nothing."

"What are you suggesting?"

"I'm going to join the Restoration," Afshar said.

Through tear-blurred eyes, Zhelica stared at him. He was no Yavan: he was too afraid even to acknowledge her on the base. But her heart warmed at his determination.

"But how? Do you know others involved?"

He nodded. "I've been doing a little undercover work," he said with a nervous smile. "I have an appointment to meet with one of the Restoration leaders."

"Afshar, is this a good idea?" Zhelica asked. She dried her face.

"I don't know. But I feel like, for Yavan's sake, I have to do it."

Something tugged within Zhelica. *If I can do something to give Yavan's death meaning, even if it is risky, it would be worth it.*

In a small voice she said, "I want to join too."

Afshar shook his head. "No, Zhelica, Yavan would want you to be safe."

Zhelica kicked a rock at her feet. "Afshar, my whole life other people have been making decisions for me – what I should be allowed to know, what risks I should be allowed to take. It's time for me to do what's right. If you think Yavan was on the side of good, then I want to be there, too. Let me go with you to your meeting."

Afshar hesitated. "The leader told me to come alone," he said. "But I'll talk to him about you, and let you know how you can be involved."

For the first time in weeks, Zhelica felt the weight of loss lift a little.

The watchman had not yet arrived when they reached Marjon's. Afshar pulled the bell cord. Marjon appeared at the door in an instant.

"Oh, Zhelica!" she cried. "I see you've brought Afshar!"

"Actually, he brought *me*," Zhelica said. "Could we stay for dinner?"

"Of course. Come in." Afshar helped Zhelica down and tied up his horse before following the women into the kitchen. "I just need to put a little extra food on. Talk to me while I work."

Zhelica told her how the children were growing and amusing things they had said in the past week. She told her about the walk to and from the base and about her daily routine outside work. As she spoke, she realized this time she felt like a peer, not a juvenile.

"Let's go into the front room," Marjon said. She moved her quilting off the chairs and they all sat down.

"So how are you *really?*" Marjon asked, patting her hair and looking earnestly at Zhelica.

"I'm doing all right. It was hard to sleep at first, but that's gotten better. I like the work," she added. "It keeps me busy so I don't have too much time to think."

"And what exactly do you do?"

"I'm in the mailroom," she said.

Marjon looked amazed by this. "I would have thought they'd have given you a less trustworthy position, since you are -" she stopped herself.

"An *alloy?*" Zhelica said. "That's just what –" she didn't want to say *Azara,* so finished, "another friend said."

Marjon lifted an eyebrow in interest but said nothing. She took up her quilting and her needle flew in and out of the cloth, a pattern forming. "Spring's really begun," she said.

"Yes, and am I glad!" Zhelica said. "My apartment is so cold when I get home."

Marjon looked as though she wanted to offer Zhelica her old room, but bit her lip. "I can imagine," she said.

"Is there anything I can do for you, Marjon?" Afshar asked. "I know you have the watchman, but I'd be glad to help if there's something you need."

"Hmm," Marjon said. "In fact, one of the boards on the roof has slid out of place and the rain has been dripping in upstairs. I wonder if you could repair it?"

"Gladly," he said. Marjon rose and fetched the tools and Zhelica could hear her upstairs giving instructions. And then her aunt reappeared.

"Good," she said. "Time for the two of us to talk."

"Yes, I have some questions for you," Zhelica said. While feeling bold in town, she now found herself reluctant to pick her aunt's mind.

"What sort of questions?" Marjon resumed her stitching.

"I want to know more about my parents," Zhelica said. "Someone in town told me there had not been a plague at the time of their deaths, so I figured you created that story to protect me."

She clasped her hands in her lap to keep them from shaking. Marjon seemed to concentrate harder on her quilting. Calmly, she responded.

"You're right, Zhelica. I thought if you knew the truth, it would change the kind of life you lived." She looked up and said sadly, "But that has happened despite my attempts to keep you from it."

"So, how *did* my parents die?"

Marjon sighed. "It was a terrible time," she said. "They were happy about *you,* of course. What a beauty you were, with your little red curls! Your mother was torn between wanting to care for you and being active in the Restoration." She scrutinized Zhelica's expression. "You know about the Restoration, don't you?"

"I've heard a little," Zhelica said.

"They were rounding up Darzians and shooting them. Your father hid in the forest." Marjon's stitching slowed. "Your mother was staying here with me, and when she went out on missions, she left you sleeping upstairs. One day she decided to take lunch to your father. She packed up food and rode to the stone house by the river." Marjon dropped her quilt. "Someone followed her. While they were eating inside, troops surrounded the house. They threw torches through the windows and then blocked every exit so your parents could not escape." She looked at Zhelica with haunted eyes.

"They died in the stone house," Zhelica said. Suddenly, she remembered visiting the eerie home with Yavan, its shutters and door long ago dissolved in ash. "I've seen that house," she whispered, tears springing to her eyes.

Marjon nodded. "Yavan told me he had taken you there," she said. "It seemed cruel, but I think he knew that someday you would want to piece together the whole story."

Zhelica tried to wipe away the tears, but they fell hard and long. She made no effort to stop. She cried for the mother and father she had lost and for the husband who was an enigma – Yavan wanted her to know the truth yet refused to tell it.

Afshar reappeared and seeing Zhelica's distress, paced on the far side of the room, saying nothing.

"And now I will answer a question you would probably never think to ask," Marjon said. "Zhelica, I have loved you like my own child since you were born."

"I know, Auntie," Zhelica said, her sobs slowing as she dried her eyes. "I have never lacked for love from you."

"Well, I hope you will forgive me," Marjon said. "Zhelica, I am not your aunt."

Afshar stopped in his tracks. Zhelica jumped up. "What do you mean, Marjon?"

Marjon stood facing the younger woman. "Your parents were my friends. When your mother married a Darzian, her family cut her off; I was the nearest thing to a sister she had. She made me promise that if anything happened to them, I would take you to Darz. I couldn't bear the thought of leaving you in a strange country with people you didn't know. . ." Her voice trailed off. She cleared her throat and continued. "I should have told you sooner, but I was afraid...afraid of losing you. You were my last link to them, and you were like my own."

Zhelica's chest felt as though it would explode. She tried to speak, but the words choked her. Feeling faint, she dropped back into the chair. Afshar was at her side in an instant.

"I'm sorry, Zhelica," he said. "I didn't know."

Marjon wrung her hands. She looked years older in an instant. "I can't go back and make different choices," she said. "And I'm not sure I would. I love you. I did my best to care for you while keeping you here."

Finally Zhelica spoke. "In some ways, you and Yavan are the same," she said. "You both deceived me about who you really were. And you both justified keeping me in the dark, telling yourselves you were protecting me."

She turned to the soldier. "Afshar, after you have eaten, would you please take me home? I'm just going to rest now." She leaned back in her chair and closed her eyes. At that moment, she never wanted to open them again.

Eleven

Zhelica met Afshar in the woods beyond view of the base and they walked together toward Hyarani.

"I can't tell you much about the leadership," he apologized. "They arrange it so that you're in contact with only two or three people. That way if there is infiltration, only a few people are caught."

"That makes sense," Zhelica said.

"They were pretty happy to hear about your position in the mailroom. Since all the correspondence goes through that building, you are in a position to intercept anything sensitive."

"Like what?"

Afshar listed them off on his fingers. "Letters between military leaders that might involve raids. Coded mail sent between Restorers. Anything coming from Darz."

Zhelica stopped. "How can I possibly get those? Rakshan is the one who sorts and censors things like that."

Afshar shrugged. "They didn't give me any ideas on *how* to do it. That's up to you to figure out."

She began walking again. "It will never work," she said. Rakshan had begun to trust her more; maybe she *could* somehow get him to explain the system. Then at least she would be able to report what mail was coming through. But the task seemed daunting.

"Zhelica, anything you can do to help will be appreciated. Start small."

"What do I do if I find something important? Pass along the information to you?"

"No! This is the only time I can talk to you about this," Afshar said. "I'll show you where to leave messages."

He glanced both directions and then motioned her to follow him off the road. Once they were past the row of trees nearest the pavement, Zhelica could see that there was a well-worn footpath paralleling the road. This branched off, one arm leading deeper into the woods.

"Not too much farther," Afshar whispered. He stopped in front of what appeared to be an old wooden bird house. He pushed on the bottom, and the floor dropped open.

"You can leave any messages in here," he said.

Zhelica looked at it skeptically. "Isn't it a bit obvious? It must be the only bird house out here."

"They're scattered throughout the forest," he said. "During the days of Darzarada, birds were brought from the north to populate the woods. They were all killed after things fell apart. Only the native birds are left."

"Well, I don't know if I'll have anything to report," Zhelica said. She did not feel hopeful about her assignment. "But I'll try."

"That's all any of us can do," Afshar told her. He accompanied her back to the main road. "I better go my own way now. We can't risk being seen together." He put his hand over his heart. "Until all things are restored."

Afshar then hesitated uncertainly before giving Zhelica a quick hug and running off into the woods opposite the direction she was going.

The next morning Zhelica watched Rakshan, looking for ways to get access to all the mail. His method was simple: He would scan every address, take out the significant letters, and then toss the rest in a pile for Zhelica to sort. As she worked, she watched him from the corner of her eye. Rakshan kept a knife at hand to slice open the envelope of each of the sensitive letters. Dumping out the correspondence, he quickly perused it, and then either put it in a box to pass on to his superiors, or glued the envelope shut and then tossed it in the pile for Zhelica to post.

Whenever he left the room, Rakshan put the box in one of the cupboards under the counter and locked it. After they finished for the day, he delivered it to the administration building before returning to the barracks.

The system seemed failproof.

As the afternoon (and the work) wound down, Zhelica watched Rakshan haul the mail bags to the door. The box with its precious letters was on the counter, within reach of Zhelica. She knew she dared not touch it or even show interest in it. Suddenly she determined what she would do.

"That's it for today," Rakshan said. He shook his hair from his eyes and crossed his arms. "You can go."

She looked down and blushed. She had not meant to do that, but realized as it was happening that it would serve her purposes.

"You invited me once to have a drink with you," she said. "Is it too late to take you up on that offer?"

His eyes flashed, but not with anger. The closest thing Zhelica had seen to delight lit his face. "Not at all."

He brought out his bottle and agitated it gently. "Not full, I'm afraid."

"That's all right," Zhelica said. "I've never had wine before. I probably don't need much to get a taste."

"You are in for a treat," Rakshan told her. He rummaged in the cupboard and brought forth a glass. Holding it up to the firelight, he grimaced. "Let me wash this," he said, and ducked out of the office.

Zhelica could scarcely breathe. She was alone with the box...but for how long? Wasting no time, she pried up the lid, grabbing a letter from the top. She pushed the lid back in place and slid the letter into the pocket of her dress. The door of the mailroom opened; Rakshan locked it behind him, and then turned to hold up the glass.

"Fit for a lady," he said. He directed her to the fireplace, pulling the chair she had been using for work over near the tiny table, then throwing a couple of fresh logs on the fire. It blazed up, sending sparks flying. The day was cloudy, the light fading outside. Despite herself, Zhelica found the mailroom cozy after hours.

"I only have one glass, so apologies for being a boor," Rakshan said. He poured the ruby liquid for Zhelica. "Let's drink to friendship and a job well done." He handed her the glass and clinked his bottle against it and took a hearty swig. Zhelica watched. The wine in her glass beckoned, glowing like a jewel in the flickering firelight. She lifted the glass to her lips and took a sip.

It startled her. It was not hot, but it seemed to burn her tongue and the back of her throat as it went down. Seeing the expression on her face, Rakshan laughed.

"What do you think?"

Zhelica set the glass on the table. "I have never tasted anything like it."

"Have some more," he urged her. Reluctantly, she picked up the glass and took another tiny sip.

"You'll be here all night if you drink like that," he said. His eyes glittered.

"This is too much for my first time," she protested. She pushed the glass toward him. "You'll have to help me."

He finished what was in the bottle first. Then he leaned back in his chair. He seemed more relaxed than Zhelica had ever seen him.

"You're a funny one, you know? It seems like you never left that farm until you married Yavan."

"It was an orchard," she corrected him.

He waved his hand in the air. "Farm, orchard. Place growing food."

"I hadn't really been anywhere," she agreed. "And to be honest with you, Yavan's the first man I'd ever had a conversation with."

Rakshan stared at her, and then shook his head. "Incredible," he said. "It could have been any of us, you know, buying apples and plums. But Yavan was the lucky man."

She was not sure if he was being facetious, so she said nothing.

Rakshan took her barely-tasted glass and held it aloft. "To beautiful women," he said, and drank it down.

The room was getting darker than she thought it would in a few minutes' time. "I should probably get going," she said, starting to rise.

Rakshan grabbed her hand. "Don't go."

She gently pulled her fingers away. "Thank you for sharing your wine with me. We should do it again sometime." Quickly she stepped beyond his reach as he rose. She ducked beneath the counter and unbolted the door. "Goodnight, Rakshan."

He leaned over the counter. "Goodnight, Mrs. Yavan," he said.

Zhelica did not look back as she hurried toward the gate. A new shift had begun and although the guard did not recognize her, he waved her through. Zhelica walked quickly down the road. The letter rustled in her pocket as she moved; she was certain someone would hear it and haul her back to the base. But the road was empty. She sought out and found the footpath and half-walked, half-ran to the bird house.

Should she leave the entire letter there? If she did not make sure it got turned into the office, eventually someone would catch on. Zhelica considered the implications, and decided to take the letter home, make a copy, and leave *that* in the bird house on her way to work. She could return the letter to the mailroom the next day and no one would be any the wiser.

The family was at dinner when she arrived. "Sorry I'm late," she said, sliding into her chair. Beyman raised an eyebrow but said nothing, passing her a bowl. She served herself and made a show of engaging the older girl in conversation about her new hair ribbons. After the meal, she excused herself to her own room.

Zhelica lit the fire and found a piece of paper and a pen. Sitting at the table, she opened the letter and read it by the light of the flames:

General,

A party is planned near Arkamedi in a few days. It will be a small gathering. The guest of honor is someone you have been wanting to host for some time. Advise.

Capt. Tieron

Zhelica gazed at the note. This did not seem important; why was it top-secret? When the truth dawned on her, she shivered. Some Zaharadans were innocently planning a gathering, not knowing their movements were watched, their names taken down, one of them especially destined for arrest...and she had the opportunity to save them. She took a deep breath, and rewrote the message in block letters (to hide her distinctive handwriting).

She wondered if it was prudent to wait until morning to deliver it. But how could she possibly get it there tonight? She parted the lace curtain and looked down on the street. A soft rain was falling. Surely whoever was intercepting messages would wait until the next day. Zhelica folded her note into a small bundle and put it in her bedside table.

She smiled to herself. There was something satisfying about this work – no wonder Yavan had been involved. The image of him and his dimples flashed across her mind. *Oh, I miss you!* she thought sadly. But her determination to follow his example grew.

The next morning Zhelica left a few minutes early. Nazhin looked surprised. "I'm a little tired, so this way I can walk slower," Zhelica said softly, patting her stomach. She felt a twinge of guilt at lying to her friend. But clearly Beyman and Nazhin were not involved in the Restoration, and like her husband, Zhelica wanted to protect them.

In fact, her morning sickness had stopped and she was feeling extraordinarily good. When she looked in the mirror, her skin seemed brighter. Although the bodice of a Zaharadan dress was tight, the skirt flowed loosely; at this point her body's changes were perceptible only if she tugged the fabric close. But Zhelica knew she was curving in ways that would soon make her pregnancy obvious.

There were markers of spring everywhere, the bright new grass poking through the mud and the flowers unfurling.

Zhelica exited the road farther from where Afshar had led her onto the footpath, following this until it branched.

Looking around to make sure she was unseen, she swiftly made her way to the bird house and pressed the bottom so that the base dropped down. There was a tiny shelf in the back wall of the house, and she slipped her message onto it before snapping the base shut. With the same furtiveness, she returned to the road, arriving at the gate at her normal time.

"Look at your shoes," Rakshan commented when she came in. Zhelica did, and could not hide the horror on her face: they were covered in mud.

"It rained last night," she said.

"Never mind," Rakshan said. "This is a military base. If there's one thing I've learned, it's how to keep footwear clean. Slip them off."

Zhelica sat down and unlaced her shoes. She gingerly removed them, trying to keep the mud off her hands.

"First," Rakshan said, "We set them in the sun to dry. Then it's easy: we just brush the dirt off."

"Very clever," she said. "But I feel silly in my stocking feet."

"It's all right," he said. "Sit over here and sort, and by the time we're finished, your shoes will be ready."

She obediently positioned herself and got to work.

"So how are you feeling today?" Rakshan asked. "No headache from the wine?"

"Not at all."

"Well, we should make it part of our routine. I get tired of drinking alone."

Zhelica was not sure this was a good strategy, but she had not come up with any other plan for getting information. She smiled. "Maybe," she said.

Rakshan was a creature of habit, Zhelica realized. He automatically locked up the box whenever he left the building. She knew she could not rely on him to disappear every evening; today he deliberately pointed out the wine glass, washed and ready for her. As she sorted, she watched him peruse a letter and then reseal its envelope.

"You know, that takes a lot of time. What if you read the letters, put them back in the envelope, and I resealed them?"

He looked dubious at this. "What if one of the other officers came in? They'd think you were looking at top-secret correspondence."

Boldly, she said, "Nonsense. I'll stand right by you so you can see what I'm doing. If anyone comes in, I'll move away so it's clear I'm working on something else."

"That would save me time," he mused. "All right, let's try it. Bring your other work over here by me. But you don't need to stand." He moved her chair next to his. Zhelica grabbed the pile she was sorting and sat down.

"Look at your little feet," Rakshan said.

"Only little compared to some," she replied. They both laughed.

These were the innocuous pieces of correspondence, so not of any real value to the resistance. The letters that went into the box were harder for her to see; Rakshan skimmed a few lines before returning the sheets to their envelopes and tossing them unsealed into the guarded container.

I have to figure out a way to get a hold of those, she thought almost frantically.

"We just get faster and faster," Rakshan said, looking around at the cleared tables and filled pigeon holes. "The commander even commended me yesterday on the quick turnaround for mail. You're going to put me out of a job."

"Not likely," she said. "I'm doing the brainless work."

Rakshan stood by the pile of bags at the door. "You're too smart to do anything brainlessly."

Her heartbeat quickened. *Does he suspect me?*

"Are you making fun of me, Lieutenant?" she asked. It seemed like the best way to deflect any thoughts about her mental skills.

He leaned over the counter and gave her a grin. "Not exactly," he said.

Zhelica could feel her cheeks redden. She turned away. "Where are my shoes?" She found them on the back porch. True to Rakshan's word, the mud was caked and dry. As she pounded them against the steps, chunks of dirt flew off. They were still dusty, but much better.

"You aren't going, are you?" the soldier asked. He had crossed the room and now stood near.

Zhelica closed the door. "I should," she said.

He moved so close to her that she backed up and stumbled over a package. Rakshan caught her arm to keep her from falling but did not let go. "I know a lot of people find *alloys* unattractive," he said softly. "But not me. Maybe it's the novelty, but the color of your hair is definitely eye-catching."

"No teasing," she said lightly, hoping to avoid something more serious. She held up her shoes as she shook free from his grasp and sat down in the nearest chair, hurriedly slipping them on and tying the laces.

Rakshan leaned over her, and she could feel his warm breath on her neck. "Stay and have a drink with me."

What to do? She glanced at the box on the counter and wondered how she would ever extract a letter from it.

"Look," she said, "I have to be honest with you. I don't actually like wine."

"You barely tasted it," he protested.

"However," she continued, "I'd be happy to sit with you and talk while you drink."

Rakshan weighed this in his mind and then said, "Fine."

He retrieved a full bottle (he must have brought it in before she arrived), and uncorked it. "Come here."

Zhelica joined him again by the fireplace. She decided to get him talking...maybe he would let some information slip.

"Tell me more about your family," she said. "I know your father is a general."

He tossed his head and curls flew around him, settling like a flock of birds. "What's to tell? I have one younger brother. He's the good one," he said, lightning returning to his eyes. "Like your Captain Yavan."

She cleared her throat. For some reason, she did not want Yavan mentioned between them. "And your mother?"

"You'd probably like her," he said. "She's quite a beauty, for an old lady. My father parades her around at all the official functions. She is also a good mother," he added quietly.

"Did you spend all your childhood at the military academy?"

He took a swig. "No. We moved there when I was about ten. We were stationed at a base at the southern tip of Zaharada. It was great. Playing in the sand by the ocean, eating coconuts and pineapples...not like this wretched mud hole."

"Did you like *anything* about school?" Zhelica asked.

"Not really. All the other boys already had friends by the time I got there. I was tall and awkward and everyone was terrified of my father. I was thoroughly glad to be rid of that place."

He scowled at the fire and took another drink. Zhelica looked at the box. *Not getting anywhere,* she thought.

"What about you? Family?"

Zhelica gazed at the fire as she spoke. "My parents died when I was little. I guess my father was from Darz." She twirled a piece of loose hair with one hand. "I was raised by my...my *aunt* until I met Yavan and married him."

Rakshan was watching her closely. "I saw her at the funeral. Not really your aunt?" he guessed.

"More like a family friend."

"Hmm," he reflected, making circles with the bottle so that the wine inside formed a tiny whirlpool. "So I have a complete family, but I'm miserable. And you basically have no family, and you're –"

"Don't say, 'happy,' " she begged him, her eyes suddenly filling with tears.

Rakshan set the bottle down and leaned over, taking her hand. His was so large it swallowed hers up as he closed his fingers around it. "You must miss your husband," he said.

She brushed away her tears with her free hand. "You have no idea." She stood up, dropping Rakshan's hand in the process. "I better go," she said.

He rose, too. "I'm sorry for making you cry. I can be a dolt sometimes."

"No, it's not your fault. Could you unlock the door for me?"

To pass through the counter, he threw back the opening without realizing how close the box of high-security correspondence was. Airborne, it sent letters fluttering like leaves from an autumn tree.

"Oh, my!" Zhelica cried, and without thinking, began scooping up the envelopes and returning them to the box.

Rakshan swore and joined her, plucking up letters that had sailed to the edges of the room.

Zhelica suddenly realized what was happening, and while Rakshan was behind her, she grabbed a few envelopes and dropped them down the front of her dress.

"Thank you," Rakshan said, gathering the remaining pieces. "I better get these over to the admin building before I make a further disaster of them." He gave her a quick smile, and reached his hand out to help her up. She rose slowly, feeling the letters shift before settling on top of her baby bump.

"I'll see you tomorrow," she said. She threw her cloak around her shoulders, pulled up the hood, and slipped out before Rakshan could collect the box and lock up.

That night, after writing copies of the letters she had stolen, Zhelica dropped into bed. She was just about to fall asleep, when she felt rustlings in her belly. *I'm not hungry,* she thought. The whisper of movement came again, and she knew that it was the baby.

"Oh, little one," she whispered, her hand on her swelling abdomen, "what sort of a life will you have? How will I ever provide for you?" She pulled Yavan's pillow close. It had almost lost his scent. In her heart a sense of loss mingled with one of purpose. Wrapping her arms around the pillow, she fell asleep.

Twelve

"I felt the baby move last night," Zhelica said softly to Nazhin at breakfast the next morning. Her friend gave a restrained squeal.

"Oh, Zhelica, I know you've lost so much...but a baby! Motherhood is so wonderful." Her dark eyes danced as she looked around at her own brood.

"I don't know how we'll live," Zhelica said, lifting a spoon of oatmeal. "We can't stay here after the baby is born."

"Why not?" Nazhin demanded. "You're practically family now. And your little one will have ready-made siblings."

"But how will I provide for a child?" Zhelica asked. "I can't watch a baby and work on the base at the same time."

"Don't fret about it," Nazhin said soothingly. "Something will work out."

Zhelica ate quickly and hid the notes she had copied in the bird house. She wondered where they were transported, and if her information was received in time to make a difference.

The footpath had mostly dried, but she walked along the edges to avoid the muddy tracks in the center.

Rakshan was in a foul mood. He greeted her with a grunt, and whenever he moved something, there was noise: slamming cupboard doors, slapping down bags. Zhelica did not want to take his surly silence personally, but it was hard not to. After watching him a few minutes, she asked, "Excuse me – did I do something wrong?"

A storm brewed behind the curls. "No, *I* did something. Apparently." He did not elaborate.

Zhelica found it a challenge to slip the letters she had "borrowed" the day before back into the special box. She kept them close and while passing him periodically slid one in. Rakshan seemed distracted and barely spoke to her for most of the morning. As the workload diminished, he warmed up a bit. Zhelica decided she would not risk extracting any mail that day; it might be better if there was no pattern to her movements. She would just look for those lucky moments when the box made itself available to her.

The days were getting longer and the room warmer; there was no need to light a fire. As the work ended, Rakshan said, "Would you like a tour of the base?"

"Would that be allowed?" she asked. "I mean, is it permitted for civilians to look around?"

"If you're with me, it should be fine," he said. There was something grim in his tone, and Zhelica worried a bit. Had he figured out what she was up to? Was he turning her in?

"Let's go out the back way," he suggested. She followed him. "I'll just drop the box off first," he said. "Allay some fears coming from on high."

This comment was concerning. But she smiled and waited as he trotted down the road with the mail and reappeared a few minutes later.

"We'll do the back-roads tour," Rakshan said.

He led her behind buildings: past the infirmary and staff offices and behind the rows of beige barracks. She could see men walking between the buildings, talking. But she and Rakshan were effectively invisible: no one was looking for them on the outskirts of the property.

"I told you my father was a general," Rakshan said, as he brushed aside some weeds for her to pass behind the last structure in the row. "Besides letting me keep my hair long, he's arranged that I have my own room."

"That's unusual, isn't it?" Zhelica asked in surprise.

"Usually only the highest-ranking officers get their own quarters," Rakshan said. "But my father knows that if he throws me in with a bunch of other guys, there will be trouble."

He stopped in front of a door on the side of a small building out of view of the central barracks area. "Welcome to my home."

There are steps one takes, Zhelica reflected later, that send you on a dangerous path. If you do not take the first step, you remain safe. But once you have, it is hard to turn around.

For her, it was the after-hours drinking and talking with Rakshan. She had been encouraging his interest without desiring it. She only wanted to help the

Restoration, to avenge Yavan's death by assisting those on his side. She did not want to get involved with Rakshan.

But he stood there, holding the door open for her, and she did not know what to do.

"What's the matter?"

"I don't know if I. . ." her voice trailed off helplessly.

"I just wanted to show you where I live," he said. He looked hurt. "Never mind."

"No," she said quickly, "I do want to see. Come on."

She plunged ahead of him into the room and the door swung shut behind them.

"It's a little dark in here," Rakhsan said as he pulled open the slatted blinds. As he did so, sunlight illuminated the low-ceilinged chamber. There was little in his quarters, even if he was a general's son. The regulation army cot and a desk. Hooks across one wall on which hung his few articles of clothing. A shelf against the opposite wall holding a number of books, neatly arranged and held upright by bottles of wine. Underneath Zhelica could see more bottles, some full but most empty.

"You've found my treasure cache," Rakshan said. He pulled out a bottle. "And I actually have clean glasses here, so I can drink with style."

Zhelica stood where she had entered, not sure whether to sit or leave.

"Come here," Rakshan said, patting the bed, where he was already positioned.

Instead, Zhelica went to the bookshelf.

"I love to read. What kinds of books do you have?"

"All kinds," he said, rising. "What are you interested in?" He pulled out an old book with a battered cover. "This is poetry from Bustaan. Banned now, but I found a copy tucked behind the permitted books." He held it tenderly.

"I like history," Zhelica said.

Rakshan slipped the poetry back in place and searched until he found a thick volume. "Pick your time period."

"How about Darzarada," she said. It was a stupid thing to say, she realized instantly. Rakshan scowled.

"What do you know about that?" he asked in a low voice.

She shrugged, backing away. "Nothing, really. I just heard someone mention it once."

Her heart was pounding and she could feel the infant inside her twitching.

Rakshan slid the book back on the shelf. "I have nothing about that period."

The sun dipped low enough to shine directly into the little room. Dust motes formed a wall between them.

"I better go," Zhelica said. "Thank you for showing me around. You have a very comfortable room."

"Let me walk you back to the main gate," he said flatly. He was back to his morning mood. They said nothing as they retraced their steps and passed the mailroom and the administration building.

"Thank you, Rakshan," Zhelica said. She pulled her hood up and gave him a little wave before leaving the base. It felt like she had escaped more than one close call.

The next day, Rakshan seemed to have recovered from his frustrations. They worked at a good pace, finishing slightly before quitting time. Rakshan did not ask her to stay, which was a relief, although Zhelica felt a twinge of loss at not receiving an invitation. She got home in time to play with the children before dinner, eat with the family, and go to bed on schedule.

As she brushed out her hair, the familiar loneliness crept into the room. Nazhin seemed to think that Yavan's child would somehow compensate for his absence, but Zhelica doubted this. She closed her eyes and tried to remember his smile, the dimpled cheeks, the way his hair stood in a grove of curls. She thought about the way he lifted her chin to kiss her. *Yavan! Will I ever stop aching for you?*

She climbed into bed and held his pillow close to her chest. As she dropped off to sleep, she imagined his voice speaking to her from behind the door. As the door opened in her dream, a soldier stepped into her bedroom. It was not Yavan.

It was Rakshan.

Zhelica woke feeling guilty. Then she reminded herself that she was not responsible for her dreams; it was not her fault that Rakshan had interposed himself there. She climbed out of bed shivering. The weather seemed to have reverted back to winter: the room was cold, and only a thin light skirted the curtains.

She rifled through her drawers until she found her wool stockings. Slipping them on and pulling them up she realized they would not cover her belly. Zhelica ran her hands over her abdomen, half delighting in and half dreading its convex shape.

In the common room, Beyman was feeding the children. "Nazhin's not feeling well this morning," he said. He winked at Zhelica, and she knew what this meant: her baby really would not grow up alone in this household. Nazhin was expecting a fifth child.

"I'm freezing," one of the girls complained.

"Yes, a cold front from Darz moved in during the night," Beyman said. "Make sure you all dress warmly."

The road was slippery, and Zhelica walked carefully. When she came to the bridge where Yavan had been stabbed, she hesitated. Usually she tried not to think about its history, but she was forced to move so slowly, sliding her hand along the railing, that she could not help reflecting on her husband's last journey. At one place the railing had been broken and mended after the horse's fall; the splintered wood pierced Zhelica's hand. She yanked it back and almost lost her balance. There was a nasty sliver buried in her palm and a growing drop of blood at its entry point. Carefully looking as she clutched the rail, she worked her way off the bridge and stumbled toward the base. There was something traumatic about being injured and bloody at the place where Yavan had been attacked.

Zhelica entered the mailroom cradling her bleeding hand. She thought Rakshan would notice and offer to remove the offending piece of wood. But as soon as their eyes met, she was so stunned, she forgot her hand.

"Your hair!" she exclaimed.

He looked completely different: his mane had been cropped close with only a few regulation-length waves across his forehead. His eyes burned with anger and shame.

"Yes," he said bitterly. "Daddy ordered it removed."

Zhelica ducked under the counter and came close. Rakshan's rugged features were exposed. Zhelica knew that the curls were his badge of independence, and he was so used to flipping his head to get hair out of his eyes, or to brushing the hair out of his line of sight, that he repeated those motions still. Every time, anguish flitted across his face.

"Why?" Zhelica whispered. "Why did he make you get your hair cut?"

At that moment, Rakshan caught sight of her hand. The bleeding had stopped, but there was an ugly smear of rust across her palm.

"What happened?" he asked, uncurling her fingers so he could get a better look.

"I got a sliver on the bridge," she said. "It was right where –" She teared up and covered her mouth with her other hand to keep a sob from escaping.

Rakshan seemed to forget his own distress. He guided Zhelica to a chair and told her to wait. He ran to the infirmary and came back with tweezers, a needle, a wet cloth, and a bandage. Kneeling at her feet, he gently washed away the blood and turned her hand to see how the wood was embedded.

"This is going to hurt a little," he said. "Look out the window."

Zhelica obeyed. She watched a soldier as he crossed the street, and tried to ignore the sting of the needle going in and the tug of the tweezers pulling out the sliver. Rakshan quickly pressed the bandage in place and held her hand tightly to staunch the bleeding.

"There," he said. "That should be fine now if you can keep it clean."

He was so tall that on his knees his face was positioned directly opposite her own. His flashing eyes were filled with a look so caring, that Zhelica had to drop hers.

"Thank you," she said. "Do you want to tell me why your father made you get your hair cut?"

He shook his head. "No. Let's get to work." He checked her palm, and convinced the bleeding had stopped, wrapped a piece of gauze securely over the bandage, tying it on the back of her hand. "Will you be able to use it?"

She nodded. "I just need a task to keep me from thinking about it."

They worked in near silence. Rakshan was absorbed in his thoughts; every now and then his eyebrows compressed as though he were carrying on an internal argument. Zhelica watched him with a little worry and a small degree of affection. They had become friends, and she was sorry to see him upset.

She could not help fumbling as she handled the correspondence; it was hard to get a good grip with the fingers of one hand stiffly extended. "I'm useless today," she apologized.

"Never mind. It doesn't matter how good a job we do now anyway. I'm being transferred."

"Transferred?" Zhelica wondered what Rakshan had done to receive this consequence.

He flung a hand across the pile of letters, sending them skittering across the wooden floor. "Yes, it's back to daddy. He wants to keep an eye on me," he snarled.

Zhelica instinctively rose and stood before him. "What happened?"

He gave a caustic laugh. "I seem to have undermined army intelligence."

A chill ran through Zhelica. It was almost as though she knew what he was about to tell her.

"Somehow," he said, his words staccato, "vital information about the resistance has been leaked. Several planned apprehensions have been thwarted. Father claims the mailroom is the weak link, and I am the broken ring in that chain." He swept another stack of letters off the table. And then he looked closely at Zhelica.

"You have gone completely white!" he said. "Are you all right?"

Zhelica tried desperately to regroup. "I'm fine," she said. Actually, she felt a wave of nausea – not, she knew, from the baby, but from her own duplicity.

"Maybe it's *you*," Rakshan said. "Everyone associated with you gets caught for spying, whether they are guilty or not."

She began to tremble.

"I was just joking." He laid a hand on her arm. "No one could look at you and suspect you of anything."

She gave what felt a weak smile in response. Rakshan did not remove his hand. She could feel the warmth of it through the sleeve of her dress.

"I'm sick of being here," Rakshan said. "Let's go somewhere."

"Go somewhere? Where would we go?"

He let go of her arm. "I know how to get off base without being seen. Get your cloak."

He locked the front door and led her out back. They headed away from the barracks and other buildings. The weedy ground sloped downward; at the bottom of the dip was a wooden fence.

"I figured out pretty early on that there was a way out of here," Rakshan said. Some of the original boards had rotted and rather than replacing them, someone had leaned a few newer boards up in their place. From a distance, it looked complete. Rakshan moved them aside and motioned for her. "After you," he said.

Zhelica did not know why she was going along with him, but she did. If he was being transferred, she would probably lose her job anyway.

They followed a skinny stream running along the ditch that bordered the base. A plank had been thrown across as an impromptu bridge; Rakshan crossed and held out a hand to Zhelica. She reached her uninjured hand to him, joining him on the other side of the water.

The air was moist and cool; the sun had never managed to break through the overcast sky. In the forest new leaves glowed bright green against the black bark of the trees. The path looked like it had been well-used.

"Are we going to run into others from the base here?" Zhelica whispered.

"I don't think so," Rakshan whispered back. "I'm the only rebel here, I think."

After they had gone far enough not to be heard, Rakshan said, "I found an old house out here where I sometimes go when I want to be alone."

"Oh," Zhelica said quietly. For some reason, a voice was ringing in her head, warning her to turn back.

"Over time I have actually stocked it with a few goodies," Rakshan said, lifting an eyebrow. "You can probably guess what kind."

"Wine?" she suggested.

"Yes, but not only that," he said defensively. "I do eat, you know."

As he spoke, they turned onto a little lane. At the end of this, Zhelica could see a ramshackle cottage.

"Is that it?" she asked doubtfully. "It looks like the roof needs to be repaired."

"Yes, it may be a bit damp inside," he agreed.

He pushed on the wooden door; swollen with wetness, it resisted until he threw his shoulder against it. The inside was dappled with light from holes in the roof. Rakshan had arranged old pieces of furniture so that they would not be directly affected by the elements.

"This is kind of charming," Zhelica admitted. It was like the ghost of a home: an old sofa faced the fireplace, its cushions sagging on a broken frame. There was a table in front of it, one leg missing. On the mantel over the fireplace Rakshan had left a stack of books. Zhelica was immediately drawn to these.

"Let's see...more poetry," she said. "Have you memorized any?"

He was trying to get the door closed. It didn't want to fit back into place, so he pushed a shelf against it to prevent it from swinging open before joining her.

"No," he said. "There didn't seem any point in memorizing it when I had no one to share it with." His dark eyes fixed on hers, and she did not look away. "I could read you some, if you like."

"Maybe in a while," she said softly. "Let me see your kitchen."

Rakshan opened a cupboard door hanging on one hinge. Bags of dry lentils and rice and a few bottles of spice lined the shelf. "I try to pick up a few things when I'm in town," he said apologetically.

"Do you have a stove?" Zhelica asked, glancing around the room.

"No, I just cook over the fireplace."

"Well," she said, "I think we better have a fire then."

As she spoke, the voice in her head screamed for her to leave, but Zhelica found that when she ignored it, eventually the word of caution disappeared.

Together they collected wood that Rakshan had stacked in an adjoining room and before long a fire roared. "You just sit down," Rakshan said. "I will prepare everything."

He did. Zhelica watched him measure out lentils and water into an old pot and generously shake spices over the mixture. He hung this on the fireplace hook. Once it came to a boil, he swung the hook so that the beans would simmer over indirect heat.

Meanwhile Zhelica lowered herself onto the sofa. She doubted it could hold her; as she slid to the center, where the frame had collapsed, she laughed aloud.

"This is like falling into a pit!"

"You have to sit on the edge," Rakshan told her. She scooted to one side, near the arm of the chair, then leaned back, resting her head on the sofa, closing her eyes.

"This is actually pretty comfortable."

"I'm glad you think so."

"I think I like this better than your room on the base."

"That's why I sneak over here when I can."

When Zhelica opened her eyes, she could see Rakshan watching her. Part of her wanted to get up, but since becoming pregnant, she found she was tired mid-afternoon. She closed her eyes again.

Once Rakshan got the fire to a point where he could leave it for a few minutes, he sat down on the floor by Zhelica, his back against the seat of the couch. Zhelica was conscious of him there, and for an instant it reminded her of Yavan. She pushed that thought away.

"Do you want me to read to you now?" Rakshan asked.

"That sounds nice," she said drowsily.

He fetched a book and returned to her feet before beginning to read. The Bustaanis had perfected the lyrical style, and as Rakshan's deep voice rolled out poem after poem, Zhelica delighted in immersing herself in the words. There was one more flutter of warning in her heart before she let herself go, imbibing the poetry like Rakshan drank wine.

She reached out with her wounded hand and ran her fingers lightly over his shorn head. *It's a pity that the general forced him to trim that beautiful head of hair,* she thought.

He stopped reading, and looked at her. His bright eyes sparkled, but his voice was calm. "Are you getting hungry?"

The fire had burned down and, as Zhelica looked toward the hole in the ceiling, she could see that the sky had turned from ash to coal.

"I am," she said. In fact, the baby was wiggling in a way that indicated that he or she was hungry, too.

He fetched an old curtain from the kitchen and threw it over the table as a dining cloth.

"I don't have any dishes here. I hope you don't mind sharing."

"Not at all," Zhelica said. She was in a stupor. She did not want to move or break the spell of Rakshan's lair.

The soldier lifted the pot and set it on the table. "May I join you?" he asked. When Zhelica nodded, he carefully settled into the valley that was the middle of the couch.

"Don't move, or you might finish the sofa off," Zhelica laughed.

Together they dipped spoons into the simple meal. Halfway through, Rakshan said, "I forgot drinks," and returned with a bottle of wine, which he opened with relish. He held it to Zhelica, who took a sip.

"That won't quench your thirst," Rakshan said. Zhelica gingerly tipped the bottle and let a mouthful of the liquid warm her throat. Rakshan followed suit.

Zhelica wasn't sure wine was good for a mother-to-be, so she passed on further offers. Rakshan finished off the bottle and went for another.

He settled on the other end of the sofa and put his feet up on the table. Zhelica could see that the alcohol had relaxed him, and he began babbling.

"My father will never get what he wants from me," he said. "I'm not a very good soldier, am I? Off base without permission, letting critical information slip through my hand." He tried to snap his fingers unsuccessfully.

"That's not your fault," Zhelica said. "Someone else must have had access to that information."

"Right," Rakshan said, nodding. "Not my fault." He frowned. "And now I'm going to be sent far away and never see you again."

"Are you sure about that? Maybe he'll change his mind."

The lieutenant shook his head violently. "No, my father never changes his mind." He took a swig from the second bottle. "Come here."

Zhelica felt a little dizzy as she climbed off the sunken couch. She was not used to wine, and it had taken very little to affect her sense of balance.

Rakshan set the bottle on the floor and held his arms open. When Zhelica got near enough, he pulled her onto his lap. "Maybe you should come with me," he whispered in her ear.

He wrapped his arms around her. Zhelica did not struggle. She closed her eyes and soaked in the sensation of being held by a strong, if somewhat relaxed, man. She did not resist when he kissed her.

The taste of wine was on his breath. *He doesn't kiss like Yavan,* she thought – and then pushed that idea away. She was not going to think about him. He was dead. And Rakshan was here, right now. Zhelica kissed him again and then relaxed in his arms. She tried very hard not to hear the alarms blaring inside her head.

Thirteen

The wine was more powerful than the kiss. With the warmth of Zhelica in his arms and the soothing flicker of the firelight, Rakshan nodded off. Zhelica nestled down and tried to sleep, too. But the battle that had been raging in her heart and mind would not allow it.

Zhelica did not love Rakshan. Her heart was Yavan's, even if he was no longer there to receive or give her love. Rakshan was a substitute, and she had used him as a way to satisfy her own yearnings. Despite her every effort to push away thoughts of her husband, he insisted on seeping in. Once Rakshan's measured breathing indicated he was asleep, Zhelica was unable to avoid the shame of what she had done. She had betrayed Yavan. She had debased herself.

Rakshan's arms were still around her, so Zhelica carefully shifted a little, hoping he would move. One arm dropped limply onto the couch. Encouraged by this, Zhelica gently picked up the other and moved it aside so she could get up.

It would have looked comical, she thought, if anyone had been there to see her struggling to stand up from that sunken couch. The soldier mumbled as she finally forced herself out of his lap. She whispered, "I'm sorry, Rakshan," and tripped toward the front door.

The clouds made the night absolutely black, but the fireplace embers cast enough glow for Zhelica to at least head the right direction. She was dismayed to see the shelf pushed against the door. But with only a few screeches, it slid away enough to allow her to escape through the opening.

She stumbled to where the walkway joined the main path, turning left – she remembered that – and then picking her way slowly through the forest. The path was wide and had been cleared of most roots and larger rocks, so there was not much to trip on. But when she came to a fork, it was not clear which way to go.

She did not want to return to the base. There must be a way to circumvent the camp and find her way back to Nazhin's. But it depended on following the correct path.

While she stood hesitating – squinting to see if she could distinguish details in the dark – there suddenly appeared off the trail to the left tiny dots of white light, blinking like fireflies. They were the wrong shade for fireflies and it was the wrong time of year. But Zhelica could not resist investigating, and she headed down the left-most trail.

The lights kept flashing at intervals. When they did, they illuminated the path for an instant. Zhelica forgot about Rakshan, forgot about her shame, forgot that she was so late now Nazhin and Beyman had probably gone to bed. All she could think about was following the light.

No matter how far she went, however, they seemed to be ahead of her. Just when she began to worry that she had gone too far and was now hopelessly lost in the forest, Zhelica saw the path rise slightly and intersect the road beyond. The lights mysteriously vanished as soon as she stepped out of the trees.

She was near the town wall. Zhelica looked back to see if the lights still twinkled in the forest, but there was no sign of them. She shrugged this off. She was tired and sad, and knew that she would have to wait until morning to get into Hyarani, as the gates were bolted at sunset.

But then a second strange thing happened. As she approached, there was a grating sound, and the gate swung open. She thought at first that the guard had seen her arrival. But she could see him slumped inside his room, asleep. It felt like a dream. She pulled the gate closed herself, but the iron bolt was too heavy for her to throw. As she turned the corner of the first street, she heard it scrape in its setting. Someone – not the guard – had locked it behind her.

Despite her weariness, Zhelica ran, holding her baby bump to keep from bouncing. By now she could travel home in the maze of the town's streets even in the dark. When she arrived at Nazhin and Beyman's, she turned to look behind her. No one was following. She hastily turned her key in the lock and after securing the door, tiptoed upstairs.

The house was dark except for a flicker of light coming from the common room. *Someone must have waited up for me,* she thought guiltily. She gently opened the door and there, facing the fireplace, sat Afshar.

If she could have chosen the last person she wanted to see this night, it would have been him. Yavan's best friend. He would agree that she had behaved egregiously. Did she *have* to tell him?

He turned to look at her. His face was somber, and he motioned for her to come sit by him. Zhelica obeyed. She folded her hands in her lap and stared at them, not wanting to meet Afshar's eyes.

"The mailroom was trashed and Rakshan disappeared," he said. "You weren't seen leaving. We scoured the base looking for you. Where have you been, Zhelica?"

She swallowed hard. "Rakshan took me to a house in the woods."

Afshar sighed.

Zhelica's eyes were burning, and a single tear rolled down her face, off her chin, and onto her hands. "Oh, Afshar," she whispered. "What will I do?"

He tucked his legs under the chair and drummed his fingers on the arms of the couch. "What do you want to do?"

Run away, she thought in desperation. She brushed away her tears and looked at the soldier. "I want to keep working for the Restoration."

Afshar nodded. "You are going to have to leave Hyarani, though. I don't see how you can go back to work with Rakshan."

"He's being transferred, anyway," she said. "I doubt I could work with another soldier. If any more secrets slipped out of the mailroom, it would confirm I'm responsible."

Afshar's face had not softened during their discussion. Zhelica could tell he was hurt on behalf of his friend. Nevertheless, he spoke calmly.

"My contacts in the Restoration have made arrangements for you. I am taking you somewhere safe. Pack as quickly and quietly as you can. I'll be here when you're ready to go."

Zhelica tiptoed to her room. With little care, she threw her possessions, including Yavan's clothes, into the trunk and latched it. Fortunately, it had wheels, so she was able to pull it down the hallway. She ignored the creakings of the house this time, conscious only of the trunk as it dug a path across the carpet. Passing the others' rooms, she realized she would not be able to say goodbye.

"What about Nazhin and Beyman? Won't they wonder what happened to me?" she asked Afshar.

He carefully maneuvered the trunk down the stairs. "I told them you were being moved. They knew Yavan well enough to know not to ask too many questions."

Zhelica looked back up the stairs. There was nothing to see, just darkness. The magnitude of what she had done, and the loss resulting, swept over her. She choked back a sob and followed Afshar outside.

He locked the door. "I'll get the key back to them," he said.

He had brought a cart and loaded her trunk onto its bed. Then he gave her a hand up to the seat in front.

Mornings were coming earlier and they passed a shopkeeper sweeping outside. Afshar tipped his cap; the man raised a hand in greeting. Zhelica looked away.

The city gate was open now, and they rode through. As the countryside rolled past, Zhelica realized Afshar was taking her on the familiar road west of town. When they stopped outside Marjon's gate, Zhelica cried, "No!"

Afshar said quietly, "Zhelica, we've all made mistakes. You're not the only one. But if we want to succeed at what we're attempting, we have to be willing to go where we're directed and do what we're told."

"Marjon will never allow me to work for the Restoration," Zhelica said. "You don't know her, Afshar. All my life she has tried to keep me inside these walls, away from danger. She'll refuse to let me out."

To Zhelica's surprise, Afshar's lips curved into a restrained grin. "I don't see why she would," he said. "She's on our side."

While Zhelica tried to absorb this, Afshar pulled the bell rope, and the tiny window in the gate cracked. Then the door opened, and Marjon's watchman guided the horse in.

Her aunt appeared before Zhelica had descended from the cart. Afshar must have sent word ahead of the situation, as the older woman did not seem surprised at their arrival. If Marjon knew what Zhelica had done, chiding, anger, and shock would rain down on her so-called niece. Yet her aunt seemed unruffled as she held out a hand to balance Zhelica while she stepped down.

Marjon thanked Afshar, told the watchman to fetch down the trunk, and followed Zhelica inside.

"Why don't you have a rest, and we can talk when you're ready," Marjon said.

It felt as surreal as the opening of the city gate in the night.

"Thank you, Auntie," Zhelica said. She went to her old room and, barely noticing her surroundings, fell onto the bed and into a deep sleep.

"So *you* are involved in the Restoration?" Zhelica asked the next morning.

Marjon nodded. "That's how I knew Yavan," she said. "And that was why I wasn't very excited about him showing an interest in you."

"Did you work together?" Zhelica asked, trying to reconstruct past events in her mind in light of this information.

"Yes," Marjon said. "One member would leave messages for Yavan here, and then he carried them on to the next location. We were not supposed to know too much about what others were doing, but it was clear that Yavan was very involved. Somewhere there must have been a traitor in the system. Someone turned Yavan in."

Zhelica stirred her tea, watching the milk swirl into the brown liquid until it turned caramel.

"So who decides what happens to me now?" she asked. "Who is in charge?"

Marjon shook her head. "I can't tell you that," she said. "But I will tell you that a message came this morning with instructions for you."

This gave Zhelica some hope. Perhaps, despite her indiscretion, she could still be useful to the Restoration.

"You must leave the country," Marjon said.

Zhelica stared at her.

"It's not safe for you right now," her aunt explained. "The leaders want you to carry a letter into Darz."

Zhelica set the teacup into its saucer. Her hands shook. "Who will go with me?"

Marjon cleared her throat. "No one."

"But, Auntie –" she protested. The determined look on Marjon's face silenced her.

"You have an advantage, Zhelica," she said. "You are not invisible, but with your hair and eye color you could be from either Zaharada or Darz. While people may notice you, they won't pay much attention. You need to be careful on this side of the border, but you can travel freely in Darz, while most of us cannot."

"But I thought the Darzians were *for* Restoration," Zhelica said. "Why would they prevent you from entering?"

Marjon ran a hand over her flyaway hair. "Not all of them want reunification," she said. "Plus, how are they to know if we are sincere, or spies of Zaharada?"

"Yes," Zhelica said slowly, "I can see that."

Marjon went to her bureau and pulled out a scroll and unrolled it to reveal a map of the northernmost section of Zaharada with a band of Darz along the top.

"Can you find where we are?" Marjon asked.

Zhelica took a breath and leaned close. She found Hyarani (it looked so small in relation to everything else!) and traced the road west. "About here?"

Marjon nodded. "This is old; it marks the location of Circles of Meeting as well as cities and towns. I think you've been to this one."

Zhelica remembered her first ride with Yavan: a dot near the river showed where the Circle and the burned-out house lay.

"The main road north of Hyarani goes right into Darz," Marjon told her. "But you can't go that way."

"Why not?" The northern border was formed by a mountain range, with only this road clearly marked.

"The army will be looking for you."

Zhelica saw the worry in the older woman's eyes. "With you missing – they'll pin the information leak from the mailroom to you."

"You know about that?" Zhelica whispered.

"Yes," Marjon said. She turned away. "I am one of the local leaders, Zhelica."

"How did you ever hide this from me?" Zhelica wondered aloud.

Marjon turned back. "It wasn't easy." But rather than explaining, she continued her instructions. "If you follow the line of the mountains, you will see that they go right out to the sea."

"Yes," Zhelica said.

"Ride until you reach the coast. There is a narrow beach there...at low tide, when the water is out, it's possible to slip into Darz."

"How will I know when it's safe?"

"You'll have to watch. The low tide happens twice a day, about twelve hours apart."

"When should I leave?" Zhelica asked.

"As soon as you're ready," Marjon said. "I have packed provisions for you. There is also a change of clothing in the bag – before you go into Darz you must dress like one of their women. The message you are carrying is sewn into the pocket of the dress."

Zhelica hoped the waist was adjustable; her expanding midsection was making her own clothing tight now. Under the circumstances, she did not want to tell Marjon about the baby and kept positioning herself so her profile was hidden.

"How will I know who to give the message to?"

"That will be a bit of a challenge," Marjon said. "You need to find someone with the Restoration, but try not to arouse suspicion if you are among those unsympathetic to the cause."

It sounded overwhelming: traveling alone in unknown territory, timing her crossing so she did not get stranded or washed out to sea, finding the right person to pass along the message to.

"And when I am finished, do I return here?" she asked.

"Eventually. You might need to lie low for a while. Especially watch out for soldiers – we don't want any trouble."

Zhelica got up and hugged Marjon. "I'm sorry for the trouble I've already caused," she said.

Marjon's eyes widened as Zhelica's belly pressed against her. "Oh, child," she said. "I had no idea. . ."

She bit her lip. *I should have been more careful!*

"Even Yavan did not know," she whispered.

"I'm sorry to have to send you away," Marjon said, wiping away a tear. "But now I am even more convinced you need to get far from here."

Her aunt rolled up the map and handed it to Zhelica, then walked with her out to where the horse, already loaded, waited. The watchman would not be back until evening; Marjon, her salt-and-pepper hair blowing in the breeze, stood with her hand on the gate as Zhelica headed out.

"Until all things are restored," she said.

"Until all things are restored," Zhelica responded. Her voice sounded thin and uncertain. Thankful that Yavan had taken time to teach her the basics of horsemanship, she dug her heels into the animal's sides. They took off, west along the road.

She could not ride as fast as the soldiers who had transported her before. Plus the baby was positioned in such a way that every bounce reminded her of its presence. The main road was fairly smooth, but when she turned off onto a dirt track, the ride was even less comfortable. She slowed until the horse jogged at a pace acceptable to both of them.

Despite the heaviness of her own wrongdoing and banishment, Zhelica enjoyed the fresh air and beauty of the farms and copses she passed. There seemed to be no end to them. In the middle of the day, she stopped under a stand of trees and ate her lunch, curling up in the shade for a short nap before continuing.

A well-worn track ran parallel to the mountains. As she followed it west, the sun lowered until it shone in her face. The last farm, she realized, was now past. Trees replaced the pastures and fields. As she rode on, the forest became a dense tangle of branches and bushes, the floor so covered with plant life that she could barely find the path. At last, as the sun dipped below the horizon, Zhelica smelled a new scent: the salty breeze of the ocean. She nudged her horse forward, and within a few minutes, they stood at the top of a cliff overlooking the shore of Zaharada.

There was still a golden glow over the ocean. Zhelica marveled at the waves peeling back from the smooth, damp sand. Spotting a way to the beach, she dismounted and led the horse down.

The air flowed out from land to sea after sunset, so the temperature was still pleasant. After trying to walk on the sand, Zhelica stopped, sat down on a log, and slipped off her shoes. She carried them in one hand while keeping the other on the reins. The horse tossed his head in a motion that hinted he liked the freedom of this open space.

Zhelica could see where the mountains narrowed into a triangle of rock extending out into the water. A few trees topped the cape, which was dotted with clusters of seagulls. As she walked, the light perceptibly dimmed until only the white of the waves lit the path.

Zhelica saw someone along the shore ahead. Only his silhouette was visible. She glanced around: there was no easy exit from the beach. Spotting what looked like an even darker mouth in the rocks behind her, Zhelica headed toward it and realized there was a shallow cave here. She tied the horse to a log and removed the Darzian clothes from the bag. She unlaced her dress – it was barely tied now because of her pregnancy – and pulled it over her head. Then she slipped into the Darzian dress. It was rough against her skin, and loose. A kind of apron went over it; fortunately this tied above her waist, so there was plenty of room for the baby. There were also leggings and an outer garment warmer than the one she had been wearing. She rolled her clothes in her Zaharadan cloak and stuffed them back into the satchel. Then she attached her horse's feedbag and peeked from behind him.

While she had been busy, the man had built a fire on the beach and begun cooking something. Although Marjon had packed food for Zhelica, it was cold, simple fare. The delicate smell of fish (too expensive usually for people like Marjon and Zhelica to enjoy) wafted toward the grotto where she stood. The warm breeze had died down, and cool, damp air flowed from the sea. The fire and the food were too enticing. Zhelica tiptoed toward the man.

While she was still beyond the firelight, the traveler – without turning – called out, "Come join me! I have plenty for two."

Zhelica could not see his face and did not know if he was Zaharadan or Darzian. She held back for a moment and then stepped into the fire's circle. The man, she remembered later, was nondescript: his skin not fair but not very dark, his features not extraordinary in any way. She should have been wary, she realized later, as she was alone on the beach with a stranger. But he looked kindly, and Zhelica felt drawn to him.

"Did you catch them?" she asked. Two large fish sizzled on a grill he had laid over the fire. Flatbread was warming off to the side.

"I did," he said, poking the wood to bring coals nearer the food. He set his stick down. "There is a log here just waiting for you."

Zhelica lowered herself carefully. She felt stiff from being on the horse for so long. She wanted to be cautious, to have a plan of escape if necessary, but she was spent and sad. She said nothing.

The man seemed content with the silence.

Zhelica soaked in the tranquility of the place: the gentle caressing of wave on sand, the wisps of wind that blew across the fire, sending up small clouds of sparks, the stars beginning to stud the sky. She watched the stranger cooking and realized suddenly that she was wiping tears from her eyes so that she could focus better.

"You seem burdened," the man said.

She nodded. "I have lost so much."

He took two sticks and gently turned the fish, then looked at her. "And whose fault is that?" he asked.

She was startled. Although his voice was even, it sounded like an accusation.

"Not mine," she began. She was thinking of Yavan and his death. Then she remembered Rakshan. "Well," she added sheepishly, "some of it is mine. I made a poor choice and now I am suffering for it."

The man nodded – not sympathetically, but more in confirmation, she thought.

She shifted on the log but realized her discomfort was not physical. "I am sorry I made that choice. I have hurt people, and been exiled. . ."

"But your story is not finished," the man said gently. "Don't despair."

She took a deep breath. As though the peace of the environment was washing over her, she suddenly felt her heaviness of spirit ebb away.

Her host reached over to pull apart one of the fish to check its doneness. As he did so, his hand extended in a way that exposed his wrist. It was raw, as though burnt by a rope. This jolted Zhelica from what she had been saying, and she gasped, "What a nasty injury!"

The man, satisfied with the fish, pushed the bread off the grill onto a cloth. Deftly, he flipped one of the fishes onto the bread and handed it to Zhelica. He took the other for himself.

"Yes," he said, as she continued to stare at his wrists; they were both wounded. "I had some enemies in my last job." He gently tugged his sleeves down to cover the marks. They both ate.

Zhelica had not realized how hungry she was. The fish was warm and rich and filling, and the bread firm yet chewy. She realized suddenly that she was thirsty.

"Perhaps you would like something other than water to drink," the man said as though reading her mind. He pulled a flask from his bag and removed its lid, which served as a cup. He poured a red liquid in and held it out to her.

She hesitated. She needed all her wits about her, and drinking wine would dull them. She took one sip and knew at once it was something different from what Rakshan had served her – a juice of some kind, but not too sweet and cloying. She finished the cup.

The man poked the fire and flames licked up the fishbones, blue tongues shooting up as the skin incinerated in the coals.

"So you are on a journey," he said at last.

"Yes." She didn't want to say more than was necessary.

The man leaned his head one direction. "If you go that way," he said, "you will eventually reach the capital, Baraqan. The other way will take you to Darz."

"Oh?" she said, feigning nonchalance. "But how does one pass by the mountains?"

His eyes creased in amusement. "Most people would wait until low tide."

"When would that be?"

The man pointed to the waves. "If you watch, you can see that the tide is going out now."

Zhelica did, and he was right: with each roll, the water returned to a point farther from them.

"In about half an hour, the cape will be clear of the waves," the man said. "That would be the time to round it. If you were going that direction," he added.

"I see," Zhelica said. Then, as if to throw him off, she added, "If I *am* going that way."

He said nothing.

"And what about you?" she asked. "Where are you going?"

"Wherever I am needed," he said.

He rose from his seat and pried the grill up from the fire. It glowed red on its underside. Her host extended it with two sticks and walked out into the water. He set it down in the sea, and the grill hissed, emitting a cloud of steam.

"Who are you?" Zhelica called out.

"Some call me the Gardener," the man said. With the grill he traced a circle in the water. "Some call me the King."

"Zaharada has no king," Zhelica called back.

The steam dissipated. Zhelica blinked. There seemed to be no one there.

She rose from the log and stumbled toward the water. "Hello!" she called out. "Where are you? Are you all right?"

The fire still gave a little light. Frantically, Zhelica ran into the sea where the man had been standing. Perhaps he had been swept away by a wave. Something white floated like a cloak on the water. She reached down and grabbed its corner. When she stood up, she held something soft in her fingers. Tilting her cupped hands toward the light, she saw a giant white rose. She looked back. A trail of flowers danced on the waves.

But the man was gone.

Fourteen

The water was too cold to tolerate long. Zhelica carried the rose past the fire, which had burned to embers, to where her horse waited against the cliff. She patted his flank as she removed his feedbag.

"Who ever heard of a gardener who is king?" she asked the horse, and as the words passed her lips, Azara's story rushed back. *There were even reports that the emperor was not actually dead. I don't know how that could be, but some people believed it.*

Zhelica shivered at the memory but tucked the rose into the horse's mane and stepped on a nearby log to remount. Her thighs were sore from a day in the saddle, but she knew she had to get around the cape quickly before the tide rose again.

The moon was not yet up, but the little light from the night sky reflected off the wet sand, helping Zhelica guide her horse around the rocky prominence. They splashed through tidepools left behind by the receding waves. Zhelica could not stop thinking about the man she had seen. He seemed alive enough – he had eaten food with her. But it was crazy to think that if the emperor were around, he would stop and cook dinner for a woman out for a ride on the beach.

The change in scenery was not immediately obvious north of the border. The cliff was still thatched with dark trees, but as she rode along, Zhelica could see the bluff angling down toward the beach until at last the sand came to an end. To her relief, a rectangle of light stretched toward the shore.

She nudged the horse up nearer the building: it was a cottage. Behind and north of it the lights of a town glimmered. Zhelica walked the horse up what turned out to be the main street of this most-southerly Darzian habitation.

The night was still early and periodically a person or two would appear, glance up at her, and continue walking. Zhelica did not know if her best hope was to stop and engage one of them in conversation; she kept moving. At last she came to an inn, the only brightly lit building. She decided that might be the place to figure out what to do next.

Her unwieldy shape made it harder to dismount near the tying post. She threw her leg over the horse, but the other foot became tangled in the stirrup, and instead of descending gently to the ground, Zhelica fell.

A dagger of pain sliced through her ankle as it folded in on itself. Instinctively, she supported her belly as she went down, but let out an involuntary cry. In an instant, a small crowd surrounded her.

"Get her inside," a woman said after carefully extracting Zhelica's foot from the stirrup. Several men grabbed her (not roughly) and lifted her up the steps and into the inn. In no time she was positioned in one wooden chair with her foot elevated on another.

"Someone fetch the doctor," a man said, and a boy took off.

Her ankle throbbing, Zhelica looked around her. The room was warm with oil lamps, its décor simple and rough, the corners dark where the flickering light did not reach. The townsfolk were dressed as she was, in rough brown skirts and trousers. They were clean but unadorned. It was not their clothing or skin, however, that made her blink to clear her vision. It seemed all the eyes fixed on her were green, all the heads crowned with red hair.

"Where am I?" she murmured, rubbing her eyes.

The same woman who had spoken outside sat down and took one of her hands. "Poor thing," she said. "She's delirious."

The others nodded. Some lingered for a few minutes, but eventually they all wandered back to their places at the bar or to one of the round tables that filled the room. Conversation, eating, and drinking resumed.

"I don't think I've seen you before," the woman said, squeezing her hand comfortingly.

"No, I'm just traveling," Zhelica said. "What is the name of this place?"

"This is Zerzavy. *Alloy* town."

Zhelica was trying to think clearly, but the swelling in her leg shifted her focus. "Really? Are you all *alloys* here?"

The woman smiled. "Not all," she said. "But almost all." She stood up, dropping Zhelica's hand.

"What happened here?" came a man's voice.

When he entered her line of vision, she knew in an instant he was the doctor. One hand held a leather bag; his slacks and woolen jacket were of a finer quality than what she and the others in the inn were wearing. Zhelica could hardly take her eyes from his face as he occupied the recently vacated chair. His hair and beard glistened like gold, and eyes the blue of a summer sky met hers.

"It looks like you've taken a bad fall," he said as he unlaced the boot she was wearing. It had been tightening as her leg swelled, and she let out a yelp when he tugged it off. She winced even before his fingers began manipulating the swollen limb.

"I'm sorry about that," he said, reaching into his bag for a roll of bandage. "I'm going to wrap your ankle. I don't think it's broken, but you probably tore some ligaments."

Zhelica watched as he deftly cocooned her foot and ankle in the bandage, the blond hair on his fingers catching the light as he wound the cloth.

When the doctor finished, he sat back in the chair. His head tilted to look at her extended leg, he assessed his work. "When is your baby due?"

Zhelica's heart skipped a beat. She glanced down at her belly. In this position, slouched in the chair, the curve was unmistakable. Pulling herself up quickly, her injured foot crashed to the floor. She cried out in pain.

"Here, I didn't mean to startle you," the doctor said. He leaned over and gently lifted her foot onto the chair again. Zhelica felt a tear roll down her face.

"Let's begin again. I am Doctor Laskavosk. I know everyone in Zerzavy, but I don't recognize you."

"My name is Zhelica," she sniffed. "I'm not from around here."

The doctor again tilted his head to examine her. "And yet you blend right in," he observed.

"More than you do," she said with a laugh. She was feeling labile now, her emotions fluctuating like the ocean waves.

"True enough," he said. "And now, may I ask? When is your baby due?"

Zhelica breathed a sigh that she could feel to her core. "I don't know," she said. "A month? Two months?"

Doctor Laskavosk looked shocked. "You don't know?"

"Oh, let's see." The pulsing of the blood in her foot was like a drumbeat. "My husband died five months ago, so it would have been before that. . ."

She heard the sharp intake of breath from the doctor and looked up. His forehead was creased but otherwise there was no sign of emotion.

"Where are you staying, Zhelica?"

She looked around her. The inn was a bustling place. She had a little money, but how would she ever walk up the stairs to a room? She shrugged.

"I'm a little concerned about your child," the doctor said. "I'd like to have you where I can monitor you in case there is a problem."

Zhelica clutched her abdomen. "Do you think I might have harmed the baby?"

"There is no reason to believe that. I just want to keep an eye on you. Wait here."

He went to one of the nearby tables and came back with a couple of sturdy men. "These gentlemen are going to transport you to my carriage."

Zhelica was in no condition to resist. She allowed them to settle her onto the cushioned bench. The friendly woman waved at her from the steps of the inn.

"That's my horse," Zhelica said, pointing.

"That explains your injury," Doctor Laskavosk said. "He's huge." He leaned out the window. "Filip," he called to one of the men who had helped him, "could you feed her horse and put him in the stall? I'll come get him in the morning."

The man nodded and Zhelica watched him gently guide the horse away. The white rose came loose from its mane and tumbled to the ground; Filip snatched it up, tossing it through the carriage window. It landed in Zhelica's lap.

Doctor Laskavosk stared at the flower. "Where did that come from?"

Zhelica held it to her nose. It gave off a sweet, delicate scent. "A stranger gave it to me on the beach."

The doctor seemed uneasy. He looked as though he wanted to ask a question, but Zhelica was in no mood to answer. She closed her eyes, the rose still held to her face. Another teardrop trickled down her cheek. *It hurts!* she complained inwardly. *And I don't know where I am or who these people are or when I will ever be able to go home.* Another tear. She used the rose to brush it away and opened her eyes.

Doctor Laskavosk was watching her, his forehead again furrowed. "We are not far now," he said.

As the carriage pulled up in front of a large house, the doctor jumped down and beckoned the driver to help him ease Zhelica up the stairs. "Hold onto my arm, Zhelica." She was afraid to put any weight on her foot and balanced on the other leg while the doctor unlocked the front door.

There was no lamp in the hallway but a door at the end stood open, light pouring out. A girl about seven or eight or years old appeared at the top of the staircase in her nightgown. "Daddy? Who is that with you?"

"Gabara, I have brought a patient home," he said. He lifted so much of Zhelica's weight as he shuffled her through the hallway, she felt as though she were skimming above the ground like a bird.

The little girl scurried down the steps and watched as her father arranged Zhelica on the sofa. Dr. Laskavosk unlaced her other boot, balanced her leg up on pillows, and tucked a blanket around her.

"That's better," he said. "How do you feel?"

"My foot hurts," Zhelica said. Suddenly she was overcome with fatigue.

"Right." Dr. Laskavosk disappeared for a moment and returned with a glass of water and a tablet in his hand. "Take this. It should help with the pain."

Zhelica gladly followed his directions. Gabara stared at her.

"So this is your daughter," Zhelica murmured. "Are you the oldest child, Gabara?"

The tow-headed girl blinked her luminous blue eyes, shaking her head. "I am the *only* child," she began. "You see, my mother-"

Dr. Laskavosk cleared his throat. "Gabara, you should be in bed. Go on up, and I will come tuck you in."

The little girl kissed him on the cheek and departed walking backwards, apparently wanting to watch as long as possible.

Zhelica could see she was in a combination office and common room; the doctor's desk sat near one of the windows. Behind it were bookshelves. A fireplace was set into one of the polished wooden walls, but in the warm evening no fire had been lit.

The doctor picked up something from his desk and knelt beside her. "Zhelica, may I listen to your baby's heartbeat?"

She laughed. "How can you hear a baby's heart?"

Dr. Laskavosk held up what looked like a carved wooden horn. "Didn't your midwife ever use one of these?"

"I haven't seen a midwife," she answered.

"How could you go so long pregnant and not be seen by anyone?"

The medicine was starting to work; with her pain level reduced, Zhelica felt more in control. "Doctor, the last few months have been . . ." Her voice trailed off. She did not know how to explain, or whether she *should* explain, all that had happened. She had already mentioned Yavan's death, so she decided to stick with that part of the story. "My husband died in an accident. And life has been crazy ever since."

She motioned for him to proceed, and Dr. Laskavosk placed the bell-like end on her abdomen, moving it around. A smile lit up his face.

"That's what I like to hear," he said. He tilted the instrument toward her. "Would you like to listen to your baby?"

Zhelica leaned over and took the listening end. The swish-swishing of the baby's heart filled her head. She grasped the doctor's sleeve in amazement. "Is that really the baby?"

He nodded. "Your little one sounds just fine."

Zhelica listened for another moment and then handed the device back to the physician. *That is my baby. Yavan's child.* For the first time, she really longed to know this tiny person.

"If you're comfortable, I'll have you sleep in here tonight," the doctor said. He picked up a brass bell from his bookcase and set it on a table near Zhelica's head. "Just ring this if the pain becomes intolerable, and I'll come check on you."

"Thank you for your help, Dr. Laskavosk. You have been kind to a wounded traveler."

"That's my job," he said. "Your job is to feel better. Rest well."

Gabara suddenly appeared in the doorway. The little girl ran over and dropped a toy cat in Zhelica's arms. "Kotchka will watch you tonight so you don't get lonely," she said before turning to rush out again.

"Good night," Zhelica called. She felt oddly comforted by the fuzzy toy and positioned it next to her cheek, where it remained until morning.

When she awoke, Dr. Laskavosk was already at his desk. She could hear his pen scratching away, and she watched silently until he noticed her.

"Good morning," he said. He set his pen down. "How did you sleep?"

"Well, thank you," she said. "But I'm a little stiff. I think it's from riding so long yesterday." She scooted into an upright position and tried to wiggle her foot. "Oh," she moaned.

The doctor came over and tossed the edge of the blanket aside. "The swelling's gone down a bit," he said. "Does this hurt?"

He gently rotated her foot.

"Yes!"

"Let's keep it up," he said, helping her elevate it again. He slid his desk chair near the couch and sat down. When he rang the bell, Mrs. Milica, whom he introduced as his housekeeper and cook, appeared. The doctor ordered tea for Zhelica, and then said, "I would like to ask you a few questions."

Zhelica's hand reached for the letter which was still hidden in her pocket.

"I will answer you as best I can," she said.

"Where did you arrive from last night?"

She had hoped for something less direct. She gazed into the azure eyes fixed on her. *Maybe he is on our side.*

Maybe he can help me figure out who to take this message to.

However, she answered with a question. "Where do you think I came from?"

He shifted in his chair. "If I knew," he said, "I wouldn't have asked." But he took a moment and then said, "You have a strange accent. I think you are from Hyarani."

"You're right," she said. "I traveled here by way of the beach. At low tide, there is a dry path."

He nodded. "And the man with the rose? Where did you see him?"

"He was south of the border."

"Did he give you any...instructions?" Dr. Laskavosk asked.

The question was as peculiar as her encounter the day before. Did the doctor know this man? Why would he think the stranger had given her instructions?

"No. He just told me when the tide would be out."

The doctor leaned toward her. Quietly, he said, "But the rose...the white rose of the Restoration..."

Zhelica pulled the blanket up around her shoulders.

"I didn't know there was significance to the white rose," she said.

Now Dr. Laskavosk seemed to be weighing what he should tell her. "Those involved with the Restoration use it as a sign."

No one had told her this; if they had, she would have asked the strange man to help her. "He said some call him the Gardener, and that some call him the King," she murmured.

"That could only have been. . ." he hesitated. "There is only one person who is known by those titles."

She nodded. "The Emperor of Darzarada," she whispered. "But I thought he was dead."

Dr. Laskavosk's eyes danced. "But now you know that can't be true."

"I'm not sure what to think."

"Tell me everything...what did he say to you?"

Zhelica remembered her confession on the beach and the stranger's words of consolation. She did not want to share this part of the conversation with the doctor.

"How do I know I can trust you?"

Dr. Laskavosk was a serious man: not moody like Rakshan, but like one who seemed to be constantly evaluating things. For the first time, he gave Zhelica a smile. "That's a good question. I'll tell you my history, and then you decide if you can trust me."

Mrs. Milica carried the tray in and poured Zhelica a cup of tea. The doctor leaned back in his chair, interlacing his fingers across his chest.

"My family is not from this area originally," he said. "We come from up north. Back when the King of Darz sought to bring our land under the dominion of Zaharada, my father crossed the border. He worked as a physician in the army. When Shurash stopped allowing Darzians to serve in the military, my father stayed on to help set up cells of those who wanted to keep the countries unified. I don't know how much you know about that time."

"I have heard some stories," she said. "As you can see, I am half Darzian."

"Your father or mother?"

"My father," she said. "I only recently learned his name. Vaclav."

When she said this, Dr. Laskavosk started. "Vaclav? Was he involved in the Restoration?"

"He was," Zhelica said. "I don't remember much about him, but I was told he was a musician and was killed for being part of those pushing for reunification."

The doctor went to the window seat and lifted its lid. He extracted something from inside, and when he turned, Zhelica let out a cry.

"His instrument!"

There was no mistaking it: his name was painted on the neck. Zhelica had seen the initial "V" of it in the portrait Marjon gave her before the wedding.

"How did you know about this?" Dr. Laskavosk asked.

"My aunt gave me a picture...a painting of my parents with me. My father had that in his hand."

The doctor passed it to her. Zhelica lovingly stroked the smooth wood, running her finger over the letters. She plucked a string, allowing it to vibrate into silence. Meanwhile, the doctor had gone back to the window seat. He returned with a painting – an exact replica of her own.

"That is my father on the other side of yours," he said. "They were best friends."

As she scrutinized the painting, she could see the resemblance between the man and his son.

"Was your father also killed?"

The doctor shook his head. "He returned to Darz. Vaclav seemed to have some premonition about what would happen. He told my father to take his instrument and keep it safe here. I wonder if he knew he was keeping it safe for *you*?"

Zhelica's eyes filled with tears. She blinked them away. "Is your father still alive?"

Dr. Laskavosk ran the back of his hand over his beard. "He is," he said. "But he returned to our family home, which is far from here."

"Why aren't you there?"

"He trained me in medicine," he said. "Doctors are among the wealthiest people in Darz." He held out his hands to indicate where they now sat. With the sunlight streaming into the room, Zhelica could appreciate even more the richness of the fabric from which the furniture had been made, and the soft, thick Zaharadan rugs.

"But my father taught me that as a physician, my responsibility was to take care of the poor, to treat those who could not afford to pay me much. Do you know who those people are in Darz?"

"The *alloys?*" Zhelica suggested.

"Exactly. Even though most of our countrymen were happy to become part of Darzarada, when the emperor was killed, and after him so many of our people, the Darzians came to hate *alloys* as symbols of Zaharadan influence."

"So we're despised in both countries," Zhelica complained.

"Not by everyone. Just like in Zaharada, there are people who are fighting to reunite our two countries. Some of them are *alloys;* others, like myself, are not."

"So you *are* a part of the Restoration!"

"Yes, I am. But, Zhelica, even though you are in Darz, we still need to be careful. There are people adamantly opposed to reunification, and they could make a lot of trouble for us."

Before she could reply, there was a timid knock at the door. With her father's permission, Gabara slipped inside.

"Did Kotchka help?" she asked.

"He must have," Zhelica said, handing back the stuffed animal. "I slept great."

Gabara held the cat close. "Are you going to have breakfast with us?"

Zhelica looked at the doctor.

"Do you think you can stand up?" he asked.

He offered her an arm, and she raised herself. Gingerly, she put her sore foot on the ground, but then pulled it up again. "It hurts too much to put my weight on it."

"That's all right. Lean on me, and we'll get to the dining room together."

As they slowly edged along, Zhelica remembered her letter.

"Dr. Laskavosk," she said softly, "I came here to deliver a message, but I don't know who to give it to."

He stopped, and Zhelica carefully ripped open the inner pocket Marjon had sewn in her dress. She pulled out the now-crumpled note, still in a sealed envelope.

"I'll make sure this gets to the right person," the doctor assured her. He tucked it in his own pocket, and they resumed their trip.

Gabara, who had run ahead into the room, reappeared. "Hurry!" she cried. "Mrs. Milica made sweet rolls!"

Fifteen

The first week after her injury, Zhelica sat on Dr. Laskavosk's couch, reading Darzian history books and talking with Gabara.

"What are you doing?" she asked the girl one day as she slid the doctor's desk drawer open.

"Hiding Kotchka," she answered, scooping out some papers and affectionately placing the stuffed cat in the drawer.

Zhelica watched when Dr. Laskavosk returned, opening the drawer to retrieve something. His lips bent into a little frown as he noticed the lump in his files, and lifting them up, he found Kotchka and held it aloft.

This was a daily occurrence: he came back from his rounds holding Kotchka by the scruff of its neck and feigning disgust as he tossed the cat to Gabara. "In my medical bag?" he asked in pretend outrage. Gabara rolled on the floor, laughing.

One night Zhelica was about to lower the gas lamp to sleep, when Gabara popped into the room and flounced onto the couch.

"Wait," she said, putting a finger to her lips.

A roar from upstairs. "What in the world!"

"I put Kotchka in his bed," Gabara chortled. She gave Zhelica a squeeze before running to retrieve her pet.

Zhelica *tried* to walk, but the damaged ankle persisted in swelling whenever it was not elevated, and she and Dr. Laskavosk were both concerned she would re-tear the healing ligaments.

"This must be frustrating for you," he said one evening while checking the foot. "You're probably eager to get home."

"Actually," Zhelica said, "Marjon wants me to stay out of the country for a while."

The doctor raised one eyebrow quizzically.

"I was in some trouble," Zhelica said. "I'm not sure what will happen when I do return."

Her first full day there, the doctor encouraged her to write a note to her aunt explaining that she had arrived safely but twisted her ankle and was receiving medical care. Someone in the Restoration network carried the note to Zaharada and Marjon wrote back, relieved that Zhelica was in good hands. She told her to wait there until further instructions came.

"So what is *your* involvement in the Restoration? If I'm allowed to ask."

He leaned back in his chair, his golden beard sparkling in the sunlight, and thought for a moment. "I am mostly an intermediary," he told her. "People like yourself coming north may stay here or just pass a message along. Those on the Darzian side pick up notes or people here to carry on their work. I'm usually busy with my patients, so I don't have much time to do anything more."

She nodded. "You seem to be out every day. Why don't your patients come here?"

"It was dark when I brought you, so you probably don't realize where I live. Let me take you outside."

Dr. Laskavosk disappeared and returned with a wheelchair. "I keep this to loan to patients. Most can't afford to buy one." He helped her in and pushed her out the front door. The entire house, she now saw, was surrounded by a covered porch. Dr. Laskavosk wheeled her to the back. Once there, Zhelica could see why the physician traveled to his patients rather than vice versa.

The home was perched on a bluff overlooking the ocean and the scruffy town below.

"What a view!" Zhelica cried. The sun had just dipped below the horizon, and clouds above the ocean dazzled in gold and pink. Together they watched the colors change and the sea birds perform their twilight dance.

Suddenly, Zhelica remembered another sunset, Yavan at her side. She closed her eyes tight as the suffocating pain of loss hit her again. These onslaughts happened less frequently but still with a force that took her breath away. She grasped the arm of her chair to keep from crying.

"What is it?" the doctor asked. "Are you having contractions? It's too early."

She looked down at her belly. "No, it's not the baby. It's the baby's father."

Dr. Laskavosk's voice softened. "It must be very difficult for you," he said. "Losing a spouse and then having to face raising a child alone...the prospect can be intimidating."

For some moments they watched the sky in silence.

"How long have *you* been alone?" Zhelica ventured.

"My wife died in childbirth," he said. "I have raised Gabara alone. I won't lie to you: it is hard work."

She nodded. "But you have done a wonderful job, Dr. Laskavosk. Gabara is such a delight."

The doctor gave one of his rare smiles and said, "I think we should go in before it gets cold."

They had a sort of kinship, Zhelica thought as the doctor guided her back: they would soon be two parents trying to raise little ones without spouses. There was comfort in knowing that someone had been there before her.

Gabara ran from her bedroom when she heard the front door close behind them.

"Daddy, will you read me a story?"

"Yes," he said, resetting Zhelica on the couch. "What is it to be tonight?"

Gabara pulled a book off the shelf. "The story of the Gardener King," she said. She sat down, leaning against Zhelica, forcing her father to stand behind them.

"You'll have to turn the pages," he told her.

And then he read the tale:

In the kingdom of Zaharada there was no prince. The king and queen waited for many years. The queen drank special teas and ate dishes of meat to encourage the growth of a sturdy boy within her. The king rode his horse up and down the castle paths and lifted heavy stones to be strong so that he might father a strong son.

But the royal couple grew middle-aged, and then they grew old. And there was no child to sit on the throne of their land.

One day, the queen wandered out to the Circle of Meeting. "O great Overking," she called out, "who will reign after us? For you know we have no child and heir."

To her surprise, an answer came through the Ambassador. "The young man who is your gardener will be king," he said. "You must bring him into the palace and treat him as your own son."

Now the queen had known the gardener since she was a young woman. And although she had aged (as people do), over the years the gardener never seemed to grow older. He was still as robust as the first time she had seen him. Often when the queen walked in the royal gardens she stopped to talk with the gardener. He already had won her motherly affection, and she happily adopted him into the royal family.

There were many who loved the gardener prince as the queen did. He was a gentle man who listened to all the servants, stopped to converse with children in the streets, and always took time to examine the plants growing where he traveled.

When the king died, the gardener was crowned as monarch over Zaharada. The land had peace on all its borders and prosperity in every city and town. Nevertheless, the prince had enemies.

Chief among his adversaries was Shurash. When Zaharada and Darz joined to become one country, Shurash plotted to destroy the king.

One night, Shurash's cronies ambushed the king when he walked in the garden. They killed him and tied him by his wrists between two rose trees in a grove he had once cared for.

Shurash thought he had succeeded in conquering the Gardener King and would rule the land. He fought against all who tried to reunify the kingdom of Darzarada. Many were killed and many fled north to the land of Darz.

But stories began to spread across the countryside: the king was not *dead. When those who killed him came to retrieve his body, it had vanished from the tree. Many claimed to have seen him. His faithful citizens worked together to prepare the way for the king to come back to rule.*

Someday there would be a great Restoration.

Zhelica realized, as Gabara closed the book, that she had been holding her breath. The illustrations were stylized, as they are in children's books, but she had seen enough.

"I've met him," she whispered. "I've met the Gardener King."

Gabara's mouth fell open and she stared at Zhelica, her great blue eyes unblinking. "What was he like?"

"He seemed so ordinary," she said. "But he also appeared to know, somehow, what was going on in my heart. I can't explain it," she added, lifting her hands helplessly. "He went into the waves and then disappeared."

"Disappeared?" Gabara asked.

"Yes," Zhelica nodded, remembering the scene. "And when I went to the water, there was a river of white roses rising and falling on the waves where he had been."

She looked up at Dr. Laskavosk. He seemed lost in thought.

Gabara rubbed her eyes. "I'm tired."

"Yes, it's time you were in bed," her father replied. Gabara scooted nearer to Zhelica and gave her a hug.

"Good night, Zhelica," she said. "I'm glad you're here."

"Me, too. Good night, Gabara."

Once she was alone, Zhelica thought more about the king.

How could he be dead and *not* dead? Had they been deceived? Was he only injured?

Why had he asked her the question he did? What did it matter to him if she was at fault in the things she had suffered?

Was she really involved in the Restoration because she wanted to see the emperor back on his throne? Or had she only volunteered to somehow make Yavan's sacrifice matter?

It took her a long time to fall asleep.

Weeks passed. Zhelica managed to hobble around the house, but her ankle was slow to heal. The swelling went down, and then the flesh returned to its natural color. But whenever she pressed her foot on the floor, pain flashed like lightning through her leg.

If it were not for Gabara and Mrs. Milica, her days would have been rife with loneliness. The evenings were not bad, though: Dr. Laskavosk read aloud, or the three played games together.

When she woke each day, she peered at her belly. The size was increasing perceptibly, and she longed to be back at Marjon's in time for her delivery.

"It would be good for you to get outside," Dr. Laskavosk told her one morning as he collected his medical equipment. "I'm going into town, and I thought you might like to come along. It's market day, and you'll have a chance to start walking."

"What if my foot starts swelling?" she asked, worried. "How will I get back here?"

The doctor smiled. "I'm taking the wheelchair. If necessary, you can sit down. But," he said with mock sternness, "it's time to try walking, or you will never get better."

The road to town was steep and the carriage creaked as they rounded the switchbacks. Zhelica was too busy watching to be unnerved as the little town appeared and then disappeared with each change of direction. It looked bedraggled enough from above: roofs in disrepair were patched with old boards or fabric. The unpaved streets meandered without apparent plan through the jumble of buildings.

Closer it looked no better. Zerzavy was an ugly blot between the coast and farmland.

Zhelica was fascinated by the people, though. Men, women, and children of all ages thronged the streets and yards of the town – all topped with hair liked burnished copper. *It is the most attractive thing in Zerzavy,* Zhelica thought. Their heads glowed against the tattered wooden buildings around them.

At Dr. Laskavosk's first stop he left Zhelica in the carriage, and a horde of his patient's siblings clotted the window, peering in.

"Who's that you've got there, Dr. L?" asked one of the boys, craning his neck to see over those younger.

"That," Dr. Laskavosk said, "is another of my patients. You'll kindly step back and give her some room to breathe."

One of the girls poked Zhelica's arm and ran away, tittering. Zhelica scooted away from the window and waited for the doctor's return.

As they headed to his next patient, he said, "What is your impression of our little town?"

She did not want to say what she really thought about Zerzavy. "It's not like anywhere I've ever been," she said. "And maybe it was just that family, but the people seem a bit wild."

Dr. Laskavosk nodded. "They're outcasts from society and have begun to believe the things other Darzians say about them. And act accordingly. I think you'll enjoy my next patient a little more."

They parked near a boardwalk that ran along the main street. "This is a good place to test your leg," the doctor said. Zhelica clung almost desperately to his arm while limping toward a wooden house. The owner had obviously taken some care with it: the window frames and door were painted bright green, and flowers spilled from boxes attached in front.

An older woman answered and greeted them cheerfully. "Come in, doctor, come in."

"Thank you, Aneta," Dr. Laskavosk said. "Allow me to introduce a patient staying with us. This is Zhelica."

"Pleased to meet you," Aneta said. She looked different from the others; after a moment, Zhelica realized the woman was dressed in slightly worn but clean Zaharadan clothes.

"Like you, Zhelica is from the south," Dr. Laskavosk said.

Aneta chased a cat off an armchair and helped the doctor assist Zhelica into it.

"Let me get you some tea," she said. She disappeared into the kitchen. Despite the room's unfinished woodboard walls, it was studded with treasures of Zaharadan beauty; lace covered the windows and a multicolored glass vase set nearby captured the morning light, casting red and blue and green across a plush Zaharadan rug.

"So how are your headaches?" Dr. Laskavosk asked as he took the dainty cup his patient handed him.

"I asked the shop to order those pills you prescribed," Aneta said, brushing aside a red-and-white curl that escaped from her tidy coil of hair. "They haven't come in yet...told me they've no idea when they'll arrive."

"Let me see if I have any," the doctor said. He set down his cup and began rifling through his leather bag, bringing up a small glass jar. "You are in luck," he said to his patient.

"But, Dr. Laskavosk, that is *your* supply," she objected.

"Look, Aneta, take one of these the next time your headache comes on. When your prescription is filled, you can give me a replacement."

She smiled appreciatively and set the bottle on her mantelpiece. "Thank you, doctor. How is that little girl of yours?"

"Growing every day," he said. "And causing mischief." He glanced over at Zhelica for confirmation and his blue eyes sparkled.

"The poor motherless girl," Aneta said to Zhelica. "I keep telling the doctor he needs to remarry, but he never takes my advice."

"I don't have time to look for a wife, Aneta."

"How long will *you* be visiting, my dear?" Aneta asked, turning toward her guest.

Zhelica decided Aneta's question had nothing to do with the doctor's comment. "Just until my leg heals," she said, extending her foot. To her delight, she saw that the wrapped ankle was not swelling. "The doctor has been taking good care of me."

"Has he?" Aneta asked with interest, and Zhelica flushed. She had not meant to suggest anything by her remark.

"Zhelica will be returning to Zaharada soon," Dr. Laskavosk said. "If you have any letters, I'm sure she would be glad to see them posted in country."

"I would," Zhelica echoed.

"Thank you!" Aneta said. "I'll start writing as soon as you leave today."

The doctor finished his tea. "It's always nice to have an excuse to drop by. Let me know how those pills work.

And if the ones you ordered don't come in by next week, send word. I'll have a talk with the pharmacist."

When the door closed behind them, Zhelica said, "That was pleasant."

"I thought you'd like Aneta," Dr. Laskavosk said. "She was such a help after Gabara was born. She found Mrs. Milica for us." He pried open the death grip Zhelica held on his arm and gently rearranged her fingers. "You seem to be moving pretty well. Let's walk to the next appointment."

Zhelica timidly set her right foot down. There was a dull ache, not the shooting pain she had previously experienced. She put most of her weight on it and managed to take a step.

"There you go," the doctor said approvingly. They slowly made their way down the street under the stares of the townspeople they passed. When they entered a double-doored establishment, Zhelica looked up.

"This is the inn where I fell."

"Yes," the doctor replied. "One of the cooks got cut, and I said I'd come stitch it up."

Zhelica sat at one of the tables as she had the first night, but kept both feet on the floor. A young man poked his head from the kitchen and then came out and gave the doctor a hearty handshake.

"Look at this, doc," he said, unwinding the bandage on his left hand. A gash stretched from his thumb to his pinky.

"What in the world were you doing?" the doctor asked. "Don't you have cutting boards in there?"

The cook laughed. "I was drying a new knife and it went right through the dish towel."

"Let's go wash the wound properly, and then I'll suture it," Dr. Laskavosk said.

They ducked into the kitchen and returned to sit across from Zhelica.

"You don't mind?" the doctor asked her.

"Not at all," she said.

He removed a spool of thread from his bag and snipped a length off, threading the needle with it. Zhelica admired his handiwork as he nimbly stitched, leaving the cook with a tidy row any tailor would be proud of.

The young man opened and closed his hand. "Much better, Dr. L," he said.

"Try to keep it dry while it's healing," the doctor told him. "I'll check it next week."

He turned to Zhelica. "Would you like something to eat while we're here?"

She glanced back at the cook's hand. "No," she said. "I think I'll wait until we get back to your house."

They carried on for a couple more hours. There were a number of patients in the heart of Zerzavy with mostly minor complaints like sore throats and lacerations, but occasionally someone with a chronic illness. For these, the doctor insisted Zhelica wait in the carriage. By the end of the time, her foot was hurting, so she asked if she could just remain inside until he was finished. His forehead creased with concern. His last few visits seemed shorter than the earlier ones had been.

"I was hoping to take you to the market," he said. "But it looks like you've had enough."

Usually, Zhelica thought, the doctor appeared calm and unruffled. But she detected a hint of disappointment.

"Let's go," she said, forcing a smile. "I'll never get better if you pamper me too much."

He turned down a sandy path that led toward the beach. His was not the only carriage there; there were also a number of food carts parked, hawkers crying out the fruits or vegetables they were selling.

"Oh, fresh berries!" Zhelica said. No one grew the fragile fruit in Zaharada. They were rare and expensive, but here they were being sold by the crate.

Dr. Laskavosk helped her out and she bit her lip while stepping on her wounded ankle, turning her head so the doctor would not notice.

"What will you have, Dr. L?" asked the merchant.

"I will take a crate of the strawberries," the doctor said. "It looks like the blueberries are still a little green."

The farmer obligingly lifted the top crate. "Shall I put it inside your carriage, sir?"

"Yes," Dr. Laskavosk said. He fumbled around his waistcoat pocket and brought out a bag of coins, counting out the right number into the merchant's palm. "I hope you are saving some for your girls," he said. "They're good for them, you know."

"Yes, sir," the man nodded.

As they walked away, the doctor said softly to Zhelica, "They are surrounded by farmland here, but most of the people are too poor to eat what they grow. Notice what they are buying."

Zhelica tried to think past her own discomfort and observe the people around her. Their clothes sported holes and many of the children were barefoot. The women, who were doing most of the shopping, carried baskets filled with a few potatoes and leeks. Some had a carrot or two on top. Although a butcher was calling out the price of his freshly hung meat, there were few takers.

"This is so sad," Zhelica murmured. "If I lived here, I would be in poverty, too, I guess."

"No, Zhelica," he said. "You are literate. If you lived here, you would probably be a tutor for some of the wealthier families."

It was an interesting idea. *I guess I could do more than sort mail if I had to,* she thought.

The doctor purchased a few more items – Mrs. Milica had given him a list – and returned Zhelica to the house on the bluff. She was more than ready to put her foot up. When she peeked under the bandage, she could see her ankle turning purple again.

Gabara ran to the carriage as soon as they arrived. "Daddy, guess who's here!" she cried. As she said the word, the man himself appeared on the front porch. "Grandpa!"

Dr. Laskavosk waved to his father. "Well, here is someone you may want to talk to," he said to Zhelica.

He called the older man over. Zhelica could see right away the resemblance between the two, although the father's beard and hair were shot through with white. He looked more expressive than his son, the corners of his eyes lined from smiling. At Dr. Laskavosk's bidding, he provided support for Zhelica so she could stagger indoors between the two.

"Let's settle in the parlor," her host said. Zhelica had not been in this room. Once the curtains were opened, she could see it was little used. The knick-knacks placed on end tables and shelves hinted at a woman's touch.

The doctor gave his father a hearty embrace and then sat down on a stool with Zhelica's foot in his lap.

"That looks painful," the older man said, peering over his son's shoulder.

"She took quite a tumble her first night in town," the younger doctor said. "It is not healing as quickly as she would like."

"What are you doing to treat it?" his father asked. Glasses in thin wire frames rested on his forehead, and as he examined her ankle, he pulled them down so he could see more clearly.

"Rest and wrapping," the younger man answered. He looked up at his father. "Do you have any suggestions?"

"Ice would be good."

"Where would we get ice?" his son answered. "People here can't afford it."

The older physician pulled a chair over. "May I?" he asked.

The younger Dr. Laskavosk passed off Zhelica's limb as though it were an inanimate object. The father manipulated her foot gently, and then said, "I would like to give you an exercise to work on."

Zhelica looked at her host. He nodded approvingly.

"I want you to write the alphabet with your toe," he said. Zhelica looked at him blankly, so he demonstrated with his own foot. Zhelica traced three letters and then groaned.

"You need to do the whole alphabet three times a day to strengthen your ankle."

"Probably start tomorrow," the younger doctor added. "I had you on your feet a lot today."

Gabara had been watching with interest. Her father said, "Could you ask Mrs. Milica to serve our dinner in here? I hate to move Zhelica again."

"Thank you," his patient said appreciatively.

The men sat in two high-backed chairs opposite the couch where Zhelica and Gabara were situated. The younger doctor propped Zhelica's foot up on the stool.

"So, father," he began, "what brings you here?"

Instead of answering, the older man called Gabara back. "Run out and get the package I left in the hallway," he said.

Gabara returned in a flash and tried to hand it over to her grandfather. He pushed it back. "Grandma sent it for you."

The little girl sat on the sofa next to Zhelica and ripped open the brown paper. Inside were three new dresses, each soft cotton printed with flowers. "Oh, look, Zhelica!" she exclaimed, holding one up.

"Very pretty," Zhelica said.

"Mother's been sewing again," said the younger Dr. Laskavosk. Zhelica glanced at him: his tone was not happy.

"Yes," his father said. "The other grandchildren are close, but we hardly get to see Gabara. In fact, your mother wondered if I could bring her back for a visit."

Gabara tossed the dresses aside and ran to her father. "Please, Daddy," she begged, her arms around his neck.

Dr. Laskavosk sighed but gave his daughter a squeeze. "I suppose I could do without you for a week. But it will be hard," he added.

Gabara squealed with delight and threw herself into her grandpa's arms.

"You do know, though," her father said, nodding toward the new clothes, "that none of the girls here dress like that."

"She's a doctor's child," the older man said. "They'll understand."

Mrs. Milica appeared with a trolley of food, and served them each a plate before excusing herself.

"I've had a whole medical consultation with you and I still haven't been introduced," the elder Dr. Laskavosk said to Zhelica.

The corners of the younger man's mouth turned up slightly. "Someone you've been waiting to meet for a long time."

His father looked surprised.

"This is Vaclav's daughter."

The older man's blue eyes fixed on her for a moment. "Yes," he murmured. "Yes, I see it now – her father *and* her mother.

"I hoped to adopt you right after the partition of Darzarada," he told Zhelica. "Marjon was supposed to bring you, and I waited – first near the border, then in my own home – for months. How have you come to be here and I didn't know?"

Zhelica felt guilty, but knew it was not her fault she had not come sooner. "I'm sorry, doctor. Marjon only recently told me that my parents wanted me brought here. She could not bear to part with me."

"No, of course she couldn't," he said. He straightened his glasses, which had begun slipping off his head. "Where have you lived all this time?"

"Marjon has an orchard not far from Hyarani. She kept me there until I married."

The doctor acknowledged her pregnant state with a smile. "Congratulations. Is it your first?"

His son cut in almost harshly, "Her husband was killed for his involvement in the Restoration."

The older man's mouth pinched into a sympathetic frown. "I am sorry."

"This *is* my first," Zhelica answered, placing her hands on her belly. The baby was active, and she could feel something sharp – an elbow or a knee perhaps? – gliding under her palm.

"He or she will change your world," the older Dr. Laskavosk said. "I'm sure you and Matyas have talked of his experience."

"Matyas?" she repeated, confused.

"That's my first name," the younger doctor said. "It's probably time you used it."

"Especially with two Dr. Laskavosks in the house!" his father laughed. He grew serious again, and reached over to lay a hand on Zhelica's. "It will be all right," he reassured her. "The community will help you."

This flustered her. *What community?* She was not staying. A protest rose but then died before passing her lips. It was hard to imagine what her future would look like. She felt like a dandelion seed, wafting around with no clear place to land.

As they ate, the older Dr. Laskavosk told Zhelica about his time as an army physician and about his friendship with her father. "I wish you could remember him, Zhelica," he said. "He had a wonderful sense of humor and was absolutely fearless. Everyone loved him. I've never met a better man," he mused.

"Sounds like my husband," Zhelica said wistfully.

"Hmm, is that so? The only person I've ever met that reminded me of him was Matyas' wife." They both looked at the younger doctor. He was pushing a piece of meat around his plate without any apparent intention of spearing it. "Yes, that young lady knew how to have fun. This house was full of so much laughter and song –"

"Father." The word was uttered like a demand, request, and entreaty all at once. The older doctor immediately dropped the subject. He had finished his meal, and beckoned Gabara to come sit on his lap while she nibbled a bread roll.

"So how is Marjon? Feisty and strong-willed as ever?"

Zhelica laughed. "You must have known her well. Yes, she runs a thriving business single-handedly and has managed to keep me from view for most of my life."

The older man chuckled, bouncing Gabara on his knee. "If you see her again, give her my greetings. I understand why she never sent you to me," he added. "But who knows what advantages you missed out on not being raised here."

"My observation," Zhelica said, "is that *alloys* have a pretty rough life in Darz. I suppose if you had been my guardian, though, things would have been better for me. And Matyas" (she hesitated before speaking his name) and I would have been playmates." She smiled teasingly at the young doctor. He looked uncertain and flashed a feeble grin in response.

The room had grown progressively dark during their dinner. Matyas rose to light the lamp.

Dr. Laskavosk senior stood. "It's been a long day for me, so I'd like to turn in. I'll take the couch in the den."

"That's my bed," Zhelica informed him. "I'm afraid you'll have to sleep in a bedroom."

"Come on, Grandpa," Gabara said. She wasn't willing to let go of his hand to give Zhelica her nightly hug. "I'll take you to the guest room. Goodnight, Zhelica."

"We can talk more in the morning," Matyas' father said. The last thing Zhelica saw was a farewell wave as his granddaughter dragged him out the door.

Sixteen

Zhelica extended her leg and began her exercise. *A...B...C...* Her ankle was not as sore today and she slowly worked through the alphabet. She tried to stand on her foot, though, and it was still too tender to bear her full weight.

Gabara, clad in one of her new dresses, sat proudly next to her grandfather at the breakfast table.

"I slept so well last night!" he said. "The window was open, and I fell asleep and woke up to the sound of the sea."

"Will you take me down to the beach today, Grandpa?" Gabara asked.

"After your tutor is gone," her father said.

Gabara gave a playful pout. "I can learn at the beach, too, Daddy."

"Your father is right, child," the older doctor said. "I will sit in on your lesson today, and then we will go down to the beach."

"When are you thinking of heading home?" Matyas asked.

"In a couple of days," his father said. "I want to make sure my patient is making progress before I go." He winked at Zhelica.

"I wonder what I should do while I wait for word from Zaharada," Zhelica said. "Gabara's been entertaining me, but once she's gone. . ."

"You could come with us," the older doctor said. "I know my wife would love to meet you at last."

"That's a kind offer," Zhelica said. "I want to be ready to leave as soon as I get my next assignment, so I should probably stay in Zerzavy. If that's all right," she said to Matyas.

"Of course," he told her. "I'd like to have you around long enough to see that you can resume normal activities."

Four weeks, Zhelica thought. That is how long she had been in Zerzavy. She accompanied the doctor every day, and had taken to walking with a cane. She tripped, and even though the doctor caught her, the reinjury set her back. The first day that she was able to walk the entire perimeter of the house without her cane, the message came.

Mrs. Milica found her in the back, watching clouds scuttling over the ocean and thinking about the Overking, who (Gabara told her) lived on an island far across the water.

"A letter was dropped off for you," Mrs. Milica said.

Zhelica ripped open the envelope; there was another, smaller one inside wrapped in a note. She unfolded the paper and read:

Carry this message to the town of Baraqan. You must find Mr. Koosha and deliver these instructions to him. He is known as a tutor for the students at the military academy. Be careful not to speak to any of the students or staff at the academy.

Zhelica flipped the paper over; there was no signature.

The name seemed familiar...Mr. Koosha...This was the man Yavan visited on his trips to Baraqan – Mr. Koosha was his former tutor and friend. When Mr. Koosha heard about Zhelica, he sent the beautiful peacock scarf as a wedding gift. The recipient of this note was one who had a connection to Yavan.

She carried the message back indoors and found Dr. Laskavosk at his desk.

"Look at you," he said as she slowly crossed the room. "You are doing very well."

Zhelica sat down nearby and held up her note.

"My instructions have come."

He looked puzzled for a moment and then said slowly, "Ah. Restoration work." He did not ask her to explain her assignment.

"I must go," she said. "This message needs to be delivered quickly."

Matyas said nothing. Zhelica pressed him.

"Do you...do you think it's all right for me to travel now?"

"What do *you* think?" he asked her. He was so still, she could read nothing from his body language.

"I did just make it all the way around the porch without my cane," she said. "But there is still pain. I don't know how far I am able to walk at one time." She also could not help but look at her belly, which was massive.

"So you think you should wait?" Matyas asked. "I could find someone else to deliver the message."

"Well, I don't know," she stammered. "You're my doctor; tell me what to do."

Matyas responded, "Zhelica, I am *not* going to tell you what to do. If you feel you must go, I will do what I can to help you on your journey. If you want to stay, I'll find someone else to carry the message."

Zhelica stared at him. She was so used to others organizing her life – where she could and could not go, who she could and could not talk to – it seemed strange to have options.

"I suppose. . ." she began. Matyas was completely attentive.

"I suppose I could still ride, and try to minimize my walking."

"It will be hard for you to mount and dismount right now. Let's take your horse down to town, and we'll get you fitted up with a surrey. That should make your travel a little easier."

Does that mean he thinks I should go? Zhelica wondered. Or did Matyas mean it would be easier whenever she *did* decide to leave? Or, she thought, did he really have no opinion and was leaving the choice up to her? He was a hard man to read.

Matyas took her to the workshop where wagons and carriages were constructed. The owner greeted him heartily.

"My little one is thriving," he told the doctor. "And her mother. You did a fine job delivering the baby, Dr. L."

"I thought you had midwives do deliveries," Zhelica said.

"The mother had a long labor and was getting weak," Matyas told her. "I just came to give a little assistance at the end."

"He saved her life," the man told Zhelica. He pointed to her abdomen. "He'll do the same for you, if you get into a fix."

Zhelica blushed. She had no desire to have Dr. Laskavosk deliver her baby.

Matyas explained to the carpenter what he wanted. The man led them inside the barn-like building where his apprentices were working.

"We have one made to order," the carpenter said. "Is this what you were thinking of?"

Matyas ran his hand over the wooden sides and footrest. "I think this would work for you," he said to Zhelica. "Do you think you can climb in?"

He gave her a hand and she stepped up with her sore foot, quickly dropping into the seat.

"I can get in," she said with a grin. "Let's see if I can get out."

The doctor again held his hand to her, and she carefully stepped on the stair and then the ground.

"That's easier than getting in a saddle," she admitted.

Matyas turned to the carpenter. "I know you said you made this to order, but would you be willing to sell it to me? I'll pay extra so you can get your workers to make the replacement."

The carpenter ran fingers through his tousled red curls. He looked thoughtfully at the surrey and at Dr. Laskavosk. "You have done things for me that could never be repaid. I think my client can wait a few days."

"Excellent!" Matyas shook his hand. "We'll bring the horse down this afternoon?" he looked at Zhelica for confirmation. She nodded. "And then you can show us how to attach the surrey."

Matyas helped her back into his carriage. "Would you like to do my rounds with me today? Or would you rather I take you home first?"

"I would like to accompany you," she said. There was something pleasurable in watching this man interact with the sick (and well) of Zerzavy. And it would be her last opportunity to do so.

They visited Aneta last. "I have been writing letters since you left," she said. "I hope you can carry these back without any trouble."

Zhelica counted them as Aneta passed them – there were five. "I would be glad to," she said.

"If you make it to Hyarani and have time, please deliver the one on top to my sister in person."

Zhelica looked at the name and address. "Really? She's your sister?"

"Yes," said Aneta. "Why? Is her name familiar?"

"She was my friend when I lived in Hyarani. I will do my best to get this to her," she promised. Zhelica could see the resemblance now; although much younger, Aneta looked like a calmer version of Azara, the restaurant owner. "How is it that you ended up here, and she remained in Zaharada?"

"She married a local man," Aneta said. "I stayed as long as I could, but other than my sister, there was nothing to hold me there." She sighed. "I miss her."

"I can imagine," Zhelica said.

In her moving around, her heart had expanded to encompass the new people in her world. She missed Marjon, Nazhin and Beyman and their children, and even...she realized she had reddened. She did miss the camaraderie she had with Rakshan.

Zhelica blushed again when she saw Matyas looking at her curiously. *He probably thinks I am remembering my husband,* she thought. She was ashamed of her own feelings.

When they returned to the doctor's house, they were greeted by the elder Dr. Laskavosk and Gabara, who had just returned from the north. The men immediately returned to town to procure the surrey while Zhelica rested her ankle. Gabara could sense change coming, and she sat near Zhelica on the couch with Kotchka on her lap.

"Tell me about your visit to your grandparents," Zhelica said, smoothing the girl's hair. Just as she felt with Aneta, regret at leaving mingled with her desire to be back in Zaharada.

"They are so rich!" Gabara exclaimed. "You should come with me next time. Everything's pretty at Grandma's house." She fixed her brilliant eyes on Zhelica's and said, "Why are you sad?"

Zhelica dropped her hand onto her abdomen. "I have to go, Gabara."

"Oh, I just got here!" the girl complained. "When will you be back?"

Zhelica shrugged. "I don't know," she said. *Maybe never,* she thought.

"You should have your baby here," Gabara told her. "My daddy can help you deliver it. He delivered me," she added.

"We'll see," Zhelica said. "Meanwhile, I hope you'll study hard while I'm away."

The plan was for Zhelica to leave after breakfast the next morning. Her Zaharadan dress had been waiting in her closet; she rose early and called Mrs. Milica to help her into it. It stretched taut against her midsection.

"This looks terrible!" Zhelica cried, looking into the mirror.

"It looks like you're pregnant," the housekeeper said. "Nothing terrible about that."

Zhelica threw on her cloak and held it like a tent. "Room for two," she said, twisting her lips into a half-smile.

Dr. Laskavosk told Zhelica the best time to skirt the coastal cliff and how to find the road south of the border. Matyas demonstrated hooking and unhooking her horse from the surrey.

"Try to keep your injured ankle propped up if you can," he suggested. He continued running his hand over her horse after he was done showing the features of her new vehicle.

"Thank you for your generosity and all your help," Zhelica said. "You've been indispensable as a physician and gracious as a host. I can't tell you how much talking to your father and daughter have meant to me during this difficult time."

His eyes met hers, and she saw something there she was not expecting...a loneliness, a sadness that he usually concealed. He looked away.

"I'm glad we could assist you. If you're ever sent this way again, you are welcome at our house."

"Thank you, Dr. L," she said.

He laughed. "Not you, too." Then, more seriously, he held out a hand to her. "Until all things are restored," he said. She echoed his farewell.

The town was vacant and wet when Zhelica entered it. Heavy mist lay over the coast, its fingers reaching along the muddy streets of Zerzavy. *It really is an awful little town,* Zhelica thought. Matyas had definitely made a sacrifice in choosing to work here.

The tide was on its way out as the horse lumbered across the shore. Its task became easier when they reached the harder sand near the water. Zhelica waited a few minutes until the waves were safely back from the protruding cliff. She gave the reins a jerk, and her horse plunged forward, stepping around tidepools and rock half-submerged in the sand. Within a few minutes they were safely to the other side. She was back in Zaharada.

Zhelica's heart sank, and at first she was not sure why. And then she knew: for some reason, she hoped she would see the man they called the Gardener King perched on a log by a roaring fire. But nothing broke the bank of fog clinging to the coastline.

Zhelica looked for the place Matyas's father had mentioned, an area where a dirt road had been cut into the bluff angling up to the main road. Soon she saw its gash against the sea grass, and she guided the horse up the bumpy path until they reached the hard-packed road.

They followed this for some time. As the morning progressed, the fog broke into patches of white and the pale blue of a summer morning emerged behind it. Zhelica found this cheering. An hour after the mist had totally burned away, she saw the road Dr. Laskavosk had told her of ascending to Baraqan.

Long ago, he explained, what was now a military academy had been the primary royal residence. Because of that, the road transitioned from earth to red brick. The surrey rattled over this; Zhelica clutched her abdomen. The baby kicked and twisted inside her. Hopefully, she thought, this would not go on too long.

Soon she passed a cluster of houses built into a wooded hillside. They thickened until she arrived at the center of a large town. This must be Baraqan.

Zhelica was not sure how to find Mr. Koosha without talking to anyone affiliated with the school. She slowed her horse to a walk and scanned the shops and other buildings along the main street. Like Hyarani, there were restaurants and tailors. She passed a musical instrument store. And, set back from the surrounding buildings, she saw a boxy stone structure that had a sign planted in its front lawn with "Historical Society of Baraqan" painted in curly script.

Zhelica pulled the horse up and thought for a moment. It seemed a less direct way to find the tutor. She tied the horse to a post and stepped down, still favoring her weak ankle.

The curator opened the door as she approached. Zhelica nodded and smiled. The elderly man seemed startled by her presence.

"May I help you?" he asked, squinting.

"I am passing through Baraqan and wondered what I could discover about the history of the town."

Zhelica entered the dark building.

"Let me get the blinds," the man said, tottering over toward the windows. The sound of creaking was followed by transformation of the room into a small library. By the time the curator had flipped all the blinds, a soft warmth filled the chambers of the historical society.

He seated himself at a desk by the front door. "What sort of information are you looking for?" he asked, again squinting as he looked up at her. "We don't get many *alloys* in these parts," he muttered.

Zhelica realized at once that she would be painfully conspicuous in the town. How to get in touch with Mr. Koosha...that was the object. Slowly, she said, "I saw an old Circle of Meeting with a picture of what looked like a castle, and somehow got it into my head that palace was here in Baraqan."

The curator folded his hands. They were thin, almost skeletal, and the veins bulged through the skin.

"The palace was here once," he said. "It's now a school for the military."

"Do they permit tours?" she asked.

He snorted. "Not for someone like you. But if you want to know more about it, you should talk to a local historian."

This seemed promising. "Is there one that would be willing to talk to an *alloy?*"

The curator snorted again. "This one seems to meet with all kinds." He pulled a sheet of paper from his desk; dipping his pen into the inkwell, he began to write. When he finished, he blew a feeble breath over the paper and handed it to Zhelica. "Here's his address. He should be able to tell you all about the old palace."

"Thank you, sir," Zhelica said. "Good day to you."

He waved her away and flipped open a book on his desk. She was probably the only person who would interrupt whatever reading he was intent on that day. Zhelica tried to keep the front door from falling noisily shut as she exited.

Once she was back in the surrey, she looked at the paper. "Peruz Koosha, 231 Oak Grove Road."

Yes! she thought triumphantly. This was a good start to her day. She looked around the street; there were people at work sweeping, opening shops, fanning braziers full of charcoal into flame. Zhelica threw her hood over her hair – there was no point in being memorable here – and drove by a man stacking fruit decoratively in front of his shop.

"Excuse me," she called. He turned, a melon in hand. "Is this the way to Oak Grove Road?"

The shopkeeper nodded. "Keep going uphill. In two blocks, turn left and you will be on Oak Grove."

She thanked him and tried to ignore his stare as the horse hauled her up the street.

It was easy to find Mr. Koosha's house, an older cottage set back among the trees. He might not be home, Zhelica knew, but she parked the surrey near the side of the house.

She remembered with a twinge of regret the beautiful shawl he had sent her; she wished she had it now. But there was nothing to be done. Carefully, she made full use of the railing as she climbed the few wooden steps to the front door and rapped on it. Zhelica could hear footsteps inside, and the door opened.

Mr. Koosha's black hair was tipped with white around his temples; his goatee was also salt-and-pepper. He had a friendly face, and Zhelica immediately felt a connection.

"Mr. Koosha?"

He kept one hand on the door as though ready to shut it quickly as he answered, "Yes. Who might you be?"

Zhelica pushed her hood off and they stood for an instant evaluating the other.

"You must be Zhelica," he said. He broke into a big smile. "My dear! Please come in." He opened the door wider and ushered her inside.

Somehow Zhelica had imagined this place well from the little Yavan had told her. The floors were a reddish-brown wood polished to a bright finish. In Mr. Koosha's front room were the high-backed chairs at which he and Yavan had discussed academics and life. Not so long ago, he had come here and brought back the wedding gift from the tutor...

Her hand went to her neck. "I forgot the scarf you sent me," she said apologetically. "It's beautiful."

He sat in one of the chairs and motioned for her to join him.

"How is Yavan?" he asked. "Did he come with you?"

Zhelica's heart sank. He did not know. She cleared her throat. "You didn't hear?" she asked, her voice cracking. "It's been months."

His face reflected her own. "No. What happened?"

Zhelica thought she was handling the situation better with each retelling. But something about Mr. Koosha's sympathetic nature and relationship with Yavan brought her again to tears.

"He's gone," she wept. "He died at the base." She dropped her head, brushing the tears furiously away.

"Oh no," Mr. Koosha said in a tone of grief. "Oh no."

He lay a hand on her arm in comfort, and then left and came back with a handkerchief. Zhelica held the cloth to her face and sought with all her might to bring her emotions under control. *This is not why I came,* she told herself. *Yavan... Yavan...*

Mr. Koosha waited patiently for Zhelica's crying to cease. Finally, the sobs gave way to tears and then to dry chest heaves and the extraordinary calm that comes after a good cry.

"I'm so sorry," she said, smiling weakly. "I haven't wept like that since the first days."

Mr. Koosha said, "I wondered why he hasn't been to see me in so long, but I can't believe he's gone." He shook his head. "He was so young. And such a remarkable young man! I can't believe it."

"He told me about you," Zhelica said. "He said you were his friend."

Mr. Koosha's dark eyes brightened at this. "Yes, I was glad he could come back and visit so often. He was one of my favorite pupils, the kind that makes you glad to be a tutor. I am truly sorry for your loss. Do you feel up to telling me how it happened?"

She shook her head. "I'm sorry...no."

Mr. Koosha acknowledged this. He seemed neither unduly curious nor unfeeling.

"I am glad to meet you," Zhelica said. "I know he enjoyed spending time with you." She reached into her pocket and brought out the envelope she had transported from Darz. "But this is the real reason that I came."

An almost imperceptible tremor passed over Mr. Koosha as he glanced at the envelope.

"Ah," he said, his eyes fixed on Zhelica. "Would you excuse me while I read this?"

He scanned the note, and then looked up at her in surprise.

"You are part of the Restoration?"

She nodded. "I couldn't help myself after what happened to Yavan. Before that, I didn't even know he was involved."

"Really?" Mr. Koosha seemed astounded.

"I know that sounds crazy," Zhelica said. "I think he wanted to protect me somehow."

Mr. Koosha nodded. "Yes, he was that kind of man."

"Do you have a reply for me to carry to someone? I'm pretty new at this, so I don't really know what I'm doing."

"I would be most grateful if you could," Mr. Koosha said. "It might be days before one of my regular messengers shows up." He went to his carved wooden desk and scratched out a note. He addressed it in the same ornate script he had used on the card he had sent her, slid it into an envelope, and sealed it with a drip of wax. After blowing on it, he brought the note back to Zhelica.

"I would like you to carry this to Hyarani," he said. He looked at her blooming belly. "You are faithful to the cause, doing this kind of work when it looks like a time you should be resting."

"Nothing is going the way I would have planned it," she said with a sad smile.

"That's the way life is," Mr. Koosha said. "You never know what will happen next."

Zhelica tucked the note away. "Hopefully the next thing that occurs will be better than all we have suffered until now," she said.

"Let us hope," Mr. Koosha agreed.

Seventeen

The tutor served Zhelica stew before sending her on her way, regaling her with stories of Yavan as a student. She was not sure how to get back to Hyarani from Baraqan; Mr. Koosha gave her clear instructions.

"On this route, you will pass the old palace," he told her. "I thought you might like to see where your husband went to boarding school."

Although she had claimed a search for the palace as a ruse to find Mr. Koosha, she actually *did* want to see the building. The road wound around the old palace garden, now steps of lawn leading up to the main building. Only a few trees remained in the original garden. An iron fence kept passersby from entering the grounds; two soldiers stood by the main gate. Their expressions were menacing enough to keep Zhelica moving. She could only see one side of the military academy, the rosy stone pillars shading its porch. Yavan and Afshar had spent years in that place. And Rakshan. But before that, the king of Zaharada and his foreign bride...

As the road curved, the academy disappeared. The view from here, down the forested slopes, was breathtaking. It was a grand perspective, whether for a palace or a military establishment.

Mr. Koosha told Zhelica the shortest road would take her through the capital. She looked forward to seeing it, knowing it was newer than any city she had yet been to. As she approached Sandazh, Zhelica remembered the drawings she had seen in the children's book at Nazhin's. The buildings were boxy, built of stone, with very little ornamentation. Trees had been planted equidistant from one another along the wide boulevards of the city. Like Hyarani, there were commercial areas filled with shops. But there was very little to distinguish one from another; she had to see the signs set inside the large windows to know what kind of merchandise each sold.

Zhelica was disappointed. She thought the capital, of all cities, should be the most beautiful.

As she followed the main street through Sandazh, a flash of blue against all the gray caught her eye. A few boys, dressed in blue robes, were running toward a side street. Zhelica slowed her horse and stopped along the curb so that she could see where they were going.

The avenue was filled with boys, all similarly clothed. They were laughing, running, and dancing on the sidewalks and packing the street. At the end of the road, a huge building loomed. The spires on each corner glittered as the sun reflected off the tiny bits of sapphire-like glass covering them. The massive structure, painted a deep azure, seemed strangely familiar.

The House of Shurash.

She remembered the book now. The golden statue in the market of Hyarani must be a tiny replica of the great figure inside that building. Zhelica had an overpowering desire to see the statue.

She found a post where she could tie her horse and stood still among the whirling throng of boys. Two caught her hands. "Come with us!" they cried. Although they could not move fast, the crowd surged onward, approaching the great building. Boys were rushing in one door and out another, all the time noisy and jubilant. They did not seem to care that Zhelica was a woman or an *alloy*. Her guides continued to drag her forward.

The artist who had created the book Zhelica read must have spent a long time inside the building. The details – the braziers, blue smoke swirling from them, the golden man, stretching to the ceiling ...it was all there. But so much more alluring, so much bolder and more intoxicating than she could have imagined. Zhelica blinked. The glory of the golden figure glowing in the torchlight was too much to look at long. The outstretched hands, their shackles broken, seemed to reach out to her. *Break the chains of the Overking!* the boys were chanting around her. *Serve Shurash instead!*

Those in front of Zhelica prostrated themselves, forming a sea of curly, dark heads and arched blue backs. She could not move in any direction. Those who held her now fell to the floor, still grasping her wrists. She almost lost her balance, and the boys let go. Zhelica felt an arm link through one of hers, stabilizing her. Part of her wanted to join the youth around her, to yield to the beauty of Shurash. The arching walls, the rhythmic cries, the tendrils of blue ascending like flowers in praise of Shurash all called her to surrender.

But as she turned to look at the one who was holding her up, the whole scene seemed to change.

I know you, she thought. Dressed in a drab cloak, the small, dark-haired man held Zhelica's eyes. It was the Gardener King.

"Come along, Zhelica," he said gently. The sound of the boys seemed muted somehow, his own voice clear. "You do not belong here."

"But Shurash –" she began. She glanced back at the statue. It no longer looked a luminous, living thing. It reminded her of a cheap vase she had seen once in a shop in Hyarani. Hollow, flimsy, ugly. The shackles seemed to mock.

The Gardener King did not pull Zhelica. He waited. She turned away from the statue and followed her rescuer. The crowd of boys parted as they passed through. *We almost seem invisible,* Zhelica thought. Although the journey into the building had seemed long, it took no time to return to her surrey.

"Why are you here?" the Gardener King asked.

Zhelica ran a hand over her forehead. Her mind felt muddled. "I don't know," she answered. "I was on my way to Hyarani, and I saw the boys . . ."

The King gave her a hand up to her seat. "It is late, my friend, and you seem weary. Stay on this road. Just outside Sandazh you will see an inn called The Little Forest. I know the owners. Tell them I sent you, and you can rest there for the night. Go on to Hyarani in the morning. You will be safe as long as you stay on the main thoroughfare."

"Thank you," Zhelica said. She looked back toward the boys still crowding the side street. "How did you get in there?" she asked. "I didn't see you."

He smiled. "You didn't *want* to see me. I hope you are glad to see me now."

"You saved me. I might have been crushed or the baby injured in that crowd. And there is something strange about Shurash."

He nodded. "He is my great enemy, Zhelica. I think you have seen enough to know that you should avoid him at all costs. But don't be afraid. If you need help, it will come."

Zhelica's horse startled and she grabbed its reins. When she turned back, the King was nowhere to be seen. Zhelica looked for him among the crowd of boys. But he was gone. A splash of white caught her eye on the seat. A single rose lay on the cushion beside her.

That man has a penchant for appearing and disappearing, she thought as she headed on her way. But her own heart seemed at peace. She was glad to be free of the House of Shurash.

The day was still young when Zhelica arrived in Hyarani, well-cloaked to avoid drawing attention. Mr. Koosha's note was addressed to a house in a corner of the city where she had not spent much time. Farthest from the city gates, it appeared to be built into the wall and was strangely tall and narrow. The garden outside, neglected, was full of thistles that had grown across part of the path to the front door. Zhelica lifted her skirts, carefully choosing where to step. She had to stop twice to tug her dress free from the briars.

She rapped on the door and through the cloudy glass could see a head. The sound of a chain being pulled tight accompanied the opening of the door a crack. Only the sliver of a young woman could be seen.

"Yes?" she asked. "What are you selling?"

"I'm not selling anything," Zhelica said. "I brought a message for someone here."

She held out the envelope. The young woman glanced at it, and her hand shot out from behind the door and snatched it. "Wait here."

Zhelica did not want to sit on the rusty metal chair near the stairs. So she stood, supporting her belly and swaying. Gabara had pointed out to her recently that she did this, apparently in preparation for rocking her baby. Zhelica smiled at the thought.

The chain scratched from inside (it sounded as corroded as the outdoor furniture, Zhelica thought) and the door opened fully. With the girl was an older man. Despite the ragged appearance of the house, he was dressed in fine clothes. He held Mr. Koosha's letter.

"So, you must be Zhelica," he said. "Mr. Koosha wrote that you would probably be willing to carry a response back to him."

Zhelica's heart sank. She was tired from the previous day's travel. She had hoped to sneak by the restaurant to catch a glimpse of Nazhin or Beyman or their children. But she shook her head, considering this. It was dangerous for them to be in her company.

Misinterpreting this, the man said, "Oh – you cannot return to Mr. Koosha?"

"I'm sorry," Zhelica said. "Of course I can take a message back."

The man did not invite her into his house. "Stay here, and I will write a note."

Zhelica looked around her. "Do you mind if I wait in the surrey?"

"Not at all," he said. "It will only be a moment."

Instead of returning, he sent the younger woman. She seemed in a hurry, running back inside and slamming the door shut while Zhelica watched.

Strange, she thought. They did not behave like others she had met in the Restoration. *But they must also want the return of Darzarada.* It struck her as odd that Mr. Koosha had given her name in his note. Marjon, Afshar, and the others were reluctant to share identifying information within the group.

Visiting Nazhin was out of the question, but Zhelica remembered that she had a letter for Azara from her sister. She directed her horse back to the main street and the café. Since the restaurant owner had warned her about appearing at the front, she turned down the side alley and let herself in through the door to Azara's private rooms.

"Azara?" she called softly.

She could hear multiple conversations of diners; no doubt the older woman was working. Zhelica sat down at the tiny table in the apartment's kitchen and waited a few minutes. Azara suddenly popped in, letting out a cry.

"Oh! I didn't think I'd see you again after so long," she said, giving Zhelica a hug. "What are you doing here?"

"I have brought you a letter," Zhelica told her, handing her the envelope. Her friend held it at arm's length to focus.

"From my sister?" she asked in amazement.

"There's no time to explain right now," Zhelica said, getting up. "But she is well and living in a tidy little house near the beach in Darz."

Azara's eyes filled with tears as she turned the envelope over.

"Thank you, child," she said, sniffing. "But can't you stay?"

Zhelica shook her head. "I have to go to Baraqan. I'm just hoping to get there by dark." She pulled out the other letters Aneta had given her. "Could you mail these for your sister?"

"Of course," Azara said while giving her a hug. "You look about to burst, Zhelica," she added, placing a hand on her belly.

"Not long now," Zhelica answered. "Goodbye, my friend. I don't know when I will see you again."

She slipped out the back and made her way quickly through Hyarani, not daring to look around for fear she would see someone else she knew.

Zhelica was ready to retrace her trip of the morning, but a thought came into her head. *I could go by way of Marjon's house.*

Yavan had traveled to Baraqan by that route. Perhaps it was no longer, and she could take a few minutes to see Marjon.

She had traveled the road enough times to remember all the landmarks as she rolled along. She watched the farms pass with pleasure: the trees thick with leaves, the fields laden with melons and squash.

As she approached Marjon's property, Zhelica saw that the gate was unlatched and stood open. She tied the horse and squeezed through.

She could tell immediately that something was wrong. The guard house was abandoned. She walked quickly, supporting her belly to keep from bouncing, and stopped at the front door. It, too, was ajar.

"Auntie?" she called, pushing her way in. The afternoon light angled into the kitchen, giving some illumination to the house. She glanced into the sitting room. No one was there.

"Aunt Marjon!" Zhelica cried, and gripped the hand rail as she mounted the stairs. Here, too, all was desolate. Zhelica looked with dread into her aunt's bedroom. The bed still bore the impression from Marjon's last nap, but the woman herself was gone. Zhelica looked into her own former bedroom.

Here there was a difference. The bureau's drawers were pulled out, its contents tossed on the floor. The cupboard where she had kept the precious storybook had been ransacked. She reached in to the place where she had last hidden it: the book was missing.

Zhelica stood, mystified. This did not look like the work of her aunt. Someone had been here...maybe was still here...She listened, but only the usual sound of birds in the trees filled the quiet.

As quickly as she could, Zhelica descended and went into the kitchen. On the counter were vegetables Marjon had cut, ready to cook for the evening meal. They were drying out. Some hours must have passed since her aunt had left.

There was something so terrible in finding the house like this that Zhelica felt compelled to discover the reason for it. She went into the back garden. There was no one there, nothing to show what had happened. She walked around the building, calling her aunt. She paced the orchard. There were no clues.

Zhelica was truly exhausted now, and she sat down on one of the chairs in the front yard. Her eyes filled with tears. Where was Marjon? What had happened to her? Should she go to the nearest neighbor, the guard boy's house?

As these thoughts swirled through her mind, Zhelica knew she needed to leave. Marjon was part of the Restoration; if harm had come to her, it was a result of Shurash's league. She must go as quickly as possible to Baraqan and deliver the message to Mr. Koosha.

Before departing, she pumped some fresh water into a trough to let her horse drink. Then she found some dried fruit in the pantry and tucked it into her pocket for later.

"We need to fly," she said to her horse, heading him on the road toward Baraqan. She drove the beast as fast as she felt she safely could.

The road up to Baraqan this direction went through an ancient town full of wooden cottages. No one paid attention to her as she rushed through and followed the brick road that led up into the forest. The sun was so low that Zhelica felt pressed by the darkness of the surrounding trees, and even passed a pair of deer feeding in grass alongside the road. In her fretting about Marjon, even this innocent sight seemed ominous.

Zhelica was so spent she had to hesitate when she came to the center of town, trying to remember which way she had come from Mr. Koosha's house. At last she reached the bungalow. Like other things from that day, it looked darker than she remembered as she climbed to the front porch.

When she knocked, Mr. Koosha came. A blue light emanated from his parlor, casting an odd glow in the hallway.

"Ah, Zhelica, you have returned. Come in, my girl."

She stepped inside. "Here's the reply to your message," she said, holding it out.

Mr. Koosha looked closely at her. "You look worn out. Come sit down and I will get you something to drink."

She collapsed gratefully into one of the high-backed chairs by the fire. She could hear Mr. Koosha rattling dishes in the kitchen. Zhelica looked around as she waited. The blue glow she had seen when entering came from a book standing open on the mantel. Zhelica got up and went to see what it was.

She touched the volume – an ordinary book – and it fell. Zhelica caught it as it tumbled from the mantel. The light was much brighter now, and Zhelica stared at it in shock.

A row of candles in blue glass flickered. In front of them stood a golden statue. A statue of Shurash. Mr. Koosha must have quickly covered it with the book when she arrived at his house.

Zhelica's skin prickled. *Mr. Koosha is not part of the Restoration.*

In an instant, she knew what this meant. He had betrayed Yavan. He may have been involved with Marjon's disappearance, too...and this was a trap.

Zhelica whirled around, ready to escape, but Mr. Koosha was back, a tray in his hands.

"I see," he said with a smile, the white in his hair and beard blue in the candlelight, "that you have found me out."

"But," she began, her voice cracking. "Yavan. He was your friend!"

Mr. Koosha set the tray down on the table. "Would you like some tea?" he asked pleasantly.

Zhelica stamped her foot. "How could you?" She was trembling, too stunned even to cry. She tried to push past the tutor, but he grabbed her arm.

"I'm sorry to detain you, but we have to wait a few more minutes until the soldiers arrive. A messenger came earlier to tell me you were on your way from Hyarani," he explained.

Zhelica's heart thumped like cannon fire in her chest. The baby was moving, too, and she put one hand on her abdomen. "Please, don't hurt me," she begged. "The baby."

Mr. Koosha firmly led her to the chair. "Have a seat." He poured a cup of tea and handed it to her. She looked at it suspiciously, so he poured himself a cup and sat down across from her.

"No one wants to hurt you or your baby," he said. He sipped the tea.

"But you are responsible for Yavan's death."

Mr. Koosha said, "Hmm. Not *personally* responsible. I was here. I did report some information he gave me."

"-Which led to his death," Zhelica said.

Mr. Koosha nodded. "Very possibly."

Zhelica looked toward the door.

"You can't get away," Mr. Koosha said. "Just relax."

Zhelica leaned back in the chair, leaving her eyes open just enough so she could see what the man was doing. She was not going to ask or answer any questions; the less she said, the less she might implicate herself or others she had been in touch with.

They did not have to wait long before the tramp of feet on the porch indicated the soldiers had arrived. Mr. Koosha called, "Come," and they flooded into the parlor accompanied by a draft of the cool evening air.

"So many?" Mr. Koosha asked, looking around. Zhelica fully opened her eyes and sat up.

She had worked on the base long enough so that she no longer viewed soldiers as terrifying non-entities: she knew these were young men doing what they were obliged to do. She almost felt sorry for them. But she realized she was clutching her belly as though to hide and protect her child.

"Get up," one of the soldiers said, not unkindly.

Zhelica struggled to stand – it was getting harder to move her bulk around but she suddenly realized that her ankle only gave a slight twinge.

As soon as she was upright, soldiers grasped her arms and led her forward. Over her shoulder as she was taken out, she managed, "You've made a terrible mistake, Mr. Koosha. Shurash is nothing compared with the King."

"Hush," the soldier on her right said. Then he whispered, "Don't make any more trouble for yourself than you have to."

They had brought a military carriage; the soldiers eased her into it, closed the door, and pulled away from Mr. Koosha's house.

The streets were colorless, trees dense along the edge of the road. Zhelica did not know how she would ever get away. She murmured, "Oh, your Majesty, if you could see where I am! I could use your help now!" Somehow, just uttering the supplication aloud gave her some peace, and she waited to see what would unfold.

They were headed to the military academy. Zhelica heard the guards at the gate scrape open the iron doors and the carriage pulled into the former palace grounds. They rolled past the lowest level of the terraced garden and around the back of the building to a round paved plaza. As soon as Zhelica stepped out of the carriage, she could hear the thunder of the waves below.

Around the plaza's edges torches were planted in pots, their blue flames jumping and sparking in the sea air. On the side closest to the academy, a man sat, flanked by two soldiers. He was watching the proceedings. Zhelica's escorts prodded her toward him and stopped when told. Her fear evaporated. She looked into his eyes as he took her in. Finally, he spoke.

"So this is the face of a traitor," he said. The soldiers near him chuckled.

Boldly, Zhelica said, "That's not true, General." (She knew enough about rank to see who he was.) "I am a faithful citizen of Zaharada."

He leaned forward. "You are the wife of Yavan?"

"I was," she said. She chose not to add, "until you killed him."

"And you have been carrying messages for the resistance," he pointed out. "It was brazen of you to ask for a job on a military base after his death. Didn't you know you were put in the mailroom so we could find out who your contacts were? As soon as our plans began to go awry, we knew you were a spy, just like your husband."

Zhelica was shaking, hoping she had not compromised others. "You can understand why I might want to follow in my slain husband's footsteps."

"Slain," he repeated. He stood up. "Do you know the penalty for treason?"

She folded her own arms above the dome of her belly. She was not going to answer.

"The penalty," the General continued, "is death." He watched her. *Is he hoping for a particular response?* Zhelica wondered. She was not going to gratify him.

"Mr. Koosha said you were not going to hurt me or my child," she said more calmly than she felt.

"Koosha," the General said. He paced. "Yes, well, he is right. I have other plans for you." He turned to his guards. "Take her away."

To Zhelica's surprise, they did not touch her. One went before her and one followed. It would be futile to try to run away from here, and Zhelica was too tired to try it anyway. She matched her own steps to that of the soldier in front. He headed toward the academy and opened one of the heavy doors.

"Go in and up the stairs," he said.

Zhelica obeyed.

Although the administrators had tried to turn the palace into an educational institution, the beautiful red stone of the walls, the corridor punctuated with planters and fountains, all testified to the building's true identity. Zhelica touched a frond of a hanging plant as she mounted the staircase.

At the top were two brass doors, ornately decorated and polished to the shine of a mirror. For a moment Zhelica feared that inside would be a smaller version of Shurash's house. She resisted when the soldiers urged her on.

"Please," she said, "please do not do this."

They looked at each other and laughed. Then one opened one of the brass doors and took Zhelica's arm, leading her inside. In an instant, he let go, returning to the hallway. The door fell shut with a muffled thud.

Zhelica's eyes needed to adjust to the low light. After a moment, she realized the only illumination came from a window in the ceiling, a half-sphere of multi-colored glass that was letting in moon and star light. At a table not far from the middle of the room, Zhelica could see the silhouette of a man.

She backed away. *What were they thinking?* she asked herself in a panic.

But he spoke, and she knew his voice. "Zhelica," he said, in a low, pleading tone.

She sighed with relief. "Rakshan? Is it you?"

The soldier rose and came to her. She could see that his hair was growing back and hung in curls over his face and ears. Those eyes – the ones that flashed like bolts in a summer storm – were fiery but sad. He took her hands and enclosed them in his large ones. Zhelica swallowed hard.

"Why did you leave me?" he asked. "I thought my heart would break. I spent the entire next day tracking you, trying to find you. They tell me you were spying for the resistance, but I couldn't believe it."

"Rakshan, I . . ." how could she explain? "I wronged you. I am sorry."

What she meant was, *I should not have been in that cottage with you. I should not have shown affection for you in the way that I did.* But she knew he was interpreting her words differently than she intended them.

He squeezed her hands. "Well, never mind what you have done in the past. You are here now."

Zhelica did not know what to say. She glanced around. "What is this place?"

"The old library," Rakshan said. He kept hold of one of her hands. "Come and sit with me."

Along the wall was a cushioned seat, and he led Zhelica to it. Then he found an oil lamp on one of the tables and lit it, sending a warm yellow glow to flood the empty space. It was a remarkable library, and in other circumstances, Zhelica would have taken interest in the thousands of books.

"Why did the general send me to you here? Are you going to imprison me?"

Rakshan knelt beside her so that their faces were even. "No, Zhelica," he said. "The general is my father, and he has agreed that rather than executing you, you will become my bride."

Eighteen

Although she understood the words, their meaning was incomprehensible. Zhelica just stared at Rakshan.

The soldier seated himself next to her on the cushion. "Zhelica," he said, "after I went missing from the base, my father was furious with me. Information communicated by mail was leaked and he held me responsible. Then I left with you, and he decided he'd had enough. He ordered me back here."

He was still holding her hand, and he turned it over so he could look at the back of it. Zhelica followed his gaze. Her white skin against his dark palm showed like a lotus in a pond. She tried to pull it away, but again he closed his around it.

"I am a terrible soldier," he admitted. He offered a half-smile, but she could not return it. Zhelica was still stunned, the idea of becoming his bride sinking in. "He is the great general. He wanted me, his son, to follow in his steps. But I am not that man," he said to Zhelica. His eyes were flashing again. "I am not that man."

"So what have you been doing here?"

"At first he put me with the new recruits and forced me to do all the physical training they do. That was to punish me. Then we talked, and he finally listened and realized I could never be a great warrior like him."

"That's good," Zhelica said encouragingly.

He squeezed her hand. "Yes. So he offered me a political position. I am to be satrap over an area on the southern coast."

Quickly, Zhelica assessed the prudence of this choice. Rakshan was smart and could accomplish whatever he set his heart on. Until now, he had been dulling the pain of his existence with alcohol, knowing he would never escape the course plotted out for him. But maybe ...

"What do you think of that idea?" she asked.

He shrugged. "It's better than being in the military. Plus, I like the coast. That's the best thing about the academy being here in Baraqan – it's right next to the beach. The real question is: what do *you* think about the idea?"

Zhelica was flustered. Pretending she did not understand his intent in asking, she answered, "Well, Rakshan, if being satrap is what you want to do, I think you should try it."

He searched her face. "Would you like to live on the coast?"

This time Zhelica tugged her hand away from him and crossed both her arms over her belly, accentuating how large it was. "Rakshan, you weren't serious about marrying me."

He winced. "Why would you think that?" he softly asked.

"Look at me," she insisted. "In the next few weeks I am going to give birth to the child of another man."

Rakshan placed his large hand over her abdomen. "I will love your child as my own," he said.

Her heart turned over. "Oh, Rakshan," she whispered, "I can't marry you."

"Why not?" he demanded. "Why can't you marry me?"

She dropped her head and closed her eyes. *Why can't I marry him?* With Rakshan there, his warm body beside her, it was difficult to focus. He had removed his hand, and she slid her own down to cover her belly.

Then she spoke. "I have met the King."

She opened her eyes and looked at him. A puzzled expression was on his face.

"What king?"

"The King of Darzarada."

Rakshan sucked in his breath.

"Zhelica, he died years ago. They hung his body in the garden below the palace. The king is dead."

She shook her head. "No, Rakshan, he isn't," she told him. "I have spoken to him – twice – and I have met others in the Restoration."

She wondered if this was a foolish declaration. What if Rakshan was a tool to get names out of her? But she continued.

"Shurash is evil," she said. "He pretends to stand for liberty but he's got you all bound to him to destroy this country."

"I don't care anything about Shurash," Rakshan said. "I just want to marry you and move away from here."

Zhelica struggled to her feet. She stood, her hands now clasped beneath her baby. *He needs to see this!* she thought. *He cannot really want to marry me!*

Then a thought came to her. "Rakshan," she said, excitement growing, "join us. You are not on Shurash's side. You were born to be his vassal, but you don't have to be. Let's escape and work for the Restoration!"

"Zhelica, I love you," he began. He brushed locks of hair away from his face and his knees bounced in agitation. "If we don't marry, my father is going to kill you. You as my wife is part of his plan: I have what I want – a career, a wife and family – and I stop being a problem for him. When I found out they were going to seize you, I made him agree to that. I can't go back on that deal."

Although part of her was terrified that the general would force her into Rakshan's arms, she was suddenly overcome with a sense of peace.

"Yes, Rakshan, you *can*," she said. "Run away with me right now, and you can be free from your father and Shurash. The Restoration will get you to a safe place where the general will never find you."

"You don't get it, Zhelica," he said, rising. "I don't want to lose everything for another cause I don't believe in. I have the opportunity for a job that will win my father's respect plus we can be together. That is what I'm offering you. Not a life on the run, fighting against my own family and people. I know you are an *alloy* so this doesn't necessarily feel like your homeland. But this is where I belong, and I'm not going to be a traitor to Zaharada."

They stood a moment, the air between them tense. Then Zhelica walked to the door and put her hand on it.

"Where are you going?" Rakshan asked. There was desperation in his voice.

She cleared her throat. "Do you think they will let me have the baby before I die?"

As she clumsily made her way down the narrow staircase which wound around what used to be the royal family's wing, Zhelica kept her eyes on the curved plaza below her, the blue torch fire still snapping in the night breeze. Several soldiers clustered together, talking. Somehow Zhelica had to make it down to the beach and head north across the dry sand without being seen. It seemed an impossible task, but she knew it was her only hope.

The wind blowing off the sea was chillier than she anticipated and it was hard to keep her balance as each foot sank into the sand. Zhelica clung to the cliff edge. When she came to the other staircase – the main one leading up to the plaza – she stopped to make sure no one was on the steps. It was clear. She hurried past, stumbling along until the torches were well behind her, and then sat down on a log.

Zhelica was unutterably exhausted. She brushed away a tear. It seemed like a week had passed since she had left Darz. She just wanted to curl up somewhere and sleep.

Above the sound of the surf, Zhelica was startled by the neighing of a horse. She turned, covering her own mouth to keep from crying out. On the cliff she could see the outline of a man with a horse attached to an open cart.

They've caught me already! she wept. There was no point in trying to get away now, so she waited until the man, leaving his transport on the road, scrambled down the grassy hillside to stand before her.

"Zhelica."

Even in the dark, she knew who it was. Zhelica slid to her knees on the sand. "Your Majesty," she said, inclining her head.

The King held out his hand and surprised Zhelica with his strength as he pulled her upright. "It is time to go."

He led her up to the cart and somehow – she could never remember exactly how it happened – Zhelica was eased onto a bed of hay in the back with blankets tucked around her. She was too tired to question any of it. The King drove the cart along the narrow coastal road and Zhelica watched the stars.

Why did Rakshan let me go? she pondered. Perhaps he really *did* love her. The thought pained her. She knew that even if he joined the Restoration, she could not marry him. He had too far to go to be the kind of husband and father she and her child needed.

The idea that she would consider marrying again had come unasked for. Zhelica thought that after Yavan, she could never love again. The baby moved, and Zhelica curled around it. *You would probably like a daddy, wouldn't you?*

She could see the back of the King's head as they worked their way north. She did not understand history, how the King had cheated death, or how she fit into what was happening with Darzarada. But she knew that she was no longer working for the Restoration in memory of Yavan. She had come to desire the reunification and healing of the two nations herself.

Zhelica dozed in the cart, its swaying like a cradle. She woke once as they passed through a narrow divide, rock walls rising up on either side. The stars were absolutely brilliant in the slice of sky she could see.

"Your Majesty?" she called. He turned his head and she could see him smile tenderly.

"Yes, my child?"

"Where are we? I don't recognize this."

"We are passing through the mountains to Darz. This path is little known."

Zhelica, still groggy, protested. "Why are we going to Darz? Shouldn't I try to find Marjon and make sure she is all right?"

The King said nothing but continued on.

In the middle of the night, the cart stopped, and Zhelica woke again. They were outside a wooden house. A woman stood in the doorway with a lantern, the King in conversation with her.

"Zhelica, you will be staying the rest of the night here," he said, assisting her down.

Disoriented by the disrupted night, she only nodded, allowing the King to hand her off to her hostess. He prepared to depart.

"Aren't you staying, too?" she asked.

"There are others who need my help tonight," he said. "Sleep well, Zhelica."

She resisted efforts to get her inside until she had watched the King ride off into the night. But at last she was in a bed, and fell into such a long and profound sleep that she did not wake until the light of mid-morning shone on her face.

Zhelica's hostess was not an *alloy* but a native Darzian. When Zhelica finally came downstairs, she found the woman arranging flowers in a large vase. Some, Zhelica noted, were white roses.

She relit her stove and made Zhelica a pot of tea. The table in her tidy kitchen was laid out with bread, fruit, and a loaf of cheese. "Come and sit here. You should eat before you head home."

Home? Zhelica thought. The King had brought her to Darz, but this was not her home.

The woman continued, pouring amber liquid in a cup for Zhelica. "I hope you slept well? You certainly slept long."

Zhelica nodded. "I was so tired," she said, lifting a slab of fresh bread to her mouth. She was rested; now she ate to satisfaction. "Thank you for taking care of me."

Her hostess smiled. "I only did what the Overking assigned me to do," she said. "I don't want to rush you, Zhelica, but your ride will be along soon."

"My ride? Where am I going?"

"Zerzavy."

"But I thought you said I was going home," Zhelica protested. "My home is in Zaharada."

The woman sat down across from her. "I know this can all be confusing," she said. "But the King's instructions were to send you to Zerzavy. To the doctor's house."

Zhelica puzzled over this. Then she breathed a sigh of relief. "He probably has my further instructions. I stayed with him before."

Her hostess shrugged and smiled. "Perhaps," she said.

A knock at the door let them know it was time for Zhelica to go. She looked down at her clothes, wrinkled and dusty from travel and sleep, and cringed to think of seeing Matyas and Gabara in her unkempt state. She hastily rebraided her hair and, as the carriage drove toward Zerzavy, tried to smooth out her dress. At least her ankle seemed functional now, so she could move around normally.

The house looked different to Zhelica as they pulled around the last bend in the road, like an old friend. Gabara was waiting for her on the front steps. A message had been sent to the doctor informing him that Zhelica would be back that day. His daughter ran to the carriage and as soon as the door opened, clambered in to give her friend a hug.

"I am so glad you're back!" she cried. "It was boring without you here."

"That's sweet. I have had quite a couple of days, I can tell you."

The elder Dr. Laskavosk appeared at the carriage door. "Welcome back, Zhelica," he said. "Are you planning on staying outside all day?"

He lifted Gabara out and then gave Zhelica a hand. As she stepped down, a sudden cramping tugged at her insides.

"Oh!" she exclaimed.

"What is it?" Dr. Laskavosk asked. "Is your ankle still hurting?"

"No, it was. . ." she looked up into his kindly face. "The baby, I think."

He squeezed her shoulders. "Hopefully you won't have to wait long," he said.

They went into the parlor and the doctor had cold drinks brought in.

"Where is Matyas?" asked Zhelica.

"Daddy's in town," Gabara said. "I think he's arranging a place for you to stay."

Zhelica looked to Dr. Laskavosk.

"It sounds like you are going to be here for some time," he explained. "Matyas thought the office sofa might not be the most comfortable place for you."

"I was told I'd be going home," Zhelica said. "But my home is in Zaharada."

Dr. Laskavosk pulled his chair close. "Gabara, give me a few minutes with our friend." His granddaughter pouted but withdrew.

"Zhelica, think for a moment: where is your home?"

His blue eyes kept her green ones locked as she pondered this. Marjon's house? But Marjon was not there. Was it even safe?

Nazhin's house? No, she had already been sent away from there.

Her voice trembling, Zhelica said quietly, "I have no home."

Dr. Laskavosk said, "We have had news of Marjon. She got warning troops were coming for you, so she managed to be away from the orchard. Once word gets back that you are safely in Darz, we are hopeful that she will be able to return without any trouble."

"But don't they know she's part of the Restoration?" Zhelica asked. "Won't she be punished for that?"

"Marjon is a shrewd woman. No doubt she destroyed any evidence that she was connected to Darzarada or those hoping for its return."

That explained the disappearance of the book Zhelica had so loved. She was sorry she would not be able to read it again.

"So when I go back, will she be arrested again?" Zhelica asked.

Dr. Laskavosk put a hand on her shoulder. "That is the concern," he said.

"So –?"

The older man cleared his throat. "I'm sorry, Zhelica. It sounds like you won't be going back."

No! No! No! she silently cried. She would not stay here. She would find a way to return without endangering Marjon. She hated this ugly little town. She would not be an *alloy* among *alloys.*

Aloud, she said nothing.

Fortunately, the sound of carriage wheels grinding the gravel broke the path of the conversation and her thoughts. They heard the staccato beat of a man's boots on the stairs outside, and the front door swung open. Gabara ran into the room, tugging her father behind her.

Zhelica had not thought of Matyas during her ordeals, but now that he was here, she sensed a sympathetic soul. He dropped his medical bag and knelt down by the couch.

"Welcome back, Zhelica. I didn't think we'd see you again so soon." He pointed to her foot. "How is it?"

She extended her leg and did circles with her ankle.

"Only a little tender. I have been able to walk on it."

"That's miraculous," Matyas said. "Maybe excitement is good for you."

His fair eyebrows creased as he gazed into her face. "And yet I think this has been a very hard couple of days for you."

She nodded, her eyes moist. Suddenly cramping gripped her belly, and she gave a little moan.

"Is there a little activity going on? May I?" He extended his hand, and Zhelica again nodded.

Rakshan's touch was too recent to not compare it with Matyas', so she steeled herself not to flinch. The doctor urged her to recline on the couch, and he palpated her belly knowingly. While he was doing this, another pain seized her.

The elder Dr. Laskavosk said, "Is this it? Or false labor?"

Matyas stood. "This might be it. I would like to transport her to Aneta's and have the midwife join us there. Could you go get her?"

His father nodded and left the room. Matyas pulled up a chair and straddled it so that its back faced Zhelica.

"I gather that a lot has happened since we saw you, Zhelica," he began calmly. "You probably wanted more rest and preparation before having your baby, but it may very well be that that child is coming in the next day."

"Not here," Zhelica pleaded.

A brief smile flickered across his face. "Not on my sitting room sofa, I hope," he agreed. "I have arranged with our friend Aneta to put you up in her second bedroom. That is probably where your baby will enter the world."

Zhelica grabbed his hand. "This baby is Zaharadan," she insisted.

Matyas put his other hand on top of hers. "Not if its birthplace determines its nationality. Now, Zhelica, I'm going to collect a few things to take with us to Aneta's. You can rest here or walk around – the choice is yours."

He gently lowered her hand and left the room. Within a moment, Gabara peered around the door.

"Zhelica? Can I come in?"

Zhelica nodded, floundering into an upright position. With this came another contraction.

Gabara approached cautiously.

"Are you having your baby now?"

Zhelica tried to smile. "Yes, Gabara," she said. "At least, soon. Do you like babies?"

The little girl nodded. "I like their tiny fingers."

"I'll let you hold my baby after it's born," Zhelica said.

"I wish you could stay here with daddy and me," Gabara told her.

She sat down on the sofa next to Zhelica. Zhelica plucked up Gabara's braid and let it slip through her fingers. *I think I'm going to like being a mother.*

Matyas was back in a few minutes, and seeing the two of them together brought a full-fledged smile.

"Next time you see Zhelica, you will get to meet her baby, too," he said. Gabara gave a squeal of delight.

"I'm ready if you are," he said to Zhelica. He helped her stand. Another contraction gripped her. Noticing her wince, he tucked her arm through his and they walked slowly to the carriage.

The road down to Zerzavy felt rougher than she remembered, and she wrapped her arms around her belly whenever they rolled over a stone. The yanking of her insides was coming more frequently now.

Aneta assisted her into her cozy second bedroom. Zhelica glanced around. It reminded her of Nazhin's, with the lace curtains and a little fireplace on the back wall.

"This is beautiful," she said.

Aneta had her cooking apron on, and she said, "I have heard that soup is good after delivery. You make yourself at home, Zhelica."

Matyas led Zhelica to a chair by the fireplace. "You wait here. The midwife should be here soon."

"Thank you, Matyas," Zhelica said gratefully. Suddenly she was finding that her other thoughts and concerns – Rakshan, Marjon, being in Darz rather than Zaharada – all slipped away. All she could think was, *The baby is coming.*

Although Zhelica should not have been surprised, the midwife who appeared was an *alloy*. Aneta was an *alloy*, too, but like her Zaharadan sister, she dressed in the city garb of Hyarani. The midwife was clearly a Zerzavian, her skirt a brown, coarse cloth. She was large-boned, her hair tied up in a bandana.

"Hello, Zhelica," she said. "Let me see how your labor is progressing." She examined Zhelica before announcing, "Well, it looks like it might not be long before you welcome your first child."

Aneta had left her a little bell to ring for help, and the midwife gave it a brisk shake. Aneta appeared almost immediately.

"Do you have some extra pillows we could use? And some warm water would be good for bathing the child when it is born."

Aneta almost chortled with delight. She disappeared, and Matyas stuck his head in.

"How are things looking?"

"She won't have to wait too long for this child. I will send for you if there are any. . ." she dropped her voice, "complications."

Despite the steadiness in his voice and manner, Zhelica thought she detected some concern Matyas' expression.

"If you don't mind, I think I will stay and chat with Aneta for a while," he said, almost apologetically.

The midwife confidently shrugged. "Whatever you like, Dr. Laskavosk." After the door had closed, she said, "Poor Dr. L – since his wife died delivering their first, he frets over every childbirth. He should know by now," she said, shaking out a baby blanket and laying it over the back of a chair, "that mothers are in good hands with me. But it seems to make him feel better to hang around."

Zhelica tried to return her reassuring smile, but another contraction gripped her in that moment.

As the day turned to evening, the timing of the contractions grew regular. Zhelica could only doze in the short span between moments of pain. Sometimes Yavan's face floated through her mind, the dimpled charmer who had helped form this child. Sometimes she was conscious of the midwife bustling about in the corner of the room. The low voices of Matyas and Aneta occasionally punctuated the quiet of the house.

Zhelica opened her eyes at one point to see Matyas at her side. The glow of lantern and fire made his hair and beard a halo of light around his face.

"How are you doing, Zhelica?" he asked in his quiet, soothing voice.

A contraction came and went before she spoke. "I'm tired."

"Yes, you have been in here for hours," Matyas said. The midwife had left a basin of cool water by the bedside, and he dipped a cloth into it and blotted her face. He pulled out his pocket watch and began timing her contractions. "Do you feel like pushing? Because it seems like you are pretty close."

She nodded. The midwife returned and Matyas turned to leave. Zhelica reached out and grabbed his sleeve. "Don't go," she said.

On reflection later, she thought he looked relieved that she had asked. The midwife gave instructions when to push through the contractions and when to stop. Zhelica felt like her body was being torn in two with each contraction. Matyas let her hold his hand and she clutched it for dear life whenever the pains came.

The pushing seemed to go on for a long time. She did not know whether minutes or hours had passed, but she grew weaker and it was harder to make an effort; the contractions would come and Zhelica just wanted to lie still and let the pain pass. The midwife urged her on, but finally Zhelica dropped Matyas' hand and let her head fall back on the pillow.

"I'm too tired."

The doctor stood up. Zhelica could only see the back of his head as he spoke quietly with the midwife. The woman nodded, and Matyas turned to Zhelica.

His face was lined with worry. And then Zhelica remembered: his own wife, Gabara's mother, had died giving birth. Suddenly she was afraid.

"Am I going to die?"

"Not if I can prevent it," Matyas said. He was no longer the unflustered doctor she had become acquainted with over the last months. He looked like a man on a mission. He washed his hands and asked Aneta to bring a clean apron. Zhelica would have found it humorous under other circumstances: the doctor clad in a flower-printed ruffled bib and skirt. But the situation was too serious.

Matyas examined Zhelica and said, "The baby's head is in an awkward position. I am going to help turn it. Apologies ahead of time."

She felt like she was being pulled inside out as Matyas manipulated the baby. But then he cried, triumphantly, "Next contraction, give a big push, and the baby's head should be out!"

He was right. After that, the infant's shoulders and then the rest of its body slid into Matyas' waiting hands. The midwife brought over a towel to wrap the baby, who began crying, a healthy burst of protestation.

"Zhelica, you have a son!" Matyas announced. The midwife handed Zhelica her child.

Despite her previous exhaustion, as soon as she took the baby into her arms, Zhelica was wide awake. "Oh, look at him."

His head was tufted with thick black hair. He was a big boy, and the midwife had to position him for Zhelica so that she could feed him. At one point, Zhelica glanced up to see Matyas watching them. Their eyes met. The fear that had dogged his steps since the death of Gabara's mother was gone.

Nineteen

Sitting on the sofa in Aneta's front room, Gabara cradled Omeyd. The chubby-cheeked boy tightly grasped her pinky as she marveled aloud.

"Wow! He has a lot of hair," she began. "Darzians and *alloys* are usually bald. And look at his tiny fingers." She wiggled his hand back and forth. "Why does he want to suck on my hand?"

Zhelica, a week postpartum, felt like an expert. "He thinks he'll get milk there," she said. Together they laughed.

"May I see him?" Matyas asked. Gabara reluctantly handed Omeyd to her father.

Matyas unwrapped the baby. Zhelica watched him, the muscles tensed in his left arm as he supported the child. The doctor went through his mental checklist, looking into the baby's ears and eyes and mouth. He moved his plump legs in and out. He carefully re-swaddled the boy.

"Here you go, Zhelica," he said, handing Omeyd back. "He seems healthy and strong."

Matyas sat down on the sofa next to her. "And how are *you* feeling?"

"Pretty good," she said. "Aneta lets me sleep whenever I'm tired during the day, holding Omeyd even while she's doing housework."

Aneta smiled modestly. "It's so lovely having a baby in the house, Dr. Laskavosk."

"It is," he agreed. "Worth the short nights. Zhelica, are you getting any exercise?"

She shook her head. "I haven't really been out of the house yet."

"I have the perfect remedy for that," he said. "Let's go for a walk on the beach."

"I'll watch Omeyd," Aneta offered.

"No, let me carry him," Matyas said.

He tied Omeyd to his front in the carrying cloth and held out a hand to Gabara. Zhelica held her other hand.

It was a glorious summer day, sky the brilliant blue of Darzian eyes. The tide rushed out, leaving a swathe of untouched sand. Gabara tore off her shoes and ran ahead, examining every fragment of shell that had been cast up by the receding water.

Zhelica breathed deep the salty air. It felt good to walk along the shoreline without fearing capture by Zaharadan soldiers. She reflexively glanced at the bluffs: the King was not waiting there.

"How are you doing?" Matyas asked. "I'm asking as a friend now, not a doctor."

"Physically I feel fine," she said. They were walking into the breeze, and her dress flattening against her showed what remained of her baby bump. She patted it. "A bit stretched out of shape."

"Don't worry about that," he said. "You'll shrink back to normal over the next few months."

She walked backward against the wind. "Honestly, I am a little lost. I'm not sure what to do here, Dr. L."

He smiled. "Oh, so I'm Dr. L to you now, am I?"

"Well, you *are* my son's doctor. And he's a native of Zerzavy. So I guess Dr. L it is."

Playfully, he turned to walk backwards, too. Zhelica glanced nervously behind him; she didn't want him tripping while carrying her child. Seeing her concern, he faced forward again.

Gabara found an unbroken conch and hurried back to show them. They admired its delicate swirls and glossy surface. Gabara handed it to her father and ran off to find more treasures.

"Although your sleep is interrupted, he's relatively easy to care for now," Matyas said, running a hand over Omeyd's furry scalp, the only thing exposed. "You have a few months to think through your future. After that, he's going to keep you busy."

Zhelica nodded. She had hoped, long ago when she discovered she was pregnant, that her child would grow up with Nazhin's family in the little home above the restaurant. She imagined him playing with her friend's happy brood.

That was not going to happen. She was living, a widow mother, with an older, unmarried woman. This was not how she wanted Omeyd's childhood to look.

"You and Aneta have been incredibly generous," Zhelica said. "But eventually I'm going to have to support myself and Omeyd."

Matyas looked as though he wanted to say something, but did not.

"Do you know a way I can earn money with a baby in tow?"

He stopped for a moment and watched his daughter chasing the waves and leaning over periodically to examine kelp or shells. "What skills do you have, besides spying?"

She ignored this joke. "None." She threw up her hands in frustration.

Matyas stroked his beard as he walked on. "I don't believe that," he said. "How did you spend your days before you married?"

"Cooking. Working in the orchard. Reading."

He nodded, reflecting. "You are literate," he said. "Most Darzians are, too, but very few of the *alloys* of Zerzavy know how to read."

"That's discouraging," she said. "I need to get Omeyd out of here before it's too late."

He was quiet for a moment. "Or you could teach them to read."

She looked at him, puzzled. "What do you mean?"

"There is a school in Zerzavy – it was opened years ago when the first *alloys* fled Zaharada. But the teachers have wandered off to more developed cities over time. It's not an easy place to live and work."

"It's hideous," Zhelica said. A gust of wind took her words and whisked them away.

"What's that?"

"I don't know, Matyas. I don't know how good a teacher I'd be."

True to form, he did not tell her what to do. His only advice was, "Think about it."

They walked until Omeyd woke, insistent for nourishment. Matyas unwound the cloth that bound him, and handed the baby to Zhelica. She balanced on a piece of driftwood, nursing Omeyd. She watched Matyas and his daughter run and play together on the beach.

This is refreshing, Zhelica thought. Then she rebuked herself. She had lost everything: husband, home, Marjon, her chance to marry Rakshan and settle in her homeland. But into her mind crept what she had gained: a child to carry on his father's legacy, a comfortable home with Aneta, the freedom to move around without either hiding or standing out. If only she could learn to be content with a future in Darz. If only she knew how to serve the Restoration in a slapped-together town like Zerzavy.

Aneta invited Matyas and Gabara to join them for dinner, and they all squeezed around her little table, enjoying a Zaharadan stew. Gabara scrunched her nose at it, but Zhelica ate with relish. Her personal physician and friend could not resist a smile at this. "Looks like a meal Omeyd will enjoy, too," he said.

When Zhelica settled into bed that night, Omeyd already asleep in a cradle next to her, she found herself surprisingly satisfied with her day. *Maybe,* she thought, *I will find a way here.*

Zhelica rarely had vivid dreams, so when she awoke to Omeyd's crying in the night, she reviewed what seemed a vision.

She had been standing on the edge of Zerzavy. She watched a man dressed in dazzling white bent over plants in a garden. Periodically he turned and tossed away dead branches, and then returned to his labor. When he looked at her, Zhelica immediately recognized him.

"Your Majesty!" she cried, bowing. "What are you doing?"

He looked as she had never seen him before, a golden circlet on his head. Despite gardening, his hands appeared clean.

"I am tending my garden," he said proudly. He stepped back.

Zhelica moved forward to look. What she saw was a scraggly collection of weeds, some but not all with blooms. They were unremarkable plants – green, but not very pretty.

"Forgive me, Your Majesty," she said, "but it's not a very attractive garden. Would you like me to do some weeding for you?"

"These are not weeds," he said. "Look at them more closely."

Zhelica leaned down to examine the flowers. She noticed they all had a common oddity: their leaves and stems were those of one kind of plant but their blossoms of another. A morning glory glowed purple above a thorny rose base. A violet plant was dotted with daisies.

"What peculiar flowers!" she said.

"Some would say so," he agreed. "But to me they are like gold mixed with silver." He lifted one blossom and gently bent it toward her. "They are beautiful *and* strong."

Zhelica examined the flower. Its stem was sturdy, its petals like the most delicate fabric, a fluffy pink. She looked up at the King. "May I help you in your garden?"

He nodded and smiled. "This is the work of the Restoration," he said. "Many think they will bring my reign by fighting and killing. But that was never my intent. That is what Shurash wants. As you plant gardens, the people will *want* me to return. They will not need to be coerced. Cultivate the flowers," he said. "That is how you will bring my reign."

As she nestled Omeyd close, Zhelica pondered the significance of the dream. Was it actually a message from the Gardener King? What was he trying to tell her?

The next morning after breakfast, she tied Omeyd in his front wrap. It felt good to have him near where he had been for so many months.

"Aneta, I'm going for a walk," she announced.

Aneta gave a little frown. "I can't go out right now, Zhelica. I'm right in the middle of thickening a pudding."

Zhelica smiled. "You stay here. We will be fine."

She stepped out onto the boardwalk, and for an instant, she remembered her early married days, wandering around Hyarani to look into shops and see the workers sweeping and setting up wares in the open market. The image quickly faded: she was back in Zerzavy, with its drab buildings and muddy streets. With a sigh, she crossed the road and turned into a neighborhood.

Maybe the dream doesn't mean anything, she told herself. But her feet seemed to carry her on, propelling her forward. She knew she was looking for something – the King's garden – but was not sure how she would recognize it.

Zhelica traipsed through Zerzavy's battered streets. Most of the houses were shacks, boards nailed together, their cracks sealed with mud or clay. Chimneys emitted puffs of smoke: not roaring fires, but (she learned later from Gabara) dried cow patties burned in a desperate attempt at cooking food or providing warmth. There were people everywhere: standing in doorways, sitting on broken chairs in front of glassless windows, little ones making mud pies in the shade of trees.

Occasionally she passed a house as beautiful as Aneta's. These belonged to those who had left Zaharada with their wealth intact. The abject poverty belonged to the second generation, those born in Darz. It was tragic that the Darzians had left the *alloys* to themselves when they now were also natives of this land.

Zhelica turned a corner and a strange tingling filled her. This was familiar, somehow. She stopped, rubbing Omeyd's back as she looked around. Zhelica had never wandered Zerzavy alone, and she was certain that Matyas had never brought her here.

The dream! she thought. This was the place where the King had been cultivating the odd, hybrid blossoms.

Zhelica walked slowly. She passed a couple of shacks and stood still.

An open field had been turned into a playground by the neighborhood children. Their game involved hitting a homemade ball (composed of bands of rags tied around something) with a stick and then running across the field, chased by another boy or girl. It looked like fun, Zhelica thought. But it was sad, when she considered the parks of Zaharadan cities. And even *she* had had a rubber ball to play with as a child.

Zhelica walked the perimeter of the field. In her dream, there had been flowers here, she was sure of it. But in the waking world, there were only dirt and clumps of grass that had escaped the crush of children's feet.

Omeyd began fussing and Zhelica looked around. Someone had dragged a fallen log near one corner of the field. She sat down, took the baby out, and began nursing him. She gazed lovingly at his thick, dark hair, his smooth dark skin, and his gray eyes. (Matyas told her they would turn brown as he grew older.) She touched his dimpled hand. Someday he would be a boy running around this field, or one like it. It was hard to imagine now. She hoped by the time he was old enough to hit a ball, he had a better place than this in which to do it.

Zhelica watched the children play. She still marveled at seeing so many *alloys*. Although they all shared her red hair, pale skin, and green eyes, they were also different in their body shapes and sizes and their facial features. She realized with a start that these children must resemble their parents, that magical combination of a mother and father that made each unique.

She thought back on the miniature painting of her own parents. She wished they were clearer likenesses: it would be interesting to know which characteristics she had inherited from each. Omeyd was like Yavan; she wondered if as he grew, he would resemble her at all. But she, like the children around her, was a hybrid of the two different peoples – the Darzians and the Zaharadans.

Hybrid, she thought. Like a plant.

A thrill ran through her. The children – the *alloys* – the mixture more strong and beautiful than either alone...they were hybrids. They were the strange and special plants that populated the King's garden. He wanted her to cultivate the children of Zerzavy.

Zhelica was trembling. The thought was exhilarating and frightening. How could she do what Matyas had suggested – teach children? But how else could they usher in the reign of their King except by learning, growing, and thriving? There was no one else to do it.

As she weighed these thoughts, a little girl, too small to thoroughly participate in the game, ran over to see her. She screamed and clapped when she saw Omeyd.

"Your baby!" she laughed. "Your baby has black hair!"

Before Zhelica could explain, the girl ran back and grabbed a knot of friends. They all followed her over to the tree trunk and watched in amazement as Zhelica lifted Omeyd up and put him over her shoulder to burp him.

"A brown baby!" one of the girls laughed. It was not a malicious observation; she seemed truly amazed that such a thing existed.

"Why is your baby brown?" asked another girl.

"He looks like his father," Zhelica told her.

"A brown man!" the girl cried. They all laughed.

By now, the larger group had noticed the band in the corner of the field. They finished their game and wandered over. The youngest were four or five years old; the oldest around twelve. They continued calling out questions to Zhelica until she held up her hand for silence.

"Would you like to hear a story?" she asked them. "It will explain how I came to have a brown baby."

The children shouted in affirmation.

Zhelica turned Omeyd around, sitting him on her lap, and cleared her throat. "Once upon a time," she began, "in the land of Zaharada, there was a king. . ."

It was funny, Zhelica thought as she sat at her desk in the refurbished school a few months later, how different Zerzavy had come to look. Matyas's was still the most beautiful residence, with his view of the sea and the town and the farms that rolled away to the north and east. And the tumble-down houses that lined Zerzavy's back streets did not hold the order and symmetry of Hyarani's homes. But now as Zhelica carried Omeyd through the town, they were greeted by happy shouts from her students. She knew them, not as a collection of poor, miserable *alloys,* but as friends she had come to love.

Aneta agreed to join the class, helping students struggle through the texts that old Dr. Laskavosk had sent from the north. When Omeyd got fussy, Aneta plucked him from his mother's arms and walked him in the playground until he fell asleep.

Her sister, Azara, had decided to close her café in Hyarani and move north. She brought with her a letter from Marjon telling Zhelica that she was back at the orchard and all was well.

Zhelica admitted to herself, as she looked across her empty classroom, that she was beginning to feel at home in Zerzavy. Teaching had given her a sense of what she had heard in her dream: she was doing her part in bringing about the Restoration. But, she thought wistfully, it would be nice to hear that from the King himself.

At that moment, something flew in the window and landed on the desk in front of her. A white rose.

Zhelica jumped up and leaned out the window. Where was he? Was the King there?

At the corner of the playground, a man dressed in the humble clothes of the townspeople pruned a bush. When he stood upright, Zhelica knew immediately who it was. She lifted the single rose, and the Gardener King smiled. It was the sign she needed. *Beautiful* and *strong,* she thought. *Together we will cultivate the garden. Until all things are restored.*

About the Author

Melinda J. Lewis studied journalism at the University of Oregon, where she met her husband, Richard. They and their four children spent years in Afghanistan, inspiring her memoir, *In the Warlord's Garden.*

Darzarada is the second book in the *Dunyara Trilogy* and follows *The Queen of Bustaan.*

Made in the USA
Monee, IL
21 October 2024